"Don't dare miss
THE PASSION OF PATRICK MacNEILL,
*Virginia Kantra's emotional tour-de-force that
will introduce you to some of the most
compelling, most endearing, most memorable
characters you've met."*
—National bestselling author Kathleen Korbel

It just took one glance.

Before she could help herself, before she could stop and prepare, Kate looked through the glass to the tidy rows of blue upholstered chairs in the waiting room. Patrick MacNeill paced between them, too big to be contained, too energetic to stand still. He raked his dark hair with his fingers, then jammed his big hands into his pockets, straining his jacket across broad shoulders.

It was unprofessional, it was irrational, it was embarrassing, but when Kate looked at him, her jaw went slack and her knees sagged.

Kate closed her mouth and stiffened her spine. She would not let him get to her. At least, she wouldn't let it show. She'd spent too many years being patronized by colleagues to pant and sigh over some virile specimen now.

Dear Reader,

Happy New Year! And welcome to another month of great reading from Silhouette Intimate Moments, just perfect for sitting back after the hectic holidays. You'll love Marilyn Pappano's *Murphy's Law,* a MEN IN BLUE title set in New Orleans, with all that city's trademark steam. You'll remember Jack Murphy and Evie DesJardiens long after you put down this book, I promise you.

We've got some great miniseries titles this month, too. Welcome back to Carla Cassidy's Western town of MUSTANG, MONTANA in *Code Name: Cowboy.* Then pay a visit to Margaret Watson's CAMERON, UTAH in *Cowboy with a Badge.* And of course, don't forget our other titles this month. Look for *Dangerous To Love,* by Sally Tyler Hayes, a book whose title I personally find irresistible. And we've got books from a couple of our newest stars, too. Jill Shalvis checks in with *Long-Lost Mom,* and Virginia Kantra pens our FAMILIES ARE FOREVER title, *The Passion of Patrick MacNeill.*

Enjoy them all—and be sure to come back next month for more of the most exciting romantic reading around, right here in Silhouette Intimate Moments.

Yours,

Leslie J. Wainger
Executive Senior Editor

Please address questions and book requests to:
Silhouette Reader Service
U.S.: 3010 Walden Ave., P.O. Box 1325, Buffalo, NY 14269
Canadian: P.O. Box 609, Fort Erie, Ont. L2A 5X3

THE PASSION OF
PATRICK MacNEILL

VIRGINIA KANTRA

INTIMATE™ MOMENTS®

Published by Silhouette Books

America's Publisher of Contemporary Romance

If you purchased this book without a cover you should be aware that this book is stolen property. It was reported as "unsold and destroyed" to the publisher, and neither the author nor the publisher has received any payment for this "stripped book."

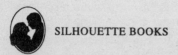 SILHOUETTE BOOKS

ISBN 0-373-07906-0

THE PASSION OF PATRICK MacNEILL

Copyright © 1999 by Virginia Kantra Ritchey

All rights reserved. Except for use in any review, the reproduction or utilization of this work in whole or in part in any form by any electronic, mechanical or other means, now known or hereafter invented, including xerography, photocopying and recording, or in any information storage or retrieval system, is forbidden without the written permission of the editorial office, Silhouette Books, 300 East 42nd Street, New York, NY 10017 U.S.A.

All characters in this book have no existence outside the imagination of the author and have no relation whatsoever to anyone bearing the same name or names. They are not even distantly inspired by any individual known or unknown to the author, and all incidents are pure invention.

This edition published by arrangement with Harlequin Books S.A.

® and TM are trademarks of Harlequin Books S.A., used under license. Trademarks indicated with ® are registered in the United States Patent and Trademark Office, the Canadian Trade Marks Office and in other countries.

Printed in U.S.A.

Books by Virginia Kantra

Silhouette Intimate Moments

The Reforming of Matthew Dunn #894
The Passion of Patrick MacNeill #906

VIRGINIA KANTRA

credits her enthusiasm for strong heroes and courageous heroines to a childhood spent devouring fairy tales. For several summers she trailed her English professor father through Europe's romantic grottoes and England's battle-scarred castles. She wrote her first stories on hotel stationery to bribe her younger cousins to go to bed.

She continued to share her love of books as a children's storyteller, and still visits local classrooms on Valentine's Day dressed as the Queen of Hearts. When her youngest child started school, Virginia fulfilled her dream of writing full-time. Her first two stories were both RWA Golden Heart finalists. She has won the Georgia Romance Writers of America's Maggie Award and the Orange County Romance Writers of America's Orange Rose.

She is married to her college sweetheart, a musician disguised as an executive. They live in Raleigh, North Carolina, with three children, two cats, a dog and various blue-tailed lizards that live under the siding of their home. Her favorite thing to make for dinner is reservations.

This book is dedicated in loving memory to
Sergeant Major Paul W. Ritchey, USMC (Ret.)

and to his son, my husband, Michael.

Special thanks to Judith Stanton, who insisted I could
write this book; to my dad, Robert A. Kantra;
and to Ernest J. Grant, R.N., M.S.N.,
and Hugh D. Peterson, D.D.S., M.D., of the
North Carolina Jaycee Burn Center.
The good stuff is all yours, the mistakes are all mine.

Prologue

The high, terrible keening of a child in pain went on and on.

Outside in the hall, Dr. Kate Sinclair narrowed her eyes, concentrating fiercely on a stack of medical charts. She wouldn't think, she couldn't think, about the five-month-old baby on the other side of the door. In six days, she was leaving Jefferson University Hospital, leaving the burn center, for a fellowship in pediatric surgery at Auburn. While her mother cried and her cat protested, she'd spent the Family Weekend from Hell packing up ten years of medical texts and mismatched dishes. If she weren't so behind in her paperwork, she'd be loading her life into a rental trailer at this very moment.

Kate rubbed two fingers between her brows, trying to erase the lines of tension that always formed over her nose. The child behind the door wasn't even her patient, she reminded herself. He had an immunologist, the attending pediatric surgeon and the director of burn medicine pulling for him. He didn't need her.

One of the interns staggered out into the corridor and leaned against the wall. "Good Lord." He blotted his upper lip with the back of his hand. "How do you stand it?"

Kate capped her pen. Emotion made ineffective doctors. She knew that, and the intern would learn it. "How are they doing in there?"

"They're almost done changing his dressings."

Sharon Williams, a burn unit veteran, paused on her way back to the nurses' station. "How's our little Iron Man?" she asked the resident.

"Who?" Kate asked.

"Baby MacNeill. Tough little guy. He was admitted over the weekend. How's he doing?"

The intern rubbed his face again. "It— He— Swaim seemed pleased."

Swaim was the burn unit director. If things went well at Auburn, if Kate's evaluations were good, there was a chance he'd call her back to the burn center to complete her training. She hoped so. Burn medicine fascinated her. The power to take a severely injured survivor along all the slow steps to new life made her feel good in a way that nothing else ever had.

She allowed herself a professional question. "Any sign of infection?"

"No."

"Good. That's good." She hesitated, and then offered, "Typically, patients who endure this kind of pain don't seem to remember much of it."

The crying broke into a series of gurgling sobs, horrible to hear.

Kate bit her lip. "Anyway, that's what they say."

The metal double doors at the other end of the hall swung open, and a tall man in green scrubs blew in like a weather system, crackling with energy, big and dark, eyes a stormy blue. In spite of his clothes, Kate didn't think he was on staff at the hospital. He wasn't the kind of man a woman, even a woman like her, could forget meeting. Instinctively, she straightened her spine.

Swift, intense, he strode toward them. "Are they done yet?"

Kate bristled at his tone, as peremptory as any surgeon's. Before she could speak, Sharon stepped forward, smoothly blocking his way. "Let me just make sure, Mr. MacNeill."

He nodded once, sharply, before she disappeared into the room.

So, Kate thought, studying him, this must be little Iron Man's father.

Impulsively, she spoke. "Can I get you anything?"

He didn't even look at her, all his attention focused on the baby's weak cries on the other side of the door. His big hands curled and uncurled at his sides.

"No."

Sharon came out, holding the door. "They're ready for you now."

He brushed past her without a word, ignoring the doctor and the assisting nurse and the procedure tray. Before he was three strides from the door, Kate heard his deep voice soften and change.

"Hey, buddy. Hey, Jack-o. It's Daddy. They're all done now, okay? You be tough, okay? I love you, buddy."

The crying stopped.

Kate looked at Sharon. Tears stood in the nurse's eyes.

"That's all that's keeping him going," she said. "All that's keeping either of them going."

The question popped out before Kate could remind herself that she had no business inquiring into a patient's personal life. And not even her own patient, at that. "The mother?"

Sharon shook her head, her usually placid face set. "Killed. In the same accident that burned the boy. Same damn drunk driver."

Kate's rubber ball of a heart bounced once, uncontrollably. She looked beyond Sharon into the room where the five-month-old lay swaddled and sightless, gasoline burns covering almost a third of his once-sturdy little body. His father hovered over his crib, big hands braced on the protective rails. Apparently he'd been warned not to touch his son because of the risk of infection. He bent down until he was almost nose to nose with the child in the crib.

Like a flower turning to the sun, the baby turned his gauze-bandaged head in the direction of his father's voice. Kate listened for the familiar strained cheerfulness of parents in a child's hospital room and heard only strength and love.

"You hold on, Iron Man. Daddy's here. I love you. It's been a tough day, huh? Maybe you should get some sleep now."

And before the door closed, she heard the man singing a rough lullaby in a soft, deep baritone voice.

"Hush, little baby, don't say a word, Daddy's gonna buy you a mockingbird..."

Kate wouldn't let it get to her. She never let this stuff get to her. Turning back to her medical charts, she was dismayed to note that her hands were shaking.

Chapter 1

Some days Patrick MacNeill hated doctors. The whole know-it-all, knows-best profession. He hated his dependence on their schedules almost as much as he hated his need for their expertise. He'd measured away too much of the last four years on the smug, uninformative faces of waiting-room clocks.

Pacing the rows of blue and green upholstered chairs, he glanced again at the clock over the nurses' station. Swaim was already twenty minutes late. Patrick wondered if their appointment with the reconstructive surgeon would even last that long. But after two years of hospital stays and another two of routine physicals, this examination was a necessary preliminary to the surgery Jack needed. And whatever his boy needed, Patrick would make damn sure he got.

"Daddy? I'm finished."

The impatience knotting Patrick's chest dissolved. He strode toward the child-sized table and chairs occupying one corner of the room.

"Yeah? Let me see."

The four-year-old pushed his art pad toward a corner of the

table, angling it so his father could see. Patrick leaned over, dropping a hand to Jack's shoulder as he studied the picture.

Eagles. His son had drawn eagles, carefully detailed and purposely composed: a nest at the top of a vertical cliff, three small bald heads with open beaks and a taloned adult with meticulously rendered feathers hanging in the sky above. At Jack's age, Patrick suspected, he'd still been drawing balloon-headed stick men and endless pictures of airplanes like hot-dogs with wings.

He cleared his throat, gently tightening his grip on the small, sharp bones and growing muscle under his palm. "Well, now. That looks fine."

Jack's hand, still curled from clutching his crayons, pointed. "That's the daddy eagle with the fish."

"I can see that. It looks good, buddy."

The boy tilted back his head and grinned at his dad from under the brim of his baseball cap. "How about great?"

"Great, huh?" Patrick rubbed the side of his nose, pretending to consider. "Yeah, okay. I think we can say this one looks great."

Jack giggled with satisfaction.

A crisp, feminine voice broke in on their rapport. "Mr. MacNeill? Can you come this way, please."

Patrick looked up. A pretty nurse in the loose white coat and scrubs worn by all the burn center staff stood in the open doorway. The sexy softness of her body under the oversize jacket contrasted pleasantly with her cool, tart voice and sharp, intelligent eyes. Surprised with himself for noticing—it had been years since he'd looked at a female with even passing interest—Patrick scooped up his son's art tablet.

"Okay, Jack-o, put away your crayons."

The nurse frowned slightly. "Please. We're running behind schedule this morning."

Patrick raised his eyebrows. "We noticed," he said, and had the pleasure of watching her flush. He waited until Jack had his crayons neatly aligned in their box before giving him a gentle push toward the door. "Let's go."

The nurse preceded them down the hall to the examining rooms, her curling light brown hair bouncing with indignation. Patrick followed, admiring the gentle sway of her backside under the limp white coat. He allowed himself a grin at his own expense. Obviously his libido was trying to make up for lost time. The little bossy nurse wasn't even his type, nothing at all like…Holly.

His heart clenched at the memory of his late wife. With practiced discipline, he shoved the vision into a closet in his mind and slammed the door.

"This way, please."

The nurse stood aside to admit them to a narrow box with hospital-approved art on hospital blue walls: anatomical diagrams and a photocopied warning to the staff to wash their hands.

"Yucky pictures," Jack commented.

Patrick heard his son's need for reassurance. "Absolutely."

Surprisingly, the nurse laughed, her face softening as she focused on Jack. "They are pretty awful, aren't they? I've been after them to get some real pictures for ages. Up on the table now."

With approval, Patrick noted she didn't try to lift the boy but let him climb up unaided. Patrick sat in the small, uncomfortable chair provided for parents, folding his long legs under the seat to avoid tripping the nurse.

"So tell me why you're here," she invited.

He opened his mouth to reply. He didn't see what good it would do—they were here to keep their appointment with Swaim, obviously—but he knew the medical drill by now. Give a history and another and another, until you finally gave it to the one person who could do something to help you.

"I have a scar," Jack piped up.

It didn't need pointing out. Patrick waited for the nurse to falter, to make some mistake, but her expression was only mildly interested. "Mmm. That's what it says on your chart. Do you mind if I have a look?"

Jack shook his head vigorously. "No." He pulled off his baseball cap.

It looked better, Patrick thought, with the detachment of experience and a father's foolish hope. And it could have been so much worse. Jack had sight in both eyes and a smile and a nose. He had eyelashes and one and a half eyebrows. A clear plastic mask worn in the first year had flattened the worst facial scars on his left cheek. His left ear was deformed, and he probably would never grow a full head of hair on that side. What he had, a soft, dark fuzz, was cut short.

"Like a fighter pilot," Patrick had told him. "Like mine."

The nurse approached the table, smiling as she touched a finger to the discarded cap. "So you're a Durham Bulls fan. Do you go to a lot of games?"

Releasing his breath, Patrick gave the nurse points for her matter-of-fact approach. Jack hated to be treated like a baby. Which was fine, but where the hell was the doctor?

Jack tilted his head to give the nurse better access to his ear. "Some. My dad takes me."

Patrick stood. "Excuse me, but when is Dr. Swaim coming in?"

The curly-haired woman flushed, looking suddenly younger and less self-possessed. "I'm sorry. I should have introduced myself. Dr. Swaim had to go out of town. I'm Dr. Kathryn Sinclair."

Not a nurse. Another doctor. And he'd just offended her with his unthinking assumption. Damn. He didn't mind alienating members of the medical profession, but he needed her cooperation.

Patrick wanted—Jack *needed*—to see Swaim. The reconstructive surgery Jack's doctor had proposed would take several operations spaced weeks apart. Patrick wanted it over and done with before Jack started kindergarten in the fall.

He accepted the hand this substitute doctor held out to him, noting it was small and strong and cool. A nice hand, for a doctor or a woman. "When is Dr. Swaim coming back?"

"I don't know." She inhaled once, sharply, and then favored him with a practiced doctor-to-patient smile. "Mr. MacNeill, I'm sorry about the confusion. We're short-staffed this morning. But I assure you I'm well qualified to examine Jack. I've been studying medicine for almost fourteen years, the last two as a senior fellow in reconstructive surgery at this hospital. I did my pediatrics training at Auburn. There is nothing Dr. Swaim could do for you this morning that I can't."

Patrick ran his hand through his hair. "Look, Dr....?"

"Sinclair."

"Dr. Sinclair." He committed it to memory. "I'm not questioning your qualifications. But I don't think anybody, however well trained, can schedule another doctor's surgery. Particularly when she doesn't know when that doctor's coming back."

The curly-haired doctor frowned, glancing at Jack. Bored with the adults' conversation, he'd opened his crayon case and sprawled on his stomach, drawing on the white protective roll that covered the examining table. His sneakers, enormous on the ends of his thin legs, waved in the air.

"What surgery?" Dr. Sinclair asked.

Patrick sighed. He'd *known* this was a waste of time. "Jack's."

"No, I mean... What type of surgery?"

Surprised he had to spell it out for her, Patrick said, "Multistage reconstruction on the external ear. Cosmetic work on the cheek."

"Now? At his age?"

The concern in her voice lifted the fine hairs on the back of Patrick's neck like a red indicator light flicking on in the cockpit. "Is there some reason why he shouldn't have this surgery at this age?"

"Well, I..." She bit her lip.

"What?"

He should have kept his mouth shut. Faced with a direct opportunity to disagree with one of her colleagues, the pretty little doctor closed medical ranks. He understood and admired loyalty, but at the moment hers was damned inconvenient.

She adjusted the stethoscope around her neck. "As you say, your son is Dr. Swaim's patient. I'm sure there's a sound medical reason for Dr. Swaim's decision."

"But it wouldn't be yours," Patrick guessed. He didn't know why he was trying to pin her down. Swaim was the director of the burn center. He'd treated Jack since the accident. This woman, wherever she'd been educated, however she'd been trained, was barely older than he was. She couldn't match Swaim's experience.

"I didn't say that. So." She left off fussing with the thing around her neck to shove her hands deep in the pockets of her white lab coat. "I'll have the nurse call you to set up an appointment when Dr. Swaim returns."

That suited Patrick fine. He wasn't getting anywhere with the lady doctor. In any way. "That'll be fine. Come on, buddy. Hop on down."

Jack sat up, the paper crinkling under him. "That's it?"

The doctor's face softened. "That's it."

"Aren't you gonna…"

"Nope."

"Cool." Jack jumped off the table, his sneakers hitting the floor with a double thump.

The two adults smiled at one another. She had a pretty smile, Patrick thought. Nice teeth. Big brown eyes alive with intelligent humor. Annoyed with himself for noticing, he concentrated on Jack.

"Don't forget your drawing stuff."

"Oh, right."

Importantly, Jack hurried back to the table and began to brush his crayons into the bright yellow box. By the door, Patrick shifted his weight, impatient to be gone.

"How long has he been doing that?" the doctor asked quietly.

Patrick straightened. "What?"

She nodded toward Jack. "Using his right hand like that."

Patrick watched closely as Jack flicked the last two crayons into the box and snapped the lid. He couldn't see anything wrong. "Like what?"

"His fingers are curled."

Patrick's heart jerked as he stared at his son's fingers. They weren't. They were fine. Scarred, sure, but straight. There had been a whole set of operations for function right after the accident. The tendon damage caused by the fire had healed.

"He always holds them like that," he said dismissively. "He's just tired. He was drawing before we came in."

Jack bumped into his legs, tugging at the pad of paper under his arm. "Do you want to see?"

She blinked. "All right. Please."

Proudly, Jack paged through his art pad and held it up. So the kid had taken a shine to the lady doctor, Patrick thought. So what? It was nice of her to take an interest. That didn't mean they had to see her again.

"That's excellent. I like the way you drew the feathers. Lots of detail."

"Do you want to keep it?"

Dr. Sinclair looked uncertainly at Patrick. He shrugged.

"Thank you," she said gravely. "I'd like that very much."

She didn't hug the boy, Patrick thought, the way Holly would have had she lived, the way his own mother might. Holly had been generous with spontaneous gestures of affection. Bridget MacNeill, Patrick's mother, was as openhanded with hugs as with spankings. He wondered if the doctor just wasn't naturally warm-natured or if she worried the kid might have something contagious. A doctor might think like that. Jack didn't appear to notice.

"Bye," he said, turning at the door.

She smiled then. She really did have nice teeth. "Goodbye.'' Over the child's head, her eyes met Patrick's. "I'll, um, speak to Dr. Swaim as soon as he gets back.''

"Good. Thanks.''

It was what he wanted, wasn't it? Only the best for his boy. So why, as he watched the doctor sashay down the hall in her sexless baggy coat, was he aware of a faint feeling of disappointment?

Frustration gnawed Kate's stomach. Perched at the desk in her dim, air-conditioned cubicle, she pressed two fingers under her breastbone, as if she could rub the burn away. Common sense and medical training told her to eat. Instead, she sipped at her third—or was it fourth?—cup of coffee, studying the file spread out before her, trying to drown her nagging dissatisfaction in hard work and caffeine. Nothing new there.

Kate took pride in her analytic intelligence. Amy got the beauty, their mother always said, and heart and charm, and Kate got the brains. Her mind dug and worried at problems with the tenacity of a trailer-park dog going after a possum.

Four-year-old Jack MacNeill was a problem.

Kate leafed back through the thick folder labeled MAC-NEILL, JOHN, trying to reconcile the clinic notes with her observations from that morning and her memories from four years ago. At the time of the accident that maimed baby Jack, Kate had been gearing up for Auburn, to be groomed for an eventual return to Jefferson's burn unit. But even in her stressed-out and sleep-deprived final days, the MacNeills had made an impression. It seemed everyone connected with the burn unit had been touched in some way by that particular patient. Iron Man, the nurses had dubbed the baby who refused to die.

The title could just as well apply to his father. Kate recalled Patrick MacNeill's stoic response four years ago to his family's devastation, his steady presence in his son's hospital room. Whatever rage or grief the father had felt, he'd been a formidable advocate, insisting that he be informed and involved in every step of baby Jack's treatment.

So maybe she had two problems.

She had a sudden vision of the man's vital hands, arrogant chin and measuring blue eyes and expelled her breath sharply. Sexual attraction was another problem she didn't need. Thumbing another antacid off the roll in her pocket, Kate popped it in her mouth, sucking furiously as she read. The chalky cherry flavor warred with the bitter taste of coffee. She crunched the tablet down anyway.

Methodically, she went through the surgery notes, progress reports and exam charts, page after page of Dr. Gerald Swaim's spiky, black writing. The burn unit's director was certainly conscientious, despite an old-boy attitude that made Kate arch like her cat. He was well established and well regarded. If he said elective cosmetic surgery was called for in the MacNeill child's case, then of course he was right. Of course he was.

She just didn't happen to agree with him.

Her gut flared again. Kate covered her groan with a cough and another sip of coffee. The last thing she wanted to do at this point in her career was antagonize the director of her unit. Burn doctors were the elite of medicine. For outsider Kate, to attain that level of excellence, to make a difference on that scale, was the culmination of fourteen years' hard work. She fully expected Swaim to offer her an attending slot when her fellowship expired in June, but she needed his goodwill. Maybe she wasn't as politically savvy as some of her colleagues, maybe she didn't play golf, but she was darn sure that second-guessing the center's director wasn't the best way to get his support.

Patrick MacNeill's eyes, blue as flame and hard as steel, burned against the background of medical records, judging and finding her wanting.

Kate swallowed. Look, she argued against the demand in those eyes, there's nothing I can do. You didn't want your son

to see me. You wouldn't let me examine him. You thought I
was the nurse. Her fault, she thought. She should have introduced herself immediately. Still, she fanned the little spark of
indignation produced by Patrick MacNeill's unthinking dis-
crimination, hoping to fuel her resolve. How could she question a senior surgeon's call on the strength of his clinical notes
and her fleeting observation?

She couldn't, Kate decided. For the child's sake, she would
mention her concern about his hand. Swaim could determine
whether to take that matter any further. But she wasn't going
to say a word about the advisability of performing elective
surgery on a preschooler. She didn't want the program director
thinking she was questioning his expertise.

Patrick MacNeill was not her problem. Jack MacNeill was
not her patient. She had no authority to interfere in his case.

Kate stared at the chart in front of her until the black lines
wavered like ants marching on a picnic. In spite of the chalky
sweet antacid, she had a sour taste in her mouth. No authority,
sure. But didn't she have the responsibility?

"Sharon, there's been a mistake," Kate complained, stalking down the hall toward the nurses' station. "I can't possibly
have another appointment with the MacNeill boy. He was in
here two days ago."

Even to her own ears, she sounded too sharp. Three days
of managing a double caseload were definitely taking their toll.
The news that Swaim was expected back early next week
didn't do a thing to chase away the worries spinning ratlike
in her head and gnawing holes in her stomach lining. Kate
knew she was considered more reasonable than some of her
colleagues, but that didn't mean she was liked. The awareness
twinged without bleeding, like an old scar. Serious Kate had
never been liked.

The burn nurse looked up from stacking sterile instruments
to peer at Kate's clipboard. "Your two o'clock?"

"Yes."

Sharon sniffed and resumed loading the cart. "No mistake. The father called and said he wanted to see you again."

Kate pressed her lips together. "Not me. Swaim."

"Not Swaim. He specifically asked for you."

"Oh." Oh, shoot. She couldn't afford to alienate the nursing staff. In spite of the natural antagonism that sometimes existed between surgeons and nurses, Sharon Williams was one of Kate's few allies in the unit. "Did he, um, mention why?"

Sharon raised her eyebrows, thrusting her chin in the direction of the patient waiting room. "No. Why don't you try asking him?"

Before she could help herself, before she could stop and prepare, Kate glanced through the wired glass to the tidy rows of upholstered chairs. Patrick MacNeill paced between them, too big to be contained, too energetic to stand still. He raked his dark hair with his fingers and then jammed his big hands in his pockets, straining his flight jacket across his broad shoulders.

It was unprofessional, it was irrational, it was embarrassing, but when Kate looked at him her jaw went slack and her knees sagged.

She closed her mouth and stiffened her spine. She would not let him get to her. At least, she wouldn't let it show. She'd spent too many years being patronized by aggressive male colleagues, too much of her life being intimidated by assured and handsome men, to pant and sigh over some virile specimen now.

"All right, I will. Thank you, Sharon."

Ignoring the nurse's amused, speculative look, Kate approached the carpeted waiting room, a professional smile pasted to her face. Young Jack MacNeill slumped in his chair, swinging oversize feet. Despite his early childhood trauma, he was going to grow up tall, Kate thought. Like his father.

Something in the child's patient, dejected posture touched

her heart. Without thinking, she spoke. "Hey, Jack. So you guys just couldn't wait to see me again, is that it?"

She regretted the stupidly flirtatious words the instant they left her mouth. But the boy brightened, smiling up at her from under the bill of his cap.

His father stopped pacing. "Dr. Sinclair. Thanks for seeing us again on such short notice."

She shook hands, noting the strength and warmth of his grip, proud of her composure. "You're quite welcome. Won't you come this way?"

In spite of the polite distance he maintained, she was too conscious of him as he followed her through the double doors and down the hall, his size, his tread, his...maleness, she supposed. And wasn't that bomber jacket a bit of an affectation? It made him look like some World War II pinup boy. When they took their seats, Jack up on the table, Patrick MacNeill in the chair by the door, she propped against the examining room's tiny sink instead of perching on her customary stool. She needed every inch of advantage she could get.

"So." She hugged her clipboard to her chest. "What's new?"

Jack turned wide eyes on his father.

Patrick smiled reassuringly at the boy before turning to Kate. "The other day you said—you mentioned you'd like a look at Jack's hand. I didn't think much of it at the time." His fierce blue eyes met hers without apology. "But that night I watched him. And yesterday. He can't—he doesn't seem to be using his thumb like he used to. I want you to take a look at it now."

Satisfaction flared in Kate. She liked being right. She'd like nothing better than to help Jack MacNeill and prove her worth as a consultant to Gerald Swaim. On the other hand, she didn't want the exalted director to think she was questioning his judgment or encroaching on his case.

She stepped to the exam table, carefully keeping her voice neutral and light. "Of course. Let's see what we've got here."

Jack's ears shrunk to his shoulders. "Is it gonna hurt?"

By the door, Patrick MacNeill's big body stirred protectively and then stilled. Kate thought of what the boy had endured, what they'd both endured, so far, and drew on her pediatrics training for a technique she sometimes found helpful with small patients. Swaim disdained her soft approach, she knew, and the boy was Swaim's case. But she was the one examining him, darn it.

"I'm going to bend your fingers. It might get a little uncomfortable. Do you want to sit on your dad's lap?"

"Can I?"

"If it's all right with your dad. You're a pretty big boy."

"All the MacNeills are big and tough. But I can take him," Patrick growled. He rose from his chair and swooped the child into the air, making him giggle with delight.

"Rough and tough and good enough!" the boy shouted gleefully. "That's what Uncle Sean says."

Good enough for what? Kate wondered dryly, fascinated by this glimpse into the masculine MacNeill clan. But Patrick MacNeill mounted the long, narrow table and held his son comfortably on his lap, waiting for her to examine him.

Goodness, Kate thought. This technique sure felt different when she used it with her patients' moms. Clearing her throat, she stepped between the tall man's knees and took Jack's hand, stabilizing it in both of hers.

"I'm going to do some exercises with you. I bet you already know a lot of them, but I don't want you to help me, all right? You can tell me if it feels uncomfortable."

Jack nodded gravely. One after the other, at different angles and degrees, Kate flexed, separated and curled his fingers, thumb, palm and wrist. The familiar exercises drew her concentration, blunting her awareness of the big man looming over them both.

Several times, in response to her touch, Jack stiffened. Once he cried out and pulled away. Kate stifled her own totally useless empathetic response as Patrick MacNeill cuddled the boy, his deep baritone soothing. Jack sighed and leaned back against that broad chest, turning his face into his father's arm.

Patrick nodded at her over the child's head. "Okay. Go on."

Appreciation welled in Kate for his support. Appreciation, and just a tingle of envy for the love that flowed from father to son. What on earth had gotten into her today? Methodically, Kate returned to testing the full range of motion in Jack's hand. The results were clear. Too clear. This time, a correct diagnosis brought her little satisfaction.

She patted Jack's hand and released it. "That's great. We're all done now."

"You did good, buddy." Patrick praised his son.

Jack squirmed. "Can I get down now?"

"You bet." Patrick's voice as he spoke to his son was cheerfully casual, in contrast to his watchful, wary eyes.

Reluctantly, Kate met the question in his gaze. "Maybe we could speak alone? Jack could go with Nurse Williams. There's a playroom attached to the—"

He held up one large palm, forestalling her. "We know the playroom. Go ahead, buddy. I'll be along in a minute."

Yes, Kate thought, they would know the playroom. She'd reviewed Jack's chart. She knew how many surgeries the boy had been through, how many hospital stays, how many days and weeks of therapy and recuperation in the first two years following the accident. She saw the cost in the quick hug the child required from his dad before trotting off, hand in hand, with Sharon Williams. She saw the burden in his father's tense shoulders, the profound weariness etched in the corners of his eyes, the doubt that all his masculine assurance could not disguise or allay.

It made what she had to say to him now doubly hard.

Chapter 2

Dr. Sinclair steered him to her office, a gray, featureless cubicle with towering files and ruthlessly organized shelves. Patrick stiffened with dislike. He couldn't imagine a less welcoming or less feminine environment. No pictures, no photographs, no nonsense. A philodendron dropped yellowing leaves in one corner.

A bad sign. He hoped the lady doctor took better care of her patients than her plants.

She leaned forward earnestly across the neat stacks on her desk. "In the majority of cases, this kind of operation is done as soon as possible and not again unless we see compromised function. Jack is very young. I wouldn't even suggest we operate except that this is Jack's dominant hand."

"Why not?"

"Frankly, preschoolers don't cooperate very well in their own physical therapy. Without a great deal of parental support—"

Patrick straightened in his ridiculous little chair. He didn't need another doctor preaching to him about the role of loved ones in the healing process. "He's got parental support. What do you need to do to fix the hand?"

She sat back, as if his response wasn't quite what she expected. "Well, we... Surgery is the first step."

He'd figured that. He was already planning how to break the news to Jack and calculating the time he'd need to take off work. If he called his mom, Patrick knew, Bridget MacNeill would hop the next available flight from Boston to be with her son and grandson. But both his parents had put their lives on hold for him after the accident. A potent combination of love and pride prevented him from asking for their help again.

He and Jack would make it on their own.

Dr. Sinclair cleared her throat. "We can replace the skin of the affected joints. But after the reconstructive procedure, you will need to exercise Jack's hand through a passive range of motion many times a—"

He appreciated her meticulous attempt to explain, but it wasn't necessary. "Who's the best person to do the surgery?" he interrupted.

"I could do it." She capped and uncapped her pen several times. The unconscious nervous gesture was oddly appealing. "But Dr. Swaim should be back soon, and your son *is* Dr. Swaim's patient. I think it would be best if we schedule the procedure for his return."

She hadn't really answered his question, Patrick noted, his brows drawing together in concern. But what she said made sense.

"Replace the skin, you said. You mean grafts?"

Holding his gaze, she nodded, her brown eyes wide and compassionate.

Hell. As clearly as if it were yesterday, he could hear the screams of his infant son as grafts were peeled from his uninjured back and stomach to replace the charred skin on head and arms and hands. Twelve days of slow and painstaking torture to combat the destruction of one drunk driver's moment of carelessness.

He retreated from her unspoken pity, sitting to military attention in his tiny chair. "How many?" he rapped. "Where?"

"It's a relatively small area," she assured him. "We'll replace little diamond-shaped pieces in the crease of these three fingers and the palm." She held out her own hand to illustrate. "And here, at the thumb. Dr. Swaim should be able to harvest what he needs in one procedure."

He forced himself to ask, for Jack's sake. "Where would he take it from?"

"The graft? He can probably get all he needs in one long strip from the groin."

Patrick winced with a grown man's reflex action and a father's sympathy.

"I know," the doctor said kindly. "But it's really a very shallow, thin piece. One skin thickness. Jack will have no visible scarring. He won't even need a dressing there."

"How long will he be in the hospital?"

"Overnight," she answered promptly. "Home the next day."

"Fine. Let's do it."

A hint of exasperation appeared on her face. "Mr. Mac-Neill, do you— You do understand the implications of what I've been saying."

He understood them, sure. She was telling him his son needed to undergo another complex, painful procedure to ready him for a protracted and even more painful course of physical therapy. Swell. Leaning back in his chair, Patrick crossed one ankle over the opposite knee. "Yes."

"There is no point to this surgery without extensive follow-up at home."

Irritation at her prodding clamped his jaw. Any time the brass wanted a job done, they sent in the Marines. If Marine pilot Patrick MacNeill said he'd do something, then it was as good as done. Enough already.

On the other hand, Patrick reminded himself, the doctor also had a job to do. And actually, he appreciated her honesty. In his experience—and it was broader and harder than he once could ever have imagined—not all doctors troubled to make sure their patients' parents were truly informed.

"Yeah, you made that clear."

"I just want you to understand—"

"Doctor," he interrupted, moderating his tone so as not to give offense to the well-meaning lady doctor, "I may not have a medical degree, but if you speak slowly and use little words, I can follow you fine. Jack is losing the use of his hand. He needs an operation and he needs physical therapy. Okay."

Her rounded chin lifted. "We're not talking about fifteen minutes twice a day. In adult patients, we tell them to go through the full range of motion every hour on the hour that they're awake. A child won't do that. You will have to do everything for him. His exercises will become the center of your relationship with your son."

The prospect appalled Patrick, but he spoke firmly. "Whatever it takes. Whatever he needs."

The doctor's face softened. She was pretty when the tight lines bracketing her mouth relaxed. He didn't want to notice that, or respond to the sympathy in her eyes.

"Your commitment to Jack is commendable. I wish all my patients had that kind of support. But I want you to realize the burden this will place, not only on him, but on you. This development has to have come as a surprise. If there's anything I can do... Anything you want to discuss... There are psychologists here on staff who can help you."

Patrick crossed his arms over his chest. Any minute now, she was going to invite him *to share his feelings,* like that misguided grief counselor he'd been forced to see after the accident. He wondered what the curvy little doctor would say if he suggested she help him work out his worries and frustrations in bed. Probably toss him out on his ear. He flashed her a smile of pure amusement at the thought.

To test his theory, to tease her, to turn her focus away from him, he lifted an eyebrow. "If you think analysis is really necessary. Your couch or mine?"

She flushed the color of his mother's wild Irish roses, but her eyes were steady. "You're joking," she said flatly.

He grinned at her, oddly pleased both by her discomfiture and her recovery. "Yeah." He could have dropped it there. He should have dropped it there. But some impulse from his Top Gun days made him push. "Unless you're free on Friday night."

"I'm never free, Mr. MacNeill. If I'm not on call or doing rounds or paperwork, I catch up on my sleep."

"And sometimes on your laundry," he guessed.

"Sometimes. How did you know?"

He shrugged. "I do the same. Only it's clients and planes, not clinics and patients. I run a charter business out of Dumont airport."

She sat back, clasping her hands together on top of her clipboard. "You're a pilot."

He nodded, wondering what had brought the reserve back into her voice.

"Doesn't that take you away from your son?"

He stiffened at the challenge. "No. That's the advantage of being your own boss. I handle the books, the lessons and the day trips. Ray—my partner—takes the longer flights, and his wife helps out with the schedule. When Jack can't come up with me, he stays with Shelby in the office." He didn't add that with Ray and Shelby's first baby on the way, that arrangement was going to have to change soon. He didn't believe in anticipating trouble. It would find him in its own good time.

The doctor fingered the edges of the thick file on her desk. "I don't mean to criticize. It's clear you've done a wonderful job with Jack. But with all the other demands on you, are you sure you can handle the kind of physical therapy he will need?"

"Sure."

"Because without it—"

"I can handle it," he interrupted. To deflect her persistence, he asked, "So, do we have a date?"

Her lips curled in a cool approximation of her pretty smile. "You don't have time for a social life," she said.

That was one way to put it. He hadn't had sex with a woman in years. Amused by her prim assessment, he relaxed in his chair. "No, I don't. But maybe I'm prepared to make an exception."

He was still teasing. Jack had been his single focus and his only passion since the accident. Of course he was teasing. But even as he kidded with the lady doctor, he realized with a sense of shock that he could mean it. Something about that tart mouth and those wary, intelligent eyes got under his skin. He didn't understand the needling attraction. He didn't want it.

And apparently neither did she, because she recapped her pen with a decisive click. "Well, I'm not. I don't date."

Intrigued despite himself, he raised his eyebrows. "Ever?"

She flushed. "Patients."

"I'm not your patient."

"Jack is."

"No, he's not. You just told me Dr. Swaim would do the operation."

She pounced on that one like a cat going after a cricket. "Yes. He'll be back next week. I've told Sharon to schedule his appointments on a need-to basis. She'll go over the paperwork with you and give you the forms for Jack's lab work. I'm sure Dr. Swaim will meet with you then to explain the procedure further and answer any questions you might have. So." She stood, straightening the edges of the already squared stacks on her desk. "Best of luck, Mr. MacNeill. I'm sure everything will go well with Jack."

I'm a busy woman. Now get out of my office. The words were as clear as if she'd spoken them out loud.

Patrick shrugged and unfolded from his chair. He had no

more time to waste than she did, and even less energy. If the doctor wanted to keep things impersonal, that was fine with him.

"Thanks," he said.

They shook hands. He turned to the door and saw what he hadn't seen coming into the room. What he couldn't see while he faced her across her neat, hyper-organized desk.

Over one of the file cabinets, where she could see it every day from the other side of that desk, the brisk, impersonal lady doctor had taped Jack's drawing of eagles.

So the man had made a pass at her. For heaven's sake, Katie Sue, get over it.

Kate jiggled her refrigerator door, staring with a total lack of enthusiasm at eggs and ketchup and a hardening loaf of bread. A suspect carton of cottage cheese occupied the top shelf. The vegetable drawer revealed a pale green stalk of celery, a limp reminder of her resolution to watch her diet.

Blackwell twined around her ankles, complaining it was late, she was bored and where was dinner?

"In a minute, Blackie."

Kate groaned. Oh, great. She was turning into a cliché: the harried professional, hip-high in her thirties, eating alone and talking to her cat.

Why on earth had he made a pass at her?

She wasn't the type of woman guys hit on. Scorned in middle school, dateless in high school, driven in college, she knew most men found her combination of brains and ambition either boring or intimidating. Even at the hospital, where frustration, exhaustion and stress made unlikely bed fellows, she held herself aloof from casual affairs. Hot glances and surreptitious brushes in the hall were not her style.

Eggs and toast, she decided. It would have to be eggs and toast again. Balancing the bread on top of the egg carton, she reached for the butter. Blackwell crouched as Kate banged the door closed with her hip. Only once in her first year of residency had Kate allowed herself to believe that a man could actually be interested in her. By her third year, she'd learned better. It wasn't a lesson she was eager to repeat.

Which made Patrick MacNeill's reaction to her, and her response to him, even more confusing. She slammed the bread into the toaster and set the butter sizzling on the stove. After the wreckage of that one romance, she'd trained herself not to send out the signals of a woman interested in or vulnerable to a man's notice. She reserved all her attention for her patients.

So why had Jack MacNeill's father come on to her?

It didn't mean anything, Kate decided, breaking eggs into a bowl. He didn't mean anything. She attacked the eggs with a fork. Obviously, he'd felt threatened enough by her assessment of his parenting skills to retaliate by turning on his flyboy charm.

Well, it wouldn't work. The days when she could be rattled by unadulterated male magnetism were in the past. Shy, plain, socially awkward Katie Sue from Blue Moon Trailer Park was Dr. Kathryn Sinclair now.

As if to give the lie to her words, the phone rang. With a sinking feeling, Kate recognized her sister's soft, plaintive voice.

"Hey, sis." She heard her own lapse into their childhood drawl and winced. Shifting the receiver to her other ear, she turned down the burner under the eggs. "No, no, it's all right. It's not too late. I was just making myself some dinner. What do you need?"

"I don't need anything, Katie. Can't I just call to say hello?"

"Sure, you can," Kate said heartily. Too heartily. "How are you?"

"Good."

"The kids? Mama?"

"They're good, too. Katie—" excitement swelled in her sister's voice like a shiny soap bubble "—I got another job."

Well, Kate thought resignedly, transferring her eggs to a

plate, at least it wasn't another man. A string of Prince Charm-
ings had ridden through her sister's life, and none of them had
stuck around for happily-ever-after. The last one hadn't even
hung on long enough to see his infant daughter born.

"What kind of job?" Kate asked.

"Waitress down at Newton's Steakhouse. Pay's not much,
but the tips are going to be good."

"Hours?"

"Four nights a week. That's all I can manage with Billy
out of school. Mama's coming over to sit."

Kate rummaged for a clean fork and tried to remember what
Amy had said the last time they'd discussed their mother.
What could she say that would be supportive without her sister
taking it as know-it-all Kate butting in again? "I thought you
didn't want her watching them any more. Something about
Jenny's formula, wasn't it? Or Billy sassed her or something."

"Jenny's on premixed formula now."

Kate backed off. "Okay."

"And Billy's going to be good. He promised."

"Fine."

"You don't have to sound so discouraging."

Kate set down her fork and pushed her plate away, old
hurts, old resentments rising like bile. Obviously, she'd said
the wrong thing. Again.

"I thought you'd be happy for me," Amy continued, ag-
grieved. "You're always telling me how satisfying it is to
work."

Kate thought of the cases she'd seen that afternoon, the
young mother maimed when a smoldering cigarette caught her
mattress on fire, the baby scalded in a hot tub. She thought
about little Jack MacNeill, and the burn director's probable
reaction when he returned from vacation next week and found
she'd put off one surgery and scheduled another. Satisfying
wasn't quite the word for it. But she wasn't about to confess
as much to her sister.

"I am happy for you," she insisted, trying to return to a

rational plane. "I just thought you didn't want Mama watching the kids."

"It's not like I have a choice, is it?" her younger sister asked.

"Day care?" Kate suggested tentatively.

"I can't afford day care."

Kate sighed. "If you need more money, Amy..."

"No! I didn't call asking for money. I don't want your money. I wanted to tell you about my new job, and all you ever do is tell me how I'm screwing up."

Kate felt a familiar kick of guilt. "Sorry. I didn't mean... I'm sure it will all work out the way you want it to. Congratulations," she added for good measure.

"Thanks. Are you coming out on Saturday? The kids would love to see you. So would I."

"Um, I don't think so." The phone line hummed. Kate tried to explain to the reproachful silence on the other end. "I'm on call this weekend, I have a paper to present on Monday, and Swaim gets back sometime early next week. I've been seeing his patients for him, and I want to make sure my paperwork's all caught up. I just can't make it."

"Sure," her sister said. "I understand."

But she didn't, not really. Kate could hear it in her voice, the disappointment that once again Kate was putting her duties at the hospital before her responsibilities to her own family. "Maybe next week."

"Sure," Amy said again.

They chatted a few minutes longer, but the chance for any real conversation was lost. Frustrated, Kate hung up. She couldn't be the friend her sister hoped for, any more than she'd ever been the daughter her mother wanted.

It was true, what she'd told Patrick MacNeill. She wasn't free to pursue emotional involvements. For one thing, she didn't have the time. But it was more than that.

Face it, Katie Sue. You're a bust at personal relationships. She should remember that the next time she was tempted to get involved with appealing little Jack MacNeill or his sexy father.

Kate pressed her hand to her stomach, staring disconsolately at her plate. It didn't matter that the toast was cold and the eggs were tepid. She wasn't hungry anymore.

"You want me to assist in the MacNeill boy's surgery?"

Kate heard the lack of enthusiasm in her own voice and struggled for control.

Gerald Swaim, director of burn medicine at Jefferson University Hospital, flicked her an impatient glance. He wasn't used to having his pronouncements questioned. A handsome man in his late fifties with a full head of silver hair and a massive medical reputation, he expected instant understanding from his students, instant compliance from his nurses, and instant adulation from women. He usually got all three.

"Do you have a problem with that, Dr. Sinclair?"

"No," Kate assured him.

Of course, she lied. Something about the boy who drew eagles and the man who flew airplanes threatened her hard-won and carefully-preserved objectivity. She didn't want anything further to do with little Iron Man or his father.

And yet her objections were completely unreasonable. She knew the procedure. In this case, she'd actually been the one to recommend it. More and more, as a senior fellow, she worked independently, but it wasn't uncommon for Swaim to request her presence in his OR. She should welcome the opportunity to observe his technique, to refine and perfect her own.

"Seven o'clock Friday morning?" she confirmed, writing it down.

"Yes. And I'll want you to scrub in on the Heller case after that."

Kate nodded and made another note. Eight months ago, when Janet Heller was severely disfigured in a house fire, Kate had been part of the admitting hydrotherapy team. Pressure garments had done their work. Now Swaim would remove the thick, swollen red scar tissue and replace it with grafts of the patient's own skin. Kate was eager to assist a process that would help restore not only Janet's face but her spirits. Burn medicine demanded a lot from its doctors, but it paid them in dividends of courage and hope.

So Kate studied both cases and read up diligently on both procedures. She scrubbed in on Friday morning prepared to answer questions and admire Swaim's expertise.

They were forty-five minutes into the first operation when all that changed. Swaim had sutured the first graft into the crease of Jack MacNeill's ring finger. He was tying the long stitches down over the glycerine-soaked cotton packed into the joint when he made a muffled sound of impatience and stopped.

Kate's heart thumped. From her vantage point, everything was fine. She glanced from the monitors to the child's face, bleached above the faded dinosaur print of his hospital gown. Jack was okay.

The delicate instruments poised above the child's hand glinted as Swaim lifted them, stepping back.

"Are you prepared to do the next graft?" he challenged Kate.

Her surgical mask helped hide her surprise. "Of course," she said, and moved smoothly to take over.

She did the graft on the middle finger, anticipating Swaim would correct her, expecting him to stop her. He did not. She relaxed into the next procedure, letting her skill and training take over, repairing and creating with tiny pressures and sensitive movements, with sure joy and confident precision. She split, grafted and packed the crease of index finger and thumb, unconscious of the passing time, uncaring of the sweat that plastered her hair under her cap and ran between her breasts to soak her bra. The burn unit was always hot, the temperature adjusted to keep their patients warm. Destroyed skin could no longer do its job of regulating body temperature.

It was almost two hours later that Kate knotted the last suture and looked up to find Swaim avidly watching her. He nodded.

"Not too bad," he said grudgingly. "Wrap it up and put a bulky dressing over the top. I'm going to talk to the father."

Kate retrieved her jaw and found her tongue. "Don't you want to wait until the patient comes out of anesthesia?"

A mottled red climbed above the strings of Swaim's mask. "Wrap up MacNeill and scrub in for Janet Heller. I want you ready when I get back."

Fine, thought Kate furiously, staring at the surgeon's retreating back. She'd prefer to see the little boy on the table settled and recovered herself. She didn't want to talk to Patrick MacNeill anyway.

"Whew," the OR nurse muttered, once the door had closed safely behind Swaim. "What bug got in his briefs?"

Kate paused her binding of Jack's small hand in gauze. It wouldn't do to let the nurse see that she agreed with her. "It's a difficult case," she said primly.

The nurse wouldn't be discouraged.

"Well, you did all right, Dr. Sinclair. Wonder why he stopped. It's not like him to turn his surgery over to another doctor."

It wasn't, Kate acknowledged. Gerald Swaim, an accomplished surgeon at the height of his powers, was proud of his skill and jealous of his prerogatives. He might assign his scut work to the residents, but he rarely relinquished command in surgery.

Her pleasure in the perfectly executed procedure ebbed, replaced by a small, hard kernel of doubt. What had happened to make the department chief abandon his customary control? Had he simply been testing her, or had something gone wrong?

And, if it had, how would Patrick MacNeill respond to the news?

Chapter 3

At one-twelve in the morning, Kate emerged from her dinky office clutching her fifth cup of coffee and an armload of charts. The unit was never totally dark or entirely silent. The halls vibrated with a fluorescent hum and the blips and beeps of monitors. From behind closed doors, she heard a cough, a moan, a muted television. Laughter and chatter drifted from the nurses' station as they celebrated somebody's birthday.

Solitary Kate hadn't been invited, though she knew that if she stopped by the charge nurse would offer her a piece of cake. She turned the other way, down the hall, toward the patient rooms.

The kernel of doubt hadn't gone away. It swelled under her breastbone, a small, indigestible lump, a tiny hot spot that upset her stomach and her concentration.

She wasn't on call tonight. Roberts, the attending, had taken the four o'clock rounds. She had no real reason to drop her sliding stack of paperwork and squeak down the brightly painted, dimly lit floor like a ghost in orthopedic shoes. No reason. Only a burning in her gut. Quietly, she depressed the handle to Jack MacNeill's room and opened the door.

A pale rectangle of light spilled across the bed to the raised footrest of the recliner on the other side. Between the tall metal guardrails, Jack sprawled with little-boy abandon, covers pushed down and arms and legs every which way. A teddy bear with a limp bow and well-loved plush supported his bandaged hand.

In the chair, facing his child, slept Patrick MacNeill.

Even relaxed in sleep, he looked hard and male and faintly dangerous. His wide shoulders crowded the oversize recliner to its limit. Ignoring her reaction to that long, well-muscled body, Kate slipped to the foot of the bed to check Jack's chart. But she couldn't dismiss the queer twist of her heart at the sight of Jack's face turned confidingly to his father, or the way Patrick's large hand protectively spanned his son's knee as they slept.

Don't let it get to you, Katie Sue. She forced her attention back to the patient chart, angling it to catch the light from the door. Blood pressure, temp, intake and output all looked normal. Good. Stepping to the side of the bed, she reached for Jack's swaddled hand.

And then something made her look up, across his out-flung legs, into the deep-set, dark blue eyes of Patrick MacNeill.

"Is anything wrong?"

His voice, soft with caution and rough with sleep, reverberated inside her. Scolding herself for both her foolish reaction and the equally unreasonable apprehension that had goaded her here, Kate shook her head.

"No, I was just...I thought I'd just see how he was doing."

Gently, she lifted the sleeping boy's hand. The bulky dressing covered everything but his fingernails. In the dim light from the doorway, his ring finger looked blue. Frowning, she snapped on her penlight.

At her swift intake of breath, Patrick straightened the recliner, dropping his long legs to the floor. "What?"

Kate didn't answer, suppressing her own alarm, concentrating on unrolling the ace bandage over the gauze. The child whimpered and was still.

"What is it?" his father demanded.

Jack's ring finger had definitely turned blue. His circulation was blocked. Kate cursed silently.

"Nothing," she said. "I can take care of it. I'll be right back."

A nurse server loaded with supplies was parked in the hall. She grabbed a pair of sterile scissors and hurried back to the room to find Jack awake and Patrick soothing him in his deep baritone voice.

"Hey, Jack-o. It's okay, buddy. Ssh, now, it's okay."

He'd lowered the guardrail to sit beside his son and hold him. The sight of the two dark heads so close together, the man's broad chest supporting the boy's narrow shoulders, made something quake inside her.

She drew a deep breath to steady herself and smiled at them both. "Hey, Jack, it's Dr. Sinclair. Do you want to introduce me to your bear?"

The child regarded her warily from under thick dark lashes. "He's Finn MacCool."

Kate blinked. She'd figured on something like Fuzzy or Teddy. "Who?"

Patrick explained, unsettling amusement in his eyes. "Fionn mac Cumhail, the Irish warrior hero. From the Fenian poems."

"He killed monsters," Jack offered.

"Oh. Well, good," Kate said. Her own childhood hadn't included Gaelic poetry or heroes, but she understood and appreciated the talisman Patrick had given his son against the monsters that must lurk under his hospital bed. "Do you think he could help me out here?"

"How?" Jack asked cautiously.

"Maybe—Mr. Cool?—could hold your left hand, like this, see? And I'm going to hold the other one. I want to take a look at your stitches."

With sure, gentle movements, Kate tucked the bear into the crook of the boy's left arm and took his right, uncomfortably aware of Patrick's warm bulk and watchful gaze. Jack didn't resist as she unwrapped the gauze dressing.

"Why?" Patrick asked from over his head.

Kate concentrated on Jack's hand, addressing her words to them both. "Well, see how this finger is a different color, like it's bruised? That means the vein has too much pressure on it from the little bandage inside. I'm just going to cut a few stitches."

The child's hand trembled in her own. "I don't want you to cut it."

"Not your finger," Kate assured him. "Just two stitches. Can you hold still while I do that?"

Patrick kissed his son's hair. "Sure he can."

"Is it gonna hurt?" Jack asked.

"No," Kate stated positively.

Jack sighed and turned his face into his father's arm. "Okay."

Patrick's dark blue gaze met hers over the boy's head. "We trust you."

His words touched her. His confidence flattered and scared her. Her breath lodged in her throat. Ignoring her stupid, totally involuntary reaction, Kate eased the thin point of the scissors under the dark thread of the first suture. "This will only take a second."

It took five. Patrick raised his eyebrows as she stepped back from the bed. "Is that it?"

Kate forced herself to smile. "That's it."

"It didn't hurt," Jack said.

Her smile came more easily this time. "Good."

"Now what?" Patrick demanded.

Her pulse was pounding, as if her own heart could somehow force the blood supply back into the little boy's finger. He was just another patient, Kate reminded herself sharply. Not even her own patient. But her heart was not convinced.

"Now we wait," she said. "If that's all it was, the finger should... Yes, see, it's pinking right up. He'll be fine."

She replaced the gauze and the bulky dressing, careful to leave the tips of the boy's fingers exposed. "All done. Now in seven to ten days the other stitches will come out, and you'll be ready to start physical therapy."

She looked at the chart hanging from the foot of Jack's bed. She ought to make a note. But what would she write? *The illustrious Gerald Swaim goofed in surgery, the attending physician missed the signs during rounds, and I saved the patient's finger and their sorry butts?*

Her stomach lurched at the thought. No. She couldn't write that. She scrawled *Removed two sutures* on the patient chart and escaped into the hall.

It wasn't enough. She knew it wasn't enough. If one of her interns skimped on his progress notes like that, she'd be all over him like bacteria in a petri dish. But she wouldn't, she couldn't, write anything that could be construed as a criticism of the senior surgeons.

Anger burned under her ribs. Absently, she rubbed two fingers just below her breastbone.

The door behind her opened, and Patrick MacNeill came out.

"Thank you," he said quietly. "You were good with him in there. He's already asleep."

Kate straightened away from the wall, reaching for her professional composure. "Children are wonderful, aren't they? It's amazing what they can bounce back from."

Patrick's long, sensitive mouth compressed. Kate realized he'd probably watched Jack bounced too often in his short life. "Yeah, wonderful." He shook his head, as if to dislodge dark memories. "Can I do anything to thank you? Buy you a drink?"

Kate's shock of pleasure was followed by an equally automatic rejection. "Oh, no." *Never get involved with a patient.* "No, thanks."

Patrick didn't appear impressed by her refusal. He didn't move, either. "Sure?"

Kate bit her lip against the tug of temptation. What about another doctor's patient? What about another doctor's patient's father? What harm could that do?

She tilted her chin to look up at this tall, dark-haired, handsome man. The fluorescent lights overhead grayed his healthy tan, emphasizing the tiny creases between his brows and beside his mouth. Lines of temper, she thought, and humor, of passions deeply felt and strongly controlled. It was an attractive combination. But at one-thirty in the morning he looked tired. Kate wondered if he carried the burden of concern all alone. She hadn't seen any other visitors crowding the family room, waiting to share his vigil beside Jack's hospital bed.

Maybe the man needed a distraction. Maybe he needed a break.

"Maybe a cup of coffee in the hospital cafeteria," she said.

He grimaced slightly. "I've had the coffee in your hospital cafeteria. Seems like pretty poor thanks for what you've done, but if that's what you want…"

"That's all I want."

He shrugged. "Okay."

They started down the hall. She had to hurry to keep up with him until he noticed and adjusted his steps.

"Was that a usual complication?" he asked as they reached the elevators.

Honesty and caution warred within her. "Not unusual," she temporized.

"Dr. Swaim didn't tell me to watch for it," he said, punching the Down button. "He didn't tell me much of anything after surgery, except that it had gone well."

"Yes, it did," Kate responded without thinking.

He stopped just inside the elevator doors and pivoted to face her. "Wait a minute. You were there?"

Challenged with a direct question, she gave an honest answer. His concern for his child deserved that much. "I did—I finished the procedure," she admitted.

She felt the tension rising in him like a gathering storm. The air in the elevator practically crackled. "And the blocked circulation in Jack's finger? Were you responsible for that?"

Kate muttered something.

"What?"

"I said, I knew having coffee with you was a bad idea."

"Is that a *yes?*"

"No."

"Are you telling me you weren't responsible?"

Fatigue and worry ate at her. She couldn't be sure anymore if she were covering Swaim's butt or her own. She didn't want to say anything that could implicate the surgeon or jeopardize her own chances at an attending post. But sympathy for Patrick's burden—and pride in her own accomplishments—wouldn't let her keep silent.

"I'm telling you I didn't operate on that finger," she said carefully. "But I watched. The procedure went well. Everything looked fine. Sometimes unanticipated complications just happen."

"Like you *just happened* to stop by."

She was thankful when the elevator doors opened and stepped through them briskly. "I like to check on my patients."

He caught up with her in two strides. She felt his gaze on her as he weighed her response and then nodded, accepting it. "All right. Dr. Sinclair..." Reluctantly, she turned to face him. "I'm grateful."

His voice was earnest, his expression, warm. Kate's cheeks heated with pleasure.

She looked about seventeen when she blushed, Patrick thought, amused. The sight of the decisive lady doctor pink-cheeked with confusion woke a dormant sense of masculine satisfaction. He was going to have to watch himself. With a little encouragement, he might start grunting and thumping his chest.

"Especially since Jack isn't really your patient," he added dryly.

"If he were, I'd still check on him. I just wouldn't have coffee with you."

Her prim attitude tickled the hell out of him. He couldn't help himself. "No? How about sex?"

"Mr. MacNeill—"

"Patrick," he said, mildly sorry about aggravating her after her competent intervention and her kindness to Jack. He must be more tired than he'd thought. He gestured toward the cafeteria line, empty except for the bored-looking server and an intern swaying on her feet. "What'll you have?"

"Coffee. Black."

She was still ticked, he realized. Well, no wonder. "Come on," he coaxed. "I owe you. And I appreciate the company. Really. Thanks."

Her smile flickered. She did have the damnedest smile. It lit her whole face and started a warm glow deep inside him. "You're welcome," she said.

She accepted a tray and a place in line, bypassing the soggy sandwiches and yogurts on ice to help herself to coffee and a cellophane-wrapped slice of Boston cream pie. His surprise must have shown, because her chin angled up again.

"I missed dinner," she explained defensively.

"I'd spring for a hamburger, you know. Even a salad."

"This is all I want."

And if she wanted to deprive herself, it was none of his business. Patrick shrugged. "You're the doctor. You do have your four major food groups there." Smiling at her blank look, he pointed to the whipped cream with the cherry on top and the spongy yellow cake. "Dairy. Fruit. Carbohydrates. And Jack's personal favorite, chocolate."

Her chuckle was warm and surprisingly husky. If a man

weren't careful, he could waste a lot of time figuring ways to hear it again.

"Yes, well, Jack can use the extra calories. Burn survivors typically need to replace a lot of weight. I don't."

Dropping his selection—chips and an apple—onto her tray, he paid the cashier. "You look fine to me." Very fine. Her blue scrubs and limp white coat didn't completely disguise her curvy shape.

"I don't need compliments, Mr. MacNeill. I have no illusions about my body type."

He shook his head over her stubborn denial of her own attractiveness. "You do if you think there's a single thing wrong with it. And call me Patrick."

"Thank you. You can call me Doctor."

For a moment, he thought she was serious. Jarred, he set the tray down on an empty table. And then he caught the buried mischief in her eyes, and his own grin surfaced in response.

"My name's Kate," she said, offering her hand.

Her clasp was like the rest of her, smooth and strong. Patrick had a sudden image of those soft, competent hands moving over his body and practically broke a sweat.

Hell. He needed sleep. He needed his head examined. And since the first was unlikely and he'd always strongly resisted the second, he released her hand quickly and sat.

"You're working late tonight," he observed. "Are you on call?"

"No. I like to work at night. It's quiet. I can get a lot done."

He surveyed her sitting across the table, small and rounded and brown like a sparrow hawk, with a raptor's keen eye and quick intelligence. She wore no rings. She said she didn't date.

"Your family doesn't object? Your roommate, maybe?"

She fluffed at that, but her eyes remained sharp and steady. "Are you asking me if I'm living with someone?"

"Yeah, I guess I am."

"I have a cat," she offered, deadpan.

He laughed.

Smiling, she elaborated. "Well, I told you I don't have time for a human relationship. Dogs need to be walked, and fish aren't great conversationalists. Blackie's there when I get home, she eats what I give her and she sleeps on my bed. See?"

The strange thing was, he did see. He saw a dedicated professional woman made for love and starved for company. He wondered what made her choose a life so different from his own, so apparently at odds with her warm nature.

"Yeah, after a tough day dealing with hospital cases, I guess nothing beats curling up with a cold beer and a cat," he teased.

Her lips tightened. "Something like that. And for the record, I find my work very rewarding. I enjoy being able to make a difference in so many patients' lives."

He didn't doubt it for a minute. And after what she'd done for Jack, he was sorry to have offended her. "Now, we have a dog," he said, turning easily back to the subject. "And a fish. Also two white mice in a cage and a snake in the woodpile."

"You're kidding."

He smiled, enjoying the stunned expression on her face and the surprisingly wistful look in her eyes. "Nope. You're welcome to come by some time and see."

"And you take care of all that?"

"Jack takes care of them. I take care of Jack. It works out pretty well."

"He's a lucky boy. My mother wouldn't even let me keep a hamster."

"She didn't like pets?" he asked sympathetically.

"It wasn't that," she said quickly. Defensively. "She just didn't have time for them. I mean, she was a single parent."

Patrick lifted his eyebrows. So was he.

Kate shook her head. "I mean, she thought I wouldn't take good care of one. I had my schoolwork and my sister and..."

He took pity on her obvious discomfort. "You have a sister?"

She took a deep, relieved breath at the change of subject. "One. Younger. Amy. She lives near here with her two children. How about you?"

"Two. Also younger. Con and Sean."

His mimicry won him another smile. "Very Irish," she commented.

"Blame my mother. My brothers even called me Paddy until we were all old enough for me to beat it out of them."

That time she laughed outright. The husky sound loosed something warm and liquid in his chest.

"Maybe I should try that with my sister. She still calls me Katie Sue."

"Katie sounds Irish."

"It's not. It's just one of those awful, double Southern names like Betty Lou or Billy Bob. I hate it."

He crumpled his chip bag. "Deserting your roots?"

Kate stiffened. There was enough truth in his mildly voiced accusation to sting. "No more than you are. Where are you from, Yankee? Boston?"

A corner of his mouth kicked up. She tried to ignore the feminine flutter produced by that fascinating quirk, tried not to admire the confident good humor with which he responded to her gibe. "Close enough. Quincy, Massachusetts."

"And what brought you from Quincy, Massachusetts, down to the Carolinas?"

"Uncle Sam. I was stationed down here. Flew Harrier jets out of Cherry Point for a while."

Everything he said brought his background into sharper focus, masculine, alien, exciting. She was out of her depth. Possibly out of her mind. Had she actually imagined that this warrior needed her comfort? That this male animal exuding sexual confidence could be interested in her stilted conversation?

Caution tugged her back. But something about the tall, dark

man on the other side of the table exerted a pull on her mind and her senses. Fascination and curiosity drew the next question from her. ''What made you give it up?''

''Jack,'' he said simply. ''My own dad served too many tours overseas when I was a kid. I wanted my child to know both his parents growing up.''

So the warrior had given up jets to fly charter planes in North Carolina, surrendering one objective for another. Compassion twisted Kate's heart. The drunk driver who had smashed into the car carrying Patrick's family had killed more than his wife. He'd destroyed his dream.

She reached across the formica table to touch Patrick's muscled forearm, shaken from her usual self-possession by her realization. ''What about other family?'' she asked, thinking of that empty waiting room. ''You mentioned your brothers, your mother. Didn't they…?''

At her compassionate gesture, he withdrew. ''Didn't they what? Come down? Yeah. Say how sorry they were? Sure. Help pick up the pieces? Absolutely.''

His blue eyes dared her to continue. Amazingly, she scraped together her thoughts and pressed on. ''No, I meant…I'm sure they helped you help Jack. A sense of family is terribly important in survival and recovery. No one can replace Jack's mother, of course, but—''

Patrick pushed the tray away in a contained, violent motion somehow more frightening for its tight control. ''No. No one. What's your point?''

For once, Kate wasn't sure she had a point. Just this terrible, futile ache to help. ''I'm just saying you're lucky to have them. Families play an important role in treatment. With Jack facing more therapy—''

''Don't worry about Jack's therapy, Dr. Sinclair. He and I can handle it. We don't need outside help. We don't need anybody.''

''Well.'' Kate drew in a deep breath, pulling her professional demeanor around her like a white lab coat to cover her hurt and confusion. "That's clear." She stood. "Jack should be discharged sometime tomorrow. Dr. Swaim will be in in the morning to examine him and go over his postoperative care with you."

Patrick stood, too, his big body tense, his fists curled at his sides. Kate thought they must resemble a pair of fighters, circling for advantage with the table in between. "Fine. Thanks. Listen, I appreciate what you did for Jack. If you hadn't come by—"

"Don't give it another thought," she said coolly. "I certainly won't. Thank you for the coffee."

She made her exit on trembling legs, her head held high.

Chapter 4

"But it hurts," Jack whimpered.

His stitches had come out only five days ago, Patrick reminded himself. This was their third physical therapy session since breakfast. No wonder the boy was near tears. Patrick felt pretty damn frayed himself.

He made an effort to keep his voice matter-of-fact and light. "I know it's uncomfortable, buddy. But you've got to do the exercises for your hand to get better."

Jack squirmed on his father's lap, his small face flushed with exertion and temper. "It's not getting better. It's worse."

"It looks worse," Patrick agreed, "because of the operation." They'd been over this many times. "But you've actually got new skin now so you can spread out your fingers and your thumb. It's going to be fine. But you have to use the hand."

"I can't use it," Jack insisted, his voice rising dangerously. "I can't do anything with it. I can't even draw!"

Patrick shared his son's frustration. In the days since Jack's operation, he too had felt hampered by the intrusive routine of therapy. He'd taken a week off, tending to the books while Ray ferried cargo and passengers, but his partner couldn't handle all the flights forever. When Shelby had their baby, Ray would be grounded for a couple of days at least.

He looked down at Jack's mutinous face, pillowed against his arm, and wanted nothing more than to give in, to give up for the day. Together in the weeks and months following the accident, they'd tackled the grueling labor of recovery many times. Only this time it was harder. This time Jack was older. This time the gains, though important and desirable, seemed less critical in the face of Jack's discouragement and pain.

But it was Patrick's job to soothe and encourage his son. He opened his mouth to say something—anything—when the telephone rang.

"You're in luck, kid. Take five." Scooting Jack off his lap, Patrick strode into the kitchen to answer the phone, relieved at the interruption and irritated with himself for his relief. He felt better when he recognized the voice of Jack's physical therapist and then worse after she delivered her news.

She wouldn't see Jack today, she informed him bluntly. She would see him at his regularly scheduled appointment on Wednesday, because she had other patients and Jack should not become dependent on his therapist.

Patrick controlled his temper with difficulty. "Fine. Did you ask Dr. Swaim about Jack's splint? Because three hours seems—"

"Three hours on, one hour off," the therapist interrupted him. Did he imagine he heard reluctance in her voice? "I'm sorry, Mr. MacNeill. But at least it's not as bad as the pressure garments."

"Jack doesn't remember the pressure garments, thank God. He was too young. Look, let me talk to Swaim."

"Dr. Swaim isn't available."

This time Patrick was sure he heard an inflection of doubt. "So who is?"

''Dr. West,'' the therapist offered. West was one of the two interns assigned to the burn unit. ''Or Dr. Sinclair.''

Patrick gripped the receiver tighter. He had a clear, unwelcome memory of Kate Sinclair's shuttered face the last time he'd seen her, the night he'd lashed out at her in the hospital cafeteria.

We don't need outside help. We don't need anybody.

He'd regretted his hasty words the minute they'd left his mouth. Against her white face, her eyes had glittered sharp and brittle as broken glass. He'd never meant to hurt the briskly efficient lady doctor, hadn't imagined he could. But neither could he lay himself open to her intelligent probing and seductive compassion.

To defend himself, he'd set her at a distance. Now, to protect Jack, he would ask for her help.

Patrick grimaced, still holding the phone to his ear. He'd be lucky if she didn't tell him to go to hell.

''Telephone, Dr. Sinclair. One of Dr. Swaim's patients.''

Kate closed her eyes against a fresh surge of pain. Her brain wanted coffee. Her stomach did not. Forced to choose between a pounding head and an acid stomach, she'd opted for the headache. She was beginning to regret her decision.

She handed Sharon Williams the chart of the twelve-year-old boy who'd thrown lighter fluid on a trash fire that morning. Carefully, because of the throbbing in her skull, she nodded to the receptionist. ''All right. I'll take it in my office.''

Sinking with relief onto her stubby office chair, she picked up the phone. Three minutes, she bargained with herself. Three minutes' peace and quiet, and then she would go out and explain to the child's anxious mother what it would take for her son to walk again.

''Kate? This is Patrick MacNeill.''

At the sound of that smooth whiskey-and-peat voice, Kate actually felt dizzy. Caffeine withdrawal, she told herself

firmly, and concentrated on the blank blue walls until the dancing black spots went away.

"What a surprise," she said coolly.

"Yeah. Yeah, I'm sorry." It wasn't clear what he was apologizing for, and Kate was too much the coward to ask. "Listen, do you have any time free this afternoon?"

Her heart bounced into her throat. Swallowing, she drawled,
"Not really. Are you offering to take me away from all this?"

"What?"

Kate sighed. "Never mind. What is it? How's Jack?"

"Do you want me to?" He sounded genuinely interested.

"Want you to what?"

"Take you away. You having a bad day?"

"No, no more than usual." *Don't let it get to you, Katie
Sue.* "How's Jack?"

"Actually..."

She was aware of an irrational disappointment and scolded
herself. *Stupid. Why else would he call?*

"We're having some problems here."

Kate straightened, wounded feelings shoved aside in her
concern for the little boy. "What kind of problems?"

He started to tell her. Kate listened, frowned, made notes.
When he was done, she stared at her own jottings, worrying
her lower lip with her teeth. She could help. She wanted to
help. But could she risk interfering with Swaim's treatment of
a patient?

"I'm not sure what you want me to do," she said carefully.
"Jack's not my patient."

"But you could still see him," Patrick pressed.

"My schedule's full."

"We could come at the end of the day."

"My day won't end until eight o'clock as it is."

Silence. Kate fought a creeping sense of guilt. The last time
she'd reached out to this man, he'd slapped her down. She'd
have to be crazy to challenge her center director for a macho
flyboy who'd spurned her help.

"All right," Patrick said slowly. "How about this. Why don't you stop by our house when you get off? You wouldn't need to see Jack as your patient. You could just watch his therapy and tell me what I'm doing wrong."

Kate wavered, disarmed by his unexpected humility. "Surgeons don't do house calls."

"We could give you dinner," Patrick added persuasively.

She slammed down her instinctive pleasure. Oh, no. She wasn't falling into that trap. She knew better than to imagine his invitation was anything other than an attempt to take advantage of her professional skills. She wasn't going to let him reject her twice.

"You don't need to pretend a personal interest in me, Mr. MacNeill. Why don't you give me a chance to discuss your concerns with the rest of Jack's medical team, and I'll return your call later this afternoon?"

"Patrick. And it would be better if you could see him yourself. Please," he coaxed. "Jack needs you. And I want you to come."

Oh, Lord. How could she resist either one of them? The suggestion of the boy's need and the man's desire tugged sweetly against her hard-won control. But it was her own need and her own desire that undid her.

"I'll see what I can do," she said crisply. "You can give me directions to your house, but dinner won't be necessary."

She waited for him to protest, to tell her the attraction between them was real, that she had something to offer a man besides her surgeon's knowledge and her overdeveloped sense of responsibility.

"Around nine, then," he said, accepting her decision. "Thanks."

She didn't want his thanks, Kate realized as she wrote down the directions. She wanted his... Cutting that thought off abruptly, she said goodbye. But her hand lingered on the receiver even after she'd hung up, as if the warm plastic could still provide a connection with dangerously handsome Patrick MacNeill. How stupid.

"Dr. Sinclair?" Sharon Williams stuck her head into the office. "Mrs. Johnson is waiting to see you."

Kate's headache surged back. "I'll be right there."

In spite of Patrick's clear directions, his place wasn't easy to find. Kate was twenty minutes from the hospital and three miles off the highway. Evening air poured through the open car windows, cool and moist, smelling of red clay and damp asphalt. Dark pines speared a deepening blue sky. Her headlights illuminated the signs for half a dozen new subdivisions and, once, the eyes of a possum at the side of the road. Finally, they flashed on a green-and-white street sign: MONTROSE. Kate checked the directions clutched against the steering wheel and turned.

She counted four rural mailboxes by the side of the road until she came to the MacNeills'. Her ancient Honda crunched and bumped down the gravelled drive. If she'd really wanted to spend the night wandering the back roads of North Carolina, Kate thought sourly, she could have visited her sister.

And then she passed a tangle of shrub roses under a hundred-year-old oak tree, and the road dipped, and the land lifted, and a white two-story farmhouse gleamed in the evening light.

It looked like welcome. It looked like home, if your name was Walton and you lived in a television world of family warmth. Even in the blue dusk, she could see the basketball hoop mounted over the gray barn. A tire swung from another ancient tree, and a trampoline occupied a corner of the fenced backyard. A large dog, pale-coated in the fading light, padded to the rails to investigate, wagging its tail in mild greeting.

Her head throbbed. She didn't belong here. And she was uneasily aware that the man waiting for her arrival was no John Boy. She pulled the car in front of the long covered porch and cut the engine, wishing briefly that she wore something more appealing than crumpled khaki slacks and a white camp shirt. Not that her wardrobe ran to man-attracting clothes. She'd never looked good in the flowing floral skirts that Amy favored, and she hesitated to try anything bright and tight. It wouldn't be professional. She dressed mostly by catalog these days, selecting upscale separates worn by models in flat shoes who looked like they summered at Nags Head.

The hell with it. It didn't make a bit of difference what she wore. Patrick MacNeill was totally focused on his son and probably still in love with his dead wife.

Kate got out of the car.

The dog barked. Before she could climb the low wooden steps, the front door opened. Patrick's tall, broad body was silhouetted against the rectangle of yellow light. His dark hair, longer on top, looked as if he'd raked his fingers through it, and his smile was quick and potent.

Kate's lungs emptied of air as apprehension punched her chest. Outside the confines of the hospital, he looked even bigger, more relaxed and more dangerous. She couldn't relate to him as a doctor here. She could only respond to him as a woman. She tightened her grip on her purse.

The screen door banged shut behind him. "You're here. Hush, Silkie. I thought maybe you'd given up on us."

"No." She hated the sound of her voice, breathless and uncertain. As if she didn't have the muscle to make it up the front steps. As if her knees would give out at the sight of him. "I don't give up."

He came out on the porch, all lean male grace and hard male muscle, and she felt a little wobbly. Maybe her knees weren't going to make it after all.

A gleam appeared in those deep-set eyes as he registered her reaction. He didn't comment on it, though, saying simply, "Well, praise God for that. We've got a bit of a problem inside."

Kate stiffened her spine and tried to ignore that the top of her head barely reached his chin. She was not a weak woman. "Lead me to it."

He stepped back politely to let her in the open door. She crossed the threshold, conscious of him falling in behind her.

His furniture, unpretentious, masculine and inviting, matched the rest of the house, Kate thought, trying to ignore his guiding hand on her elbow. She didn't like being crowded. He steered her over the old plank floor, their footsteps echoing uncomfortably close. The braided rug in front of the fireplace picked up the colors of the navy couch and battered red recliner. As he escorted her through to the dining room, she got a quick impression of wrought iron lamps glowing on maple end tables and a framed photo of some very scary modern aircraft that flew over the mantel.

Under the old farm table, knees drawn protectively to his chest, hunched Jack MacNeill.

In spite of her pounding head and her awareness of the man behind her, Kate's heart twisted. "Hey, Jack," she drawled.

Turning his head on his knees, the boy regarded her warily through a fortress of chair legs.

"Come out and say hello to Dr. Sinclair," Patrick commanded.

Jack shook his head, arms wrapped around his legs. "Won't."

"All right," Kate said swiftly, before Patrick could intervene. "How about I come see you?"

She dropped her purse on the floor and got down on her hands and knees. She wouldn't let herself think what kind of a view she was providing for Patrick, behind her. Crawling forward, she poked her head through the chairs.

"Is there room in there?"

Jack giggled. "Sure."

He scooted over. Kate wiggled in and flopped to a sitting position.

"Cozy," she remarked, looking out at Patrick's shoes. At least size twelves, she estimated. White cross trainers, with frayed laces. She craned her neck to study the boy beside her. "How are you doing, Jack?"

"Okay."

"Sure," she said. "The Code of the Macho MacNeills. Never speak under torture."

Outside the perimeter of chairs, Patrick's feet shifted and were still. Jack smiled wanly.

"I brought you something," Kate volunteered.

"What?"

"Putty." Leaning forward, she snagged the strap of her purse and dragged it under the table. "I had a talk with Peg, your occupational therapist, today. She thought you might be able to use this." Pulling out the small plastic container of exercise putty, Kate handed it to Jack.

"It's purple," he said.

"The purple is for tough guys. Wimps get yellow."

"Really?"

"Sort of. Yellow is softer, anyway. But they both make your hand stronger. Want to see how it works?"

Please, God, don't let him say no, she thought. She released her breath when he nodded.

"Great." She hoped she didn't sound too desperately enthusiastic. Pulling out a gob of putty, she started to demonstrate the simplest extension exercises she could think of.

Jack watched with interest as she wrapped a strand around her thumb and then straightened it. "It's like thumb wrestling."

"Oh, it's much harder than thumb wrestling," Kate said as coolly as she could. "You can only do this if you're really strong. You want to try?"

Jack regarded her from under thick, dark lashes like his father's. "Here?"

Kate looked to the shoes for help, but Patrick was silent. She was going to have to go with her gut on this one. "Maybe not here. Everybody should have a safe place, a place where they don't have to do stuff that bothers them. Why don't I crawl out and visit with your dad, and then when you're ready to play with the putty you can come find us. Okay?"

"'Kay."

She navigated the chairs on all fours to find Patrick regarding her with an admiration that made her blush.

"How did you do that?"

She shrugged to hide her pleasure. "It's my job."

He helped her to her feet, his large hand cupping her elbow. "Not just your job. It's you. Thank you."

His open appreciation warmed and discomfited her. She wasn't used to masculine approval. Bending, she brushed at the knees of her slacks. "Is there some place we can go to talk?"

"The kitchen."

The kitchen was another revelation, immaculately clean, with old wood cabinets and an intimidating modern range. Both the solid quality furniture and the gleaming high-tech appliances were as far outside the orbit of Blue Moon Trailer Park as Saturn.

"Sit down," Patrick invited.

She sat at the round oak table, trying to resist the pull of the room and the tug of attraction. He poured her a glass of ice water and started to assemble various refrigerator items by the stove. Puttering, she supposed, except he was far too efficient in his movements for the word to apply.

"Well." She took a sip of water, trying to ignore the pangs in her stomach. When was the last time she'd eaten? She couldn't remember. "I spoke with the other members of Jack's medical team after I talked to you. Peg thinks we can reduce his splint time to two-and-two, two hours on and two hours off."

Patrick dropped butter into a skillet, swirling the pan with the grace of a short-order cook. "Good. That won't slow his recovery?"

"Peg doesn't think so. We'll see."

If it did, Swaim was going to have Kate's head mounted and on display in his office. But two-and-two had been the therapist's original recommendation, overruled by the surgeon's insistence that the boy make rapid progress. One more success story to write up for the medical journals, Kate thought bitterly, and never mind that the kinder, more conservative approach would yield the same results.

Patrick dumped the contents of a plastic bag into the frying pan. As it sizzled, the aroma of sautéing peppers and onions filled the kitchen. Kate's stomach protested. Her mouth watered.

"I should go," she said reluctantly. "I'm interrupting your dinner."

"No, you're not. Jack and I ate hours ago."

"Then—"

"Tell me how to use that putty stuff."

"Oh. Well." She grabbed at the question like a lifeline. She needed some distraction from the tempting aromas and her hungry reaction to the neat, quick movement of Patrick's big hands as he broke eggs into a bowl and whisked them. "It's simple, really. There's a pamphlet in my purse. Peg marked the exercises you should do with Jack."

She started to describe them, her gaze helplessly following his broad shoulders around the kitchen. As she talked, he tilted the eggs into the skillet and added more ingredients from the fridge. He wrapped something else in a napkin and popped that into the microwave. His utter confidence performing the smallest domestic chores mesmerized her.

Sexist, she jeered herself. Yet, watching his muscled forearms as he slid a spatula around the skillet's edge, she actually felt her pulse quicken. And so she concentrated on the dry details of Jack's physical therapy, painstakingly reviewing each exercise as if he couldn't see everything illustrated perfectly well in the booklet she'd brought.

Removing a plate from the refrigerator, Patrick swept off its plastic wrap. Expertly, he slid the contents of the pan onto it and set the plate in front of her.

Kate blinked at a fluffy yellow omelette flanked by a green salad and a soft roll. "What is this?"

His voice was amused. "An omelette."

"No, I meant—"

"I figured you hadn't had time for dinner. It's the least I could do."

"But—"

"Eat," he ordered. "Before it gets cold."

Obediently, she took a bite. The eggs were moist and seasoned with a melting white cheese that made her close her eyes in ecstasy. Swallowing, she opened them to find Patrick watching her with a peculiar expression on his face.

She reached for her water glass in embarrassment. "This is very good."

His mouth quirked. "Don't sound so surprised. I can also make my bed and match my socks."

Kate busied herself with her omelette. "I just meant it's unusual to find a man who can cook."

"Not that unusual." With a gleam, he added, "All the MacNeill men are domesticated."

She doubted that. There was a wild streak in him that sorrow hadn't broken and fatherhood hadn't tamed. "Housebroken, too?" she asked dryly.

He laughed, squirting detergent into the sink. "Pretty much. My mom insisted we all pull our weight and keep our rooms and noses clean. Dad was overseas a lot, and she had better things to do with her time than ride herd on three rowdy boys."

She smiled. He made it sound so nice, a family working together. She forked up a man-sized chunk of red pepper, wondering if she dared to eat it. "So you learned to cook."

"We all learned to cook, but dinner was my responsibility. I was the oldest."

"Me, too. And did I ever hear about it." She heard the faint bitterness in her voice and tried to lighten it with a teasing imitation of her mother's voice. "*Watch your sister, Katie Sue, you're the oldest. Make dinner, you're the oldest. Set an ex-*

*ample. Watch your mouth. Don't make your father angry,
you're the oldest.''*

Patrick turned from the sink, eyebrows raised. "That bad?"
he asked with unexpected sensitivity.

Kate's cheeks heated as she looked away. She didn't want
his sympathy. She didn't want this fellow feeling. "No. No,
of course not. I'm sorry, I'm just tired tonight.'' She seized
on the Irish mother as a safe topic of conversation. "So. What
did your mother do?''

His smile was wry. "Trauma nurse, Quincy Community
Hospital.''

She stared at him in astonishment before she remembered
to close her mouth. "Well, that helps explain your attitude
toward doctors,'' she said.

He chuckled.

"Ready,'' Jack announced, dragging his feet in the kitchen
doorway.

He didn't look ready to Kate. He looked apprehensive and
forlorn. If she gave him half an excuse, he'd bolt.

Briskly, she nodded, pretending she had his complete enthusiasm. "Sure. You can't play for long, though. Isn't it almost bedtime?''

She held her breath as Patrick's blue gaze measured her
over his son's head. "That's right,'' he concurred. "Nine
o'clock.''

"How about five minutes with me, and five with your dad,''
Kate proposed with a warm smile. "You can do more tomorrow.''

Now that he had a definite time limit, Jack looked more at
ease. "'Kay.''

He hopped up on the chair beside her, sneakers dangling
above the floor.

Swallowing past the constriction in her throat, Kate pushed
her plate away and rummaged in her purse for the putty. "All
right. Try this.''

And for five minutes after that, Jack did try, his face

scrunched with effort. As Kate had hoped, the novelty of the colored putty made the exercises easier. With more control over his own movements, his cooperation increased. Even when Patrick took over, flexing the boy's fingers and thumb through a passive range of motion, Jack tried not to resist.

As they worked, Patrick kept up a stream of quiet nonsense to distract the boy. Kate tuned out his soothing rumble, observing his technique as his long, strong fingers pressed and stretched his son's hand. She couldn't see his face. Only the top of his dark head as he bent over his son, and the supporting curve of his broad shoulder, and the play of his hands.

He looked up, and her cheeks got hot, as if he'd caught her spying.

"Am I doing it wrong?" he asked.

"No." Her heart was pounding. She felt like an idiot. "No, you're doing fine."

His smile gleamed with satisfaction. "Good. Okay, Jack-o. Time for bed."

"'Kay." His sneakers thumped on the floor.

"This won't take long," Patrick said, standing. "He's already brushed his teeth. I'll be right back."

"I can let myself out."

"I'll be right back," he repeated firmly.

Before she could protest, he'd followed his son from the room, leaving her alone at the kitchen table. *Well.* Kate exhaled, unsure if she were amused or offended by his unthinking faith in her compliance.

"I guess I'll wait," she said to the empty room.

But she couldn't sit still. Her headache was gone. Her stomach was satisfied. But a peculiar energy had seized her. Her blood fizzed with unrest. Her skin hummed, as with static. She fidgeted with her fork and knife and then stood, depositing her dirty dishes in the sink. How long did it take to put one small boy to bed?

She prowled into the dining room, clasping her arms under her breasts, as if she could trap her skittishness inside her. As she circled the table, something gave underfoot. Kate stumbled and jerked back.

Under the chair, plush arms wide, sprawled Jack's teddy bear. She scooped it up and set the shabby bow to rights. Didn't Jack need it? Had he forgotten it?

Wandering into the hall, she glanced up the darkened stairs. She ought to take it up to him. And yet, did she really want to intrude any further? Interrupt their precious bedtime ritual? Could she risk getting closer to Patrick MacNeill and his son?

She didn't know. Supremely confident at work, she was a muddled mess of insecurities when it came to personal relationships. She couldn't escape the feeling that by going up those steps she was stepping off her chosen path and into the unknown.

She hugged the plush toy cradled in her arms: Finn MacCool, a sign of little Iron Man's bravery, a talisman against things that went bump in the night.

Don't be such a coward, Katie, she told herself, and hurried for the stairs.

Chapter 5

The carpeted steps absorbed the squeak of Kate's sensible shoes. On the landing, a lamp cast a pool of yellow light. She hesitated at the top of the stairs, reluctant to trespass beyond that lit circle into the shadowed hall.

A door clicked shut. Glancing toward the sound, she saw the dark profile of Patrick MacNeill outside his son's bedroom. He leaned against the door frame as if, Kate thought with a queer twist of heart, for that one private moment he needed its support. His strong head bowed.

Something fierce kindled to life inside her, surprising her with sudden heat. Impelled by a surgeon's need to heal, a woman's need to touch, she bustled down the hall with Jack's bear in her arms.

"Mr.—Patrick?"

He whirled at her whisper, head snapped back.

Kate stopped three feet away. "I'm sorry. I didn't mean to intrude. It's just I found this downstairs and I thought…" He regarded her impassively. She extended the toy, feeling foolish and inadequate. "Does Jack need it?"

His tense shoulders eased. His teeth glimmered in his shad-owed face. "Trying to make things all better again, Doctor?"

If only she could. "That's my job."

His long fingers reached out and plucked the bear from her grasp. "Thank you," he said, so gravely she wondered if he mocked her. "It was thoughtful."

Dismissed. She watched as he tapped on the paneled door and went in. "Hey, Jack-o, missing somebody?"

"MacCool!"

The boy's happiness reached all the way into the hall. Smil-ing, Kate leaned against the wall. She should go downstairs, she thought, listening to Jack's muffled explanations and his father's soft, rumbling reply. She would go downstairs, in just a minute.

She stayed where she was, heart beating high and fast.

Patrick backed out of the open doorway, shoulders blocking the faint glow of the boy's night-light. "'Night, now, buddy."

"'Night, Daddy. Tell Dr. Kate thank you."

"I will. Sleep tight."

He pulled the door shut, the click of the lock unnaturally loud in the stillness of the hall, and turned.

"You're still here."

Kate felt a flare in her stomach that wasn't indigestion and swallowed her excitement. "Looks like it."

"Missing somebody?" he taunted gently.

She didn't answer. He rested one hand on the wall above her, close enough for her to feel the warmth emanating from his body, close enough for his breath to touch her face. She saw his eyes, with their thick, short lashes, his pupils nearly swallowing the blazing blue. Her stomach squeezed into her chest, crowding her lungs. She couldn't breathe. She felt the warmth of his arm, close by her head. She heard her blood thundering in her ears, and the rasp of his quickly indrawn breath.

He kissed her.

It was over before she could say if she liked it, before she had time to react. He lifted his head, and she felt the absence of his mouth more keenly than she had felt its pressure a moment before.

"Well?"

She lifted her chin. She had to, to meet his gaze. "Well, what?"

His firm, well-shaped lips curved at the corners. "Are you going to object?"

She dug deep for a cool response, her hands pressed flat to the wall behind her. He was probably the most vital, potent man she'd ever met, and she was merely unattractive Katie Sue Sinclair, too smart for her own good and stupid with men. She couldn't let him see how he got to her, how she was affected by his nearness. He would eat her alive.

Maybe she wanted him to.

Greatly daring, she replied, "To what? You didn't give me much to go on."

The arm above her tensed with surprise. Good, Kate thought, savoring the heady, unfamiliar awareness of feminine power. And then his mouth came down on hers, and her brief satisfaction caught like paper and went up in smoke.

Hot. His mouth was so incredibly hot and moist. Her own temperature shot up several degrees in response. His teeth nipped at her lower lip. His tongue thrust into her mouth. With bold, lavish strokes, he fed and consumed her. Thought fled, and the darkness behind her closed lids was streaked with fire.

"I can give you more," he promised.

Muscled and heavy and hot, he pressed all along the front of her, crushing her against the smooth, cool wall at her back. The contrast made her toes curl. Her hands abandoned the painted plaster for the hard curve of his shoulders.

He made an encouraging sound deep in his throat, tangling his fingers in her hair, angling her head to take more of him. She wanted more. She wanted everything. Blanketed by sensation, covered by his body, she ignited. Her hands flashed over him, the long muscles of his back, the taut, high buttocks.

Greedy, grasping, as if she could gather him up and into her. It wasn't enough.

He widened his stance, letting her feel the ridge of his desire. Oh, glory. She was not a passionate woman. She wasn't. But as his rough hand glided up from her waist to cover her breast, she shuddered at the intimacy, arching her back to push her aching nipple into his palm.

He tore his mouth away and leaned his forehead against hers. His was damp with sweat. Maybe hers was, too. Dropping her head, she nuzzled the strong column of his throat, intoxicated by the smell of soap and skin.

"Not here," he murmured.

Reason blipped across her mind like the warning tone of a heart monitor. She opened her eyes. "What?"

"Not in the hall, Kate." He sounded patient, almost amused. She might have believed in his good humor if she hadn't felt his impatience pressing against her stomach. "Not when I've got a perfectly good bed to take you to."

Panic. She wasn't ready for this. She wasn't good at this. "Is that what you think you're doing? Taking me to bed?" Her voice was too high. Shaky. She hated it.

He eased up on her slightly so that she no longer felt him warm and close. She shivered in reaction, in longing, her body protesting the loss of his heat.

"Aren't I?" he asked coolly.

She hugged her elbows, not meeting his eyes. "No. I'm sorry. It wouldn't be... It's a completely understandable assumption for you to make, given the way I was grabbing at you. But—"

"I didn't mind," he interrupted her.

She felt the slow, betraying crawl of blood in her cheeks. "Yes, well, I shouldn't have done it. It was unprofessional. I realize I aroused, um, created expectations that I had no intentions of satisfying, but—"

His arm dropped from the wall beside her head. He took a

step back. "Kate, relax. What do you think I'm going to do? Jump my child's doctor outside his bedroom?"

"No, of course not." She drew a deep breath. "I'm sorry," she said again.

Patrick bit back his frustration. His blood pooled in his loins and pounded in his veins. He could ignore it. What he couldn't dismiss was Kate's obvious distress. He didn't like seeing the brisk and bossy lady doctor so miserable and uncertain. What bastard in her past had convinced her that his erection was her responsibility?

"Not a problem," he assured her roughly. "Let's go downstairs."

Her neat white teeth bit down on her lower lip. Patrick wanted to soothe the tiny sting with his tongue.

His hands clenched at his sides. Sweet heaven, did she have any idea what it did to a man's guts to look at her, with her tidy blouse rumpled and her wavy hair slipping free and her intelligent eyes dark and cloudy with desire?

Of course she did. No wonder she couldn't wait to get away. He jeered his eager body. In his present state, hard as a rocket and ready to burn, he wasn't fit for a first-time lover. It had been too damn long.

"Downstairs," he repeated firmly. "I'll make us coffee."

Straightening her shoulders, she nodded, still not quite meeting his gaze. She marched down the steps in front of him like she was going to her own court martial. He would have laughed if he hadn't found her discipline so endearing, if he weren't still struggling for his own control.

"You want to wait in the dining room? I'll bring it in."

She needed the space, he figured, to reestablish some professional distance between them. He needed the time to cool down.

So he waved her into the dining room while he went into the kitchen. He rinsed out the coffeemaker, counting on the small domestic routine to distract his ready body. Who would have guessed the tart-tongued, prickly doctor would have this effect on him?

He caught himself grinning like a fool at his reflection in the coffeepot. He shook his head in disbelief, jolted as much by the force of his desire as by its unlikely object. The last time the MacNeill clan had gathered—he'd flown Jack to his parents' house for Easter—his worried mother had made her oldest son's celibacy a topic of family concern.

"Four years is a long time, Padraig," she'd said in her forthright way, using his Gaelic name. "Too long for a man to do without. It's not healthy."

Sean, seeing the warning light in his brother's eye, spoke up. "That's not what you told us in high school, Mom."

And Con, closer in age, added in his cool, assessing way, "Give it time. He might surprise you. Or himself."

At the time, Patrick had appreciated his brothers' intervention without giving much weight to their words. Holly's accident had killed his desire. All his energy and attention since then had been focused on Jack. It was disconcerting to discover that all systems were go again.

Not that he was going anywhere. Kate Sinclair had called a halt to that.

Patrick spooned grounds into a paper filter, the rich aroma sharp to his heightened senses. He should be glad. He had no heart for a serious relationship, and she struck him as a woman who took most things seriously. Pushy, opinionated and probing, she was the worst woman in the world for him.

Yet he was oddly grateful to her. There was something reassuring about his body's almost painful response to that unexpectedly passionate kiss in the hall. Patrick grinned derisively. Sort of like completing a successful pre-flight inspection when you had no intention of taking off.

When the coffee finished dripping, he filled two mugs and carried them through to the dining room. Kate turned quickly from her examination of the pine breakfront to accept the proffered cup. She was wearing her doctor's face again, he noted, interested and polite.

"Black, right?"

"Yes. Thank you." She blew on the coffee before sipping. "You have some lovely pieces here," she added, nodding toward the cabinet.

He had a bowl and a jug of blue-glazed North Carolina pottery, a Waterford bud vase he'd given Holly on their first anniversary and an incomplete set of his grandmother's china. Nothing, Patrick thought, to arouse much excitement. Which probably explained the doctor's intense interest in them now.

"Thanks," he said wryly.

She actually tossed her head, so that her light brown curls danced above her shoulders, and stabbed one slim finger at the glass. "Yours?"

He moved closer to see what had brought that note of challenge into her voice. A miniature tea set was displayed on the second shelf, its delicate, creamy porcelain painted with twining shamrocks.

"My mother's."

She inspected it, her face softening. "It's very pretty," she said, almost wistfully.

Her yearning expression pulled another admission from him. "She gave it to us when Holly was pregnant. Said she hoped it would encourage us to produce a female grandchild."

"Oh, that's sweet."

Kate was sweet, Patrick thought with a shock. Her wavy hair, scented by some citrusy shampoo, brushed his shoulder. Her face was open as a child's. Her very vulnerability made her dangerous in a way her no-nonsense competence did not. He tightened his hands on his coffee mug until it seared his palms and stepped back, away from her.

"We going to talk about tea sets all night?"

"No, of course not. Actually…" She squared her shoulders. "I felt we should talk about what happened upstairs just now."

He lifted an eyebrow. He couldn't resist. The workings of this woman's mind were a mystery and delight to him. "What happened?"

"What *didn't* happen," she clarified. "What isn't *going* to happen."

Amusement loosened the knot in his gut. "Fine. What isn't going to happen?"

"We're not going to have a relationship. Apart from Jack being a patient at the burn center, I mean."

He'd just finished telling himself the same thing. So why did it irk him to hear it from her?

"And how are we not going to do that?"

"It shouldn't be difficult," she said primly, standing with her hands clasped around her coffee mug and her neat ankles close together. "You don't really want me, and I can't afford to want you."

Fascinating as he found the second half of her pronouncement, he couldn't let her casual dismissal of his desire pass. "You don't think I wanted you?"

"I think that's evident."

"Honey, I don't want to flatter either one of us, but I'd say all the, ah, evidence, pointed the other way."

Her face turned scarlet. "Obviously, physically, we respond to one another. We're both adults. And you clearly have a great deal of experience—"

"I haven't had any experience, as you put it, since Jack's mother died."

Her lips parted in surprise before she pressed them firmly together. "There you are, then. That's a long time to go without, um, physical release. It has nothing to do with me personally."

She sounded like a doctor. She sounded like his mother. "Uh-huh. How long has it been for you?"

"We're not talking about me."

"I am. How long?"

"A while," she admitted reluctantly.

"One year? Two?"

"Why does it matter?"

Damned if he knew. "I'm just trying to get a handle on your argument here. How long, Kate?"

"*Nine,* all right?" she snapped. "Nine."

"Years?" He couldn't believe it.

"Yes." She wouldn't look at him.

Hell. Dr. Perfect was practically a virgin. The burst of tenderness that knowledge produced astonished him.

"So when you kissed me," he said carefully, "it wasn't because you were attracted to me or anything. You've just done without for a couple of years, and I was handy."

Her earnest brown eyes widened. He was touched and amused by her apparent concern for his feelings. "Of course not. I find you personally very attractive."

"Yeah? Well, I find you personally very attractive, too."

Her pretty mouth dropped open at the way he'd managed to turn her argument around. "Oh."

Patrick grinned, absurdly pleased by her reaction.

She pressed a hand to her stomach before she rallied. "That's different."

"Why?"

"You hardly know me."

"You don't know *me.*"

"You don't like me."

"Not at first, not much." Regretting the hurt that flashed across her face, he paid her the highest compliment he could. "You're good with Jack."

She nodded. "That's it. Patients frequently develop crushes on their doctors."

He leaned one shoulder against the wall. "You are not my doctor."

"Still, if we... If you... It would be a transitional relationship for you. I'd be part of your recovery process."

Her clinical analysis both entertained and annoyed the hell

out of him. "So what's wrong with that? Isn't that the physician's mandate or something? 'Heal the sick'?"

"That's 'Do no harm.' I can't risk that. I'm not Jack's doctor, but I do work at the center where he's seen. Any hint of personal involvement..." She lowered her gaze to her cooling coffee. "I can't let my social life detract or distract me from my relationship with a patient."

The hell of it was, she was right. Jack came first. Patrick could no more spare the time and energy for a relationship than she could. And there was simply no way he could justify lusting after his child's doctor.

But even as Patrick acknowledged that, even as he applauded her professionalism, he was briefly, keenly sorry that all he'd ever have of her was one taste in the shadows.

He rolled his shoulders. "Fine. We'll keep it strictly business. Maybe I'll see you Wednesday."

She balked even at that, he noted with exasperation, a vertical furrow appearing between her smooth, dark eyebrows.

"Why Wednesday?"

"Jack has his therapy session that morning. And we have an appointment with Dr. Swaim to discuss his surgery."

"Oh, of course. Wednesday." But the parallel lines of concern between her brows didn't go away.

Kate lifted her head from her clinic notes. A man was reading someone the riot act down by the nurses' station. Quietly, but the intensity of his tone penetrated the hall. She recognized the timbre of his voice before she heard the anger, and registered the anger before she distinguished the words. Her heartbeat quickened. The voice belonged to Patrick MacNeill.

Swiftly, she left her cubbyhole, her crepe-soled shoes squeaking on the blue-and-gray linoleum, anticipation humming through her blood. An expected adrenaline response to the shouting, she told herself, but Patrick's voice was low and firm. He towered over the desk, palms flat on the counter, addressing Sharon Williams on the other side.

"You told me he was in a meeting. Now you're telling me he's not here. I want to know where he is and why he can't be paged."

The veteran nurse didn't back down from the tall man looming over her, but she signalled Kate for help with her eyebrows. So it was serious, Kate thought. Nothing rattled Amazon Sharon.

Adjusting her stethoscope, Kate made a grab for her professional composure and waded in. "Can I help you?"

Patrick pivoted, battle ready, relaxing only slightly when he saw her. "Yes. Where's Swaim?"

Well, thought Kate. And hello to you, too. Any secret hope that he might be haunted by the memory of their scorching kiss, that he might be experiencing disturbed sleep and lapses in concentration, that he regretted even a tiny bit her insistence that they cool things between them, withered swiftly and died.

Clearly, she was the only one suffering.

Jack poked his head around his dad's thigh, eyes bright under the bill of his baseball cap. "Hi, Dr. Kate."

She smiled warmly at his eager face. "Hey, Jack. Aren't you guys supposed to be with Peg right now?"

"We're finished. I did real good, she said. Now I got a doctor 'pointment."

"He *had* a doctor's appointment," Patrick stressed. "Only the doctor seems to be missing."

"I told him I'd be happy to reschedule," Sharon interjected.

"For the—what—third time? Fourth?"

"You can't get in to see Dr. Swaim?" Kate asked.

Patrick plowed his fingers through his already disordered hair. "No, I just felt bored and decided to pass the time by terrorizing the nursing staff."

"And very well, too," Kate agreed politely.

That earned her his vital, mocking grin. "I've had practice."

The thought of how much practice dragged at her sympathies. She looked from the sturdy little boy with the scarred cheek to his tall, dark-haired father and sighed. She ought to stay out of it. She ought to stay away from them. Interfering between Swaim and one of his patients could jeopardize her academic appointment. Exposure to Patrick MacNeill's potent charm could destroy her emotional distance. Yet she felt herself responding to the appeal in the child's smile and the challenge in his father's blue eyes.

"Why don't you come into my office," she suggested, "and we'll discuss it."

"Dr. Sinclair..." Sharon began.

It was a warning. Kate appreciated the nurse's concern even as she chose to disregard it. "I'll take care of it. Thank you, Nurse Williams."

Patrick paced the corridor behind her, trailing Jack from one hand. By now Kate was almost used to the feeling of the big man stalking her. She pointed him to the patient chair, taking care to put the desk between them.

"Where am I supposed to sit?" Jack asked, leaning against his father's knees.

"On my lap," Patrick said promptly.

"Actually, I've got another..." Kate stooped to dig under a pile of papers for her step stool. She couldn't reach the top shelves without it. "How's this?"

"Cool," Jack approved. He settled next to his father.

"Do you want some paper? I don't have any crayons, but—" Kate rifled through her desk. "How about highlighters?"

Jack held up his splinted right hand, the palm supported by a thin plastic plate, the fingers stretched back by rubber bands fastened to a loop around his wrist. His face was solemn. Too solemn for a four-year-old boy, and his voice was too accepting.

"I can't draw."

Patrick's mouth compressed, not accepting at all. Kate felt a tug of compassion for them both. "You can draw when we get home, buddy. Two hours on, two hours off, remember?"

"No, you can draw now," Kate said. Plucking more rubber bands from her top drawer, she came around her desk to kneel beside Jack. Carefully taking his hand, she inserted two markers between his fingers, interlacing them with the bands to hold them steady without cutting off his circulation. "Try that. I'll bet if you're careful, you can draw two pictures at once."

Jack giggled, waving his hand. "I look like Wolverine."

"Is that good?" she asked.

"Awesome," Patrick assured her solemnly. She looked up to find him watching her with a warm appreciation that curled her toes inside their sensible shoes. "You're good with people."

Amy had a way with people and a special touch with men. Kate was merely competent at her job. Instinctively, she rejected the compliment. "No. No, I'm not."

"You're good with Jack."

"It's because of my pediatrics rotation. I'm trained to work well with children. I'm no good with men."

Oh, lord. Had she actually said that? Kate winced, wishing she could recall her thoughtless, revealing words.

Patrick's rich, amused voice rolled over her head. "If you think that, you haven't known the right men. Or you're ignoring the available evidence to the contrary."

The evidence. Yes. She swallowed, registering that she was practically kneeling at the man's feet, her shoulder brushing his thigh. Rising hastily, she retreated behind her desk.

"I don't think we should be having this discussion in my office."

"Yes, Doctor. Where would you like to have it?"

"I brought you in here to talk about Jack."

"Yes." His expression sobered. "Look, we're having trouble getting in to see Swaim. This is the fourth appointment he's cancelled on us. What's going on?"

Kate didn't know how much to tell him about her director's recent aberrant behavior. She didn't want to tell him anything. But this was Jack, coloring on the other side of her desk. This was Patrick, fighting for his son. Faced with the boy's candid smile and the father's level blue gaze, she felt she owed them something, some explanation.

"The situation isn't unique to Jack," she began carefully. "Since he returned a couple of weeks ago, Dr. Swaim's schedule has been...erratic."

"Is he sick?"

The possibility had occurred to Kate. But the director had vehemently denied any suggestion that he wasn't up to his regular duties. "I have no reason at this time to believe so."

"Don't try to feed an ex-Marine the official line, honey. What's his problem? Drink? Drugs?"

"No. I don't think so. I don't know," she said honestly.

He nodded, accepting that. "So what are you going to do about it?"

"Besides cover for him?" The joke, if it was a joke, fell flat. Kate sighed. "I don't know."

"You should report him."

Her face drained of blood. Her lungs emptied of air. She felt almost lightheaded at the risks she was running. She could barely bring herself to hint to Patrick that Swaim wasn't at the top of his powers. She would never criticize the unit director to the chief of surgery.

"No. I don't have any reason to suspect him of doing anything wrong. I've been with him in surgery. The only observable difference is that he's leaving more of the work for me and Owen—Owen Roberts, the other attending. He's edgy, he's distracted. But he hasn't made any mistakes. He isn't hurting anyone."

"Yet," Patrick said grimly.

The single word dropped like a stone into her fluid explanation. Kate thought of Swaim's unaccountable hesitation on the day of Jack's operation and the stitches she'd removed that night. Reluctantly, she agreed. "Yet."

"I'm done," Jack announced, waving his paper.

"Let me see." Patrick took the offering, studying the bright, duplicate designs of pink and yellow. "Not bad for highlighter hands," he teased, and Jack grinned in delight. "Why don't you go show it to Nurse Williams?"

The boy hopped to his feet. "You're not mad at her anymore?"

"No, I'm not mad. Go on, buddy. I'll see you in a couple minutes."

His dark head turned as he watched his son leave. The love and pride that shone in his eyes shattered Kate's resolution. In her entire life, no one had ever looked at her like that.

She waited until her office door closed behind Jack before she said, "I'll talk to him."

The dark brows lifted. "Swaim?"

"Yes." She fiddled with her pen. Click, cap off. Click, cap on.

"What will that do?"

She tried to imagine a best-case scenario, as if wishing could make it happen. "Well, he might tell me what's going on. At least he'll know I've noticed something. Maybe he'll be more careful. Or get help."

Patrick was still frowning. He must find her assurances as vapid as she did. "No, I meant, what will that do to *you*?"

"Oh, I don't know. Nothing, maybe. Maybe he'll thank me for my concern. Maybe he'll pat me on the head and tell me I'm imagining things." She fought to keep her voice steady, proud when she succeeded. "Or maybe he'll kick me out of the program."

Patrick's expression was troubled. "Kate—"

She turned from him, turned from the sympathy he offered. If she let herself rely on him, the inevitable disappointment would only make her feel worse.

"He won't do it right away. We're really short-staffed at the moment." She smiled feebly.

Patrick stood, ramming his hands in his pockets. "What can I do?"

"Wait until I've talked with Dr. Swaim. Please. I'll have a better idea what your options are then."

He paced the narrow space before her desk. "What about Jack's surgery? Could you do it?"

Kate hesitated. She was dangerously flattered that he'd ask. "I could, yes. But I think it would be premature."

"It needs to be done as soon as possible."

"Why?"

"Jack starts kindergarten in the fall. That's only four months away."

"Yes, but why operate? The scarring on his face and ear won't stop him from functioning in school."

"Acceptance," Patrick said simply. "Functioning in class is fine, but functioning socially is even more important at his age."

"Jack functions beautifully," Kate protested.

"With adults," Patrick countered. "Yeah, he does great with the nurses and my family and my partner and his wife. All the people he's come in contact with care about him, not his face. But all that's going to change when he starts school. Kids can be cruel."

"There are reentry nurses who can go to the school and explain to his classmates about Jack's accident."

His head came up in automatic rejection. "No. He doesn't need to be singled out or explained away, like he's some sort of freak. I don't want him to feel different."

Kate sympathized with his concern. She honored him for it. But his solution—Swaim's proposed course of treatment—was no solution at all.

"Even with the surgery, Jack will look different," she said as gently as she could. "It's better for the children to understand that, to know that the difference doesn't matter, that he's a little boy just like them who's survived a terrible accident."

Patrick's blue eyes pierced her. "How can a bunch of kindergartners understand that? How can they accept it? How can they possibly believe that in one sunny afternoon drive, in a moment, in a heartbeat, your life can be changed and your mother killed and your face destroyed, and it's not your fault? How could anyone accept that?''

He wasn't talking about five-year-olds anymore, Kate realized. He was talking about himself. The bitterness in his voice struck at her heart. How could she help him? She wanted to cradle that implacable face between her hands and promise him everything would be all right. But she was no good at that kind of comfort. It wasn't what he needed anyway, not from her.

''Maybe if Jack had the opportunity to meet other children before school started?'' she suggested.

''What good would that do?''

At his dismissive tone, she put up her chin. ''Well, it would give Jack a chance to relate to his peer group.''

Patrick raked his fingers through his hair, shooting her a disgusted look. ''And what if he's hurt?''

''What if he is?'' she returned evenly. She wasn't going to feed his big, bad male ego by retreating. ''The risk would be minimized in a controlled and protected environment. And you would have the chance to observe him.''

''What environment?''

At least he was listening, Kate thought with a spurt of hope. ''What about a play group? A neighbor's child?''

''It's almost summer. That's a little late to enroll for play group. And we don't have any close neighbors.''

His reluctant consideration made her incautious. ''I have a nephew. Billy turned five in February. Maybe you should bring Jack over to play the next time I'm sitting for my sister.''

Mistake, her mind shrieked instantly. She had reasons, good reasons, for staying out of this man's personal life. Reasons not to expose herself or her family to him.

He smiled at her with wicked intent, thumbs tucked in the front pockets of his jeans, and the reasons all melted away.

''You sure you want to let us in that far, Kate? Won't it detract from your doctor/patient relationship with Jack?''

She snapped the cap on her pen and held it stiffly before her to reinforce the barriers between them. "Not at all. The visit will be good for him. I'm recommending it as Jack's doctor."

Patrick lifted an eyebrow, and the silent, masculine challenge backed her breath up in her lungs.

Sure she was.

Chapter 6

The lady doctor had saline in her veins instead of blood. Patrick shook his head, both exasperated and admiring. No warm-blooded woman could have cut him open and then examined the results, like his emotions were a smear on a microscope slide.

He accepted that the curvy little doctor got to him physically. He figured a week of heated dreams and tangled sheets was worth the discovery that he was no longer dead from the waist down. But now she was messing with his mind. Worse, she was interfering with his son. Recalling the way she'd challenged his assumptions about Jack's surgery in her cool, analytical doctor's voice made his blood pound in his temples.

So what the hell was he doing driving to her apartment with Jack buckled in the back seat?

Patrick glanced in the Volvo's rearview mirror. His son peered out the window from under the curled brim of his baseball cap, legs splayed on the wide leather bench. He looked happy. He was smiling. Every so often one of his feet jiggled excitedly.

Jack wanted to make friends.

Somehow Kate had seen that, somehow she had known. Patrick had never considered himself overprotective. But maybe he had tried too hard to shelter Jack from the inevitable reactions of children raised with the scary stereotypes of burn survivors. It seemed that in every movie villain from Freddy Krueger to Two Face, ravaged skin was an outward sign of inner decay or madness. Applied to his innocent son, that kind of prejudice made Patrick furious. And scared.

Kate wanted Jack to relate to his peer group.

Patrick exhaled, gripping the steering wheel. When she'd called last night to invite them to her sister's, his first instinct had been to refuse. How could he expose his child's fragile scars to judging eyes and careless taunts? And yet it was Kate doing the asking. Kate, whose brisk competence imperfectly disguised her caring heart. Kate, who had crawled beneath his dining room table to reach his son. Tired, tart, dogged Kate, willing to hazard her director's goodwill to protect her patients.

Patrick wasn't about to take a similar risk with his son's feelings. But maybe he could regard this play trip as a sort of test flight. He could monitor how Jack did with careful preparation in a controlled environment. And hope like hell his boy didn't need an emotional parachute before it was all over.

Pulling in front of Kate's apartment building, he undid his seat belt and threw open the door. "Okay, buddy, we're here."

"Is this his house?"

"Billy's? No. We have to pick up Dr. Kate first."

You'll never find my sister's, she'd said last night, playing it very cool. *We might as well drive over there together.*

In spite of her invitation, Patrick reflected, the lady doctor sounded almost as if she were trying to discourage him from coming. As if she were willing him to say no. Some deep-seated masculine impulse had driven him to play it even cooler and say yes.

Jack hopped out of the car, looking around curiously. The

Dumpsters were too close to the parking spaces, the buildings too close to the highway. But the apartment was convenient to the hospital, and Patrick suspected that mattered to Kate.

The cement walkway cut through worn grass and tired bushes to three identical brick units. Kate lived on the right. He knocked on the green metal door and waited. A chain lock rattled before she jerked the door open.

His mouth dried. Her bouncy hair was loose on her shoulders and smelled faintly of citrus. In place of her usual oversize lab coat and conservative separates, she wore jeans that nipped her waist and hugged her shapely hips. The soft knit of her coral shirt clung to her rounded breasts. He had a sudden memory of weighing that sweet breast in his hand, of her nipple pushing eagerly into his palm, and his body saluted.

He jammed his hands into his pockets to hide his reaction, to keep from grabbing her. "You look good."

She stepped back to admit them. "Sure. What the well-dressed baby-sitter is wearing this spring. Come on in."

It intrigued him, this habit she had of deflecting compliments. He strolled past her into the apartment. "Is it just me, or are you this prickly with everybody?"

"I'm honest, if that's what you mean. You're meeting the pretty, agreeable sister this afternoon."

"I can hardly wait," he murmured.

At his dry tone, her shoulders relaxed. She actually smiled. "Give me just a minute and we can go. Hey, Jack."

Patrick turned his head and saw his son squatting in the narrow hallway, hand extended to a huge black cat.

"Are you making friends with Blackie?" she asked.

Jack nodded.

"Original name," Patrick said for the sheer pleasure of watching her turn frosty again. He had himself under control now.

She didn't disappoint him. Her brown eyes glinted. "Her name's Blackwell. After Elizabeth Blackwell, the first woman medical doctor in the United States."

The feline sniffed disdainfully at Jack's fingers and then walked away. Patrick grinned. Even the cat had an attitude.

Kate hefted a brown paper grocery bag off a table that apparently doubled as her desk and mail repository. "All right. I'm ready."

"Let me take that."

"I can manage."

Ignoring her dismissal, he reached for the paper sack. Her forearm was trapped between them, against his belly. The back of his fingers brushed the outer curve of her breast. His stomach muscles contracted in response.

He watched her weigh her options, her feminine pride battling with her desire for dignity. She could either tussle with him or let go of the bag. She let go. "Okay. But we take my car. And I'm driving."

He hated being driven. But having won one point, he could afford to be gracious. "Fine. Come on, Jack-o, let's go."

Politely, he stood aside while she closed up and then followed her to the parking lot. Jack balanced on the curb, arms stretched wide, as she unlocked her car doors.

Patrick inspected the battered gray Honda. "I thought doctors drove Beemers or Caddies."

She took the grocery bag from him and put it in the trunk. "No, it's little red sports cars with vanity plates. And only after you're made an attending."

He beat her to the driver's side, enjoying the surprise in her eyes as he opened her door. "And when do you get yours?"

Her face shuttered. "Hard to say. I still have to pay off my med school bills."

Her hair brushed his forearm as she swung into her seat. It was incredibly soft. He remembered the feel of it tangled in his hands, the tart, ripe scent rising to his brain, and felt his body instantly respond.

Taking a deep breath of baking blacktop, he folded himself into her car. Without asking, he snapped on the radio, searching for a distraction. The strong country voice of George Strait flowed from the tiny speakers. Patrick lifted his brows. He'd pegged her as the public radio type.

Flushing, Kate fumbled with the dial until she found an adult rock station. Patrick didn't protest the change. MacNeill Road Rules dictated the music selection was the driver's choice. Besides, earnest cowboys lamenting their broken hearts made him uncomfortable.

Kate drove, her awareness of the man beside her grinding under her ribs, a constant, compelling ache. His lean fingers tapped his knee in time to a bass guitar. His right thigh flexed as his foot depressed an imaginary gas pedal.

She'd been out of her mind to invite him. If she wrapped the car around a tree, if she smacked that handsome, teasing face, if she blew up her sister's trailer home and herself with it, she could plead temporary insanity.

The thought cheered her slightly.

In the back seat Jack was smiling and commenting on topics of likely interest to the adults in the car—billboards, cows and license plates, mostly. Apparently he'd recently mastered the alphabet and was taken with the letter Q, because, he explained, you didn't see it a lot. Also J, because it was in his name, and R, for no particular reason that Kate could discern. She began to feel better. Maybe this visit wasn't such a bad idea after all.

She turned off the highway, following a sign that mentioned no major cities and a road that went nowhere, and her brief optimism faded. Dark pines gave way to red fields of new tobacco and foot-high corn. She slowed through the town of Clayton, stopping at its one traffic light, and took the right fork to the Blue Moon Trailer Park.

Nothing ever changed. A truck on cinder blocks, a dog tied in the front yard, a rusting swing set by a desiccated garden plot could have been left from her childhood. Clothes still dried on sagging lines, and incurious eyes watched from slatted windows. Kate stopped the car in front of a gray single-wide with a bicycle out front, her old surroundings resurrecting old insecurities in the pit of her stomach.

Years and accomplishments meant nothing here. Her mother's trailer—her sister's, now—boasted a shiny new television antenna and a nice view of the pine woods and creek. The only other man she'd ever brought here had taken one look around and drawled, "Kathryn, darling, you didn't tell me you knew the Clampetts."

Things had pretty much gone downhill from there, Kate remembered with a shiver. After Patrick's crack about her car and his recoil at her choice of radio station, she didn't even glance at him to see his reaction to her girlhood home.

She hesitated before turning off the engine, as if planning a quick getaway. She had never belonged here. But her years here had shaped her, marked her, made her unfit for anywhere else. Right before Wade Preston left for Baltimore, her lover had taken pains to point out that Katie Sue from Blue Moon Trailer Park could have no place in the rarefied world the Prestons inhabited by right.

The trailer's screen door opened. Like a princess in a fairy tale emerging from an enchanted cottage, Amy appeared, and Kate's transformation into a brainy toad was complete.

"Katie!"

Her sister's face was alight with pleasure. She posed a moment at the top of the rickety steps, the sunlight striking through her flowered skirt to reveal slender legs. And then she drifted down, her blond hair in perfect disarray, her hands with their sprinkling of silver rings outstretched.

"I'm so glad you finally came. Billy's been up since six waiting for you."

Inside Kate, a small kernel of warmth unfolded at her sister's welcome. The screen door screeched, and five-year-old Billy whirled down the stairs, yelling, "I saw you first! I saw your car!"

Squaring her shoulders to banish her ghosts, Kate got out of the car and smiled at her nephew. "Hey, squirt."

Billy tackled her legs.

Amy floated over to envelope her in slim, tanned arms and a cloud of True Love cologne. Her head turned as she smiled over her shoulder. "And you must be Patrick."

Heart sinking, Kate waited for the inevitable male reaction to her sister: dilated pupils, macho stance, drool. Amy never stayed in any one relationship for long. Since her divorce from Billy's father three years ago, she'd been madly in love with four men that Kate could remember. She saw in each man, each new beginning, the relationship she'd been waiting for. And every man saw in her blond prettiness the embodiment of his own fantasies.

"Nice to meet you," Patrick said blandly.

His large hand briefly engulfed her sister's dainty one before he stepped back beside Kate. His thigh, warm and solid, nudged her hip. Startled, she looked up to meet very blue, very amused eyes. Her heartbeat quickened. Confused by his reaction, by her own response, she ducked her head and hugged her nephew's shoulders.

Amy, undeterred, swooped on the last person out of the car. "And...is this big boy Jack? Oh, sweetie, your poor face."

Kate gritted her teeth. How could she ask Patrick to trust her recommendations when her own sister was so insensitive? "It's just a scar, Amy. I told you that."

"Well, I know, but—"

Billy cocked his head. "A scar? Like a pirate? Cool. Can I see?"

A muscle tensed in Patrick's jaw. Kate held her breath. Would he give the boys a chance, or would his need to protect Jack overcome his grudging acceptance of her judgment?

Jack flinched but held his ground. In respectful silence, Billy inspected his puckered face and misshapen ear.

"Yowsers. Does it hurt?"

"No. But my hand still does, a little."

Billy gave the big bandage a cursory look. "Yeah. Aunt

Katie operated on it. She told me. You want to see my space blaster? Aunt Katie got it for me.''

Jack's face lit. "Okay."

Bless her nephew. But before Kate could draw her breath in relief, Amy intervened. "Billy, did you leave the baby inside all alone?"

He squirmed. "Ma, she was fine."

"Billy." She shook her head, seemingly more disappointed than angry. "You're the oldest. You go in and get her now and bring her to Aunt Katie."

He scuffed the ground at his feet. "Yeah, okay. Be right back."

"Can I come?" Jack asked.

"Sure."

They ran into the trailer, two sets of sneakers thumping on the steps.

"Honestly." Amy turned to the other two adults. "You'd think he'd be more responsible by now. It's like some things never change."

"Yes," Patrick said dryly. "I see that."

Kate glanced at him sharply. Whether he meant to support her or not, she wouldn't tolerate him mocking her family.

He hesitated, as if searching for an inoffensive explanation. "I'm an oldest child myself."

Amy nodded, uncomprehending.

Jack banged back through the screen door and held it open for Billy. The boy trundled down the steps, precariously balancing his baby sister, her fat little legs sticking out on either side of his waist.

Rescuing her niece from Billy's slipping clasp, Kate settled the baby competently on her hip. "This is Jenny."

A girl. The punch of yearning caught Patrick unaware. A real cutie, too, with her mother's flyaway curls and her aunt's observant eyes. A lifetime ago, Patrick had wanted a baby girl. The joy of Jack's arrival had eclipsed that dream. The loss of his wife had extinguished it. But seeing Kate with her sister's child in her arms, he realized that the hope still flickered deep inside.

Two sets of pink cheeks, two pairs of brown eyes, two rosy smiles…

He jammed his hands in his back pockets to keep from reaching for them both and took a step back. "Cute."

Kate, he saw, registered his withdrawal without understanding it, bristling at the imagined slight to her niece. "Don't you like babies?"

The child lurched for a fistful of her aunt's wavy hair and stuffed it in her mouth. Nine months old, he guessed. Probably crawling, and into everything. He'd missed this stage with Jack. Jack had gone from a sturdy five-month-old just sitting up to wasted muscle on a hospital cot. By the time he was able to crawl, Jack was well over a year old.

"I like babies fine."

"But not girls."

He smiled at the challenge in Kate's voice, letting her needling prick him from his memories. "Oh, I like girls."

"I just bet you do," Amy murmured, widening her eyes at him.

"Too bad he can't go to lunch with you and Ma," Kate said, tongue planted firmly in cheek.

She was teasing him. His body responded with instant, serious intent.

"Well, now, I know Mama wouldn't mind the company. If Patrick's free…" Amy trailed off suggestively.

Damn, she was coming on to him.

"I was joking, Amy," Kate said flatly.

"I know that, but it's not a bad idea. The kids are used to you. We'll only be gone a few hours. And I'm sure Patrick wouldn't mind taking a couple of ladies to lunch."

She couldn't be serious. He was here with Kate. He looked her way, but Kate was wearing her cool doctor's face again, the one he was learning concealed a wealth of emotion. What did she want him to do? He didn't want to be rude to her sister, but he for damn sure didn't want to spend time with Amy, either.

"I can't leave Jack," he said.

"Oh, Katie's real good with kids," Amy assured him. "Mama never could figure why she didn't have a couple of her own, instead of messing around with other people's."

Her casual dismissal of her sister's abilities and dedication stunned Patrick. He waited for Kate to protest, but the prickly lady doctor had hidden her face in the baby's neck, as if drawing comfort from the soft weight and powder smell of the child in her arms.

"Well, thank God she's taking care of mine," he said curtly. "The least I can do is stick around."

Amy smiled ruefully. "That's real sweet. That's more than any man has done for me. Okay, then. I guess I'll go pick up Mama. Billy, you be good, now." She hugged her baby and kissed the air by her sister's cheek. "See y'all later."

She floated to the little blue car parked in the weeds by the trailer. With a wave of her hand and a beep of her horn, she was gone.

Hell. Patrick studied Kate, wondering at her reaction to her flighty younger sister. Wondering what his own response should be.

She straightened her shoulders, shifting the baby to her other hip. "Billy, why don't you take Jack inside and show him your space men. Patrick, could you please take that bag out of the trunk for me?"

Her brisk recovery made him grin. "Yes, Doctor."

Billy balked at the trailer steps, dragging the toe of one sneaker in the dirt. "Can we go down to the creek, instead? We'll be careful," he added quickly, anticipating his aunt's caution.

Kate's gaze sought Patrick's. He warmed at the hesitancy he found there. "Is that all right with you?"

"Where is the creek?"

Kate pointed. "Right there. You can see it from the kitchen window."

This was part of the test flight, Patrick guessed. Could he afford to let his boy try his wings? "How deep?"

"With all the rain we've had, it might be, oh, eight inches."

So they wouldn't drown. "Anything else you should warn me about?"

Kate smiled. "Muddy shoes?"

Patrick nodded, accepting both the information and the probability. He and his brothers had trashed more shoes than a battalion at boot camp.

"Fine. As long as you're both careful. Jack, stay with Billy."

Jack was pale with excitement. "'Kay, Dad."

"And stay in front of the window where I can see you," Kate added.

"Yes, Aunt Katie," Billy said cheekily.

"And keep your bandage dry!" she called after them.

Inside the trailer, Kate plunged into activity, depositing Jenny in her playpen and pulling plastic baby bottles out from one of the cabinets. Patrick had trouble reconciling the flushed, devoted aunt bustling in the cramped kitchen with the cool, decisive doctor he'd first met. The contrast fascinated him, tempted him to explore. What had driven Kate Sinclair from the trailer park to Jefferson University Hospital?

He crossed his arms, studying her. "So how much older are you than your sister?"

Her busy hands paused briefly over the bottles. "Eons," she said. "Can you reach a can of formula out of that cabinet? I want to feed Jenny and get her down for her nap. Then I'll make lunch for the rest of us."

So they weren't going to discuss her sister, Patrick thought, contemplating her averted face. That was fine with him. As she'd been so careful to insist, they had a doctor/father-of-a-patient relationship. He didn't need the details of her personal life.

He handed her the formula and then leaned a hip against the counter. "What's in the bag?"

Running water in the sink, she barely spared him a glance. "Groceries."

He raised an eyebrow. "You brought groceries to your sister's?"

She shrugged, not answering. She didn't need to. Suddenly, the way she lived, the plain apartment, the rattletrap car, made disturbing sense. Opening a cabinet door, he began to stack cans of tuna and tomatoes on the second shelf.

Leave it, MacNeill, he ordered himself. But in the Corps he'd been known for his willingness to tackle ticklish assignments. He tried a quick, conversational foray. "So when you two were growing up, did she steal all your boyfriends?"

Bottles rattled in the sink. "What boyfriends?"

He lowered his hand, studying her uncompromising back. "There had to have been boyfriends."

"Why?"

Nine years since she'd had a lover, Patrick thought. Surely that wasn't the pattern of her life? He remembered the frame house in Quincy, the girls dropping by through long, hot summers to watch the MacNeill boys mow the grass and wash the car. He could almost taste the tang of sweat, the smell of excitement, as they experimented at love in the back seats of cars and under the bleachers in the high-school gym. Between chores and Holly, he'd never had the success Sean boasted of, but still...

"I just figured that sort of thing was part of growing up."

Kate shook her head. Her hair slipped forward to veil her face, and he felt his groin tighten. "Not for me. I never even went to my prom."

"Too busy studying?"

"Never asked."

He felt a vague need to apologize for the inadequacies of teenage boys. "They were probably intimidated."

"Not intimidated. Just not interested."

He tried to imagine Kate at sixteen. She'd been a brain, he figured. Con had gone for that type. She probably wore dark baggy T-shirts that couldn't disguise her developing breasts. He pictured her with plain nails and loose hair and big, serious brown eyes.

"Honey, I don't believe that for a minute."

Water splashed as she set another bottle on the drain board. "It's true. I was fat, I was ugly, I didn't know how to dress, and I talked too much."

Her vulnerability fissured his control. "Fat, huh?" He pushed away from the counter and came up behind her. "You probably matured early. You've got great curves."

He put his hands on her hips and pulled her back against him, ignoring her swift intake of breath, letting her feel just what those curves did to him. "What's a poor, dumb kid gonna do with a girl his age who's built like a woman? I'm telling you, they were intimidated."

Between his hands, she trembled. He dragged in a breath, fighting to keep his touch easy on her hips. He wanted to span her ribs with his fingers. He wanted to sneak his palms up over her round, firm breasts. Remembering the way her nipple had risen to his touch, his body surged.

"I still wasn't pretty," she insisted.

Tenderness swelled in him, almost crowding out desire. Almost. He turned her to face him, leaning her back against the sink.

"You look okay to me." He lifted one hand to play with her pretty hair, loving the way it curled around his fingers. "You've got nice hair. Nice eyes." She kept them lowered, as if his collarbone was a medical anomaly. "Did you have pimples when you were a kid?"

That brought her gaze up. "No!"

He smiled. "Nice skin." He let his palm cup her cheek, warming his hand on her blush as he continued to catalog her features. "Your nose is pretty straight. Your mouth…"

Her mouth quivered. She bit down on her lower lip to punish it, and he was undone. "Damn, you've got a sweet mouth, honey."

He bent to taste it. He used his tongue to comfort her poor lip and then to dip inside. Warmth and welcome greeted him. He traced the slick inner surface of her lip and the smooth, sharp edge of her teeth, getting to know her, learning the textures of her mouth. She pressed closer, seeking more. He widened the kiss, widened his stance, dipping deeper. She sucked on his tongue, and his blood pressure shot through the roof.

He lifted her, so the sink supported her sweet, lush backside, and found a place for himself between her thighs. Her breath came shallow and quick against his lips as she strained against him. Her wet hands trailed up his arms and grabbed his hair. He smelled lemon dish detergent and something sweeter, wilder, distilled from the hollows of her skin. Groaning encouragement, he thrust back into her mouth.

Her calves wrapped the back of his thighs. Her knee knocked the counter, and something clattered and fell. Jenny's bottle rolled on the floor.

Wild-eyed, Kate pushed at his chest. Patrick let her go, using his strength to gentle her, to ease her down from the edge of the sink, to support her until her legs could do the job on their own.

"I can't believe...I never meant..."

"Spit it out, honey."

Glaring, she took a deep breath and tried again. "I thought we agreed it was in Jack's best interest to keep our relationship completely professional."

She meant it, too. He raked a hand through his hair. "Yeah, we did."

Better that way, he thought. Safer that way. Only the bulge in his jeans and the empty feeling in his chest were telling him different.

He took a step back, hooking his thumbs in his back pockets, trying to lighten the tension between them. "I just figured maybe you could use a different perspective on your high-school years.''

He admired the way she lifted her chin and attempted a smile. ''Gee, thanks.''

He couldn't help himself. He had to say it. ''You were right about one thing, though.''

She blinked at him owlishly. ''What?''

''You do talk too much.''

Chapter 7

"This whole visit," Kate announced in the car going home, "was a mistake."

The yellow caution markers flashed in her headlights, rushing down the current of a dark river. Concentrating on the road, she didn't look at Patrick, but awareness of him beat through her body like a pulse. He crowded her car, his knees almost touching the glove compartment. He turned to check on Jack, sleeping in the back, and his arm stretched along the top of her seat. She felt its heat against her neck, imagined the brush of his fingertips.

"Lunch was good," he offered mildly.

Kate snorted. "Lunch was sandwiches. And about five hours too long."

"Your sister said she lost track of the time."

"Sure."

"She always take advantage of you like that?"

"I..." Kate sighed. "No, of course not. She's just started a new job, and she probably needed to get away. She's had a busy week."

"Yeah, and being a doctor is a walk in the park, right?"

It was so rare for someone to take her part that Kate actually smiled before shaking her head. "I still should never have invited you."

"The kids got along okay."

"The *kids*... Well, yes. I was talking about us."

He lifted one dark eyebrow. "Honey, if we weren't getting along, I'd love to be around when you're feeling friendly."

Kate bit her lip. She could handle the man's sex appeal. Maybe. Once she got used to it. So what if his attention made her feel like a fourth grader who'd gotten more Valentines than anybody else, or a duty date suddenly presented with a wrist corsage by her escort? She'd been taken in by a man's flattering interest before.

But she was a sucker for his humor. No one before Patrick had ever bothered to tease with bookish, serious Kate. And she was discovering the urge to laugh with him was even greater than the need to freeze him out.

How could a man who'd been through all Patrick MacNeill had endured still have the heart, the guts, the nerve to make her smile?

"We got along too well, and you know it."

"Lighten up, Kate. It was just a kiss."

"Like a subdural hematoma is just a bruise."

His eyes gleamed. "Don't get medical on me now."

"I don't know any other way to be. I'm a doctor."

"And kissing me makes you less of a doctor?"

She wasn't sure. "You're missing the point. Jack—"

"Likes you."

In spite of her defensive attitude, his words warmed her. Of course, Jack was such a wonderful little boy, he probably liked everybody. But it was nice to be liked. She relaxed her grip on the steering wheel.

"I think I've been effective with him," she admitted cautiously.

"Effective. Yeah, you could say that." Patrick shifted to

face her, and the scent of him, soap and sweat and some spicy aftershave, drifted through the dark. ''I still think Jack should have that surgery this summer, but you were dead-on about his needing kids his own age. He really took to your sister's boy.''

In spite of the doubts started by his mention of the surgery, she smiled, pleased. ''He did, didn't he?''

''Yeah. The visit was good for him, Kate. But not for some medical reason. Not because you're his doctor. Because you invited him into your family and gave him a friend.''

It was too tempting, too dangerous, to believe him. If she wasn't a doctor, she was nothing. ''All the same, he's my patient.''

''He's Swaim's patient.''

''And Dr. Swaim is my boss.''

''So.'' He studied her face in the dim glow of the dashboard. She fixed her gaze firmly on the road. ''It's political?''

''Yes. No. But I am attached to the hospital where Jack is a patient. It's not unethical, precisely, for me to see you, it's just…unwise.''

''Come off it, Kate. You said it yourself. You're a doctor, first and last. I can't see you letting any relationship compromise Jack's recovery.''

''Not on purpose, no. But—''

''And I'm not conceited enough to suppose I'd be the man to distract you from doing your job. I've seen you with Jack. I've seen you at the hospital. Hell, I've seen you with your sister's kids. You're not going to neglect your patients' care for a stunt roll and a loop-the-loop. So what is it exactly that you're afraid of?''

Of you, she almost said, but that wasn't true. He'd proven his essential kindness, his basic decency, over and over again. She was afraid of herself. Not that she would be less of a doctor for Jack, but that she wouldn't be enough of a woman for Patrick.

She signalled her exit. The car's tires rumbled through the

long, slow turn. "I've worked very hard to get where I am," she said as steadily as she could. "I don't want to compromise my position at the hospital because of a temporary attraction, and I don't have time for anything else."

Patrick leaned back against the passenger side door, but there was nothing relaxed about his pose. She could feel the weight of his interest, like the building air pressure that forecast a storm.

"Our involvement doesn't have anything to do with the hospital. It's the other one that's the kicker. No time, no energy. No sex for either of us."

Patrick MacNeill without sex? The mind boggled. His masculinity proclaimed itself in a dozen ways: his coiled intensity, his controlled strength, the obvious ease with which he inhabited his broad-chested, long-boned body. How had this potent, passionate man managed since his wife died?

Her own case was different, Kate thought. Her ex-lover had always accused her of a lack of enthusiasm in bed. She was honest enough to acknowledge that it was the intimacy she'd craved in that brief, disastrous relationship, not the physical gymnastics. Since their breakup, she'd sometimes wondered if the fault had been at least partly Wade's, but, frankly, going without sex had never been a problem for her.

Until now.

Her grip tightened on the wheel as she guided the car into the parking lot and under a light. The overhead glow threw Patrick's face into sharp relief: dark eyes, strong nose, sensitive mouth. Her insides contracted. She turned the key in the ignition.

"We're here," she said unnecessarily, and fumbled with her seat belt.

"Kate."

Her hands stilled on the shoulder strap. She looked out at the moon- and fluorescent-washed parking lot. "What?"

He shifted on the seat beside her, checking to see if Jack

still slept, and his knee brushed her thigh. With the engine shut off, the car's interior was warm and close and very silent.

"I respect that you don't have room for a grand passion in your life. Neither do I. Thing is," he continued slowly, "I'm already spending too much time thinking about you. Wanting you. Imagining how it could be between us. Maybe it would be less…distracting for us both if we found out."

She turned to face him, choosing indignation over the quaking in her stomach. "Are you suggesting we sleep together to get it out of our systems?"

"That's one way to put it. Neither one of us wants a complicated relationship in our lives."

With an effort, she kept her voice low, to avoid waking the child in the back. "And am I supposed to be flattered by this limited offer?"

He shook his head, his smile gleaming in the darkness. "Not flattered. Interested, maybe."

She was interested, all right. More tempted and more scared than she'd ever been in her life. She folded her hands tightly together in her lap to disguise their shaking. "I don't know. I'll have to think about it."

"Kate." His deep voice was gentle. "I don't want to hurt you. I like you. But you need to know up front how things are with me. I may want you until my teeth ache with it, but Jack is the center of my life right now. If that's not enough for you, if I misunderstood you, just tell me no."

Her nails dug into the backs of her hands. Kate had long ago accepted that she wasn't the kind of woman men wanted to marry. Wade, brutally breaking their understanding, had gone so far as to suggest she wasn't the kind of woman men wanted, period. But Patrick wanted her. And maybe she owed it to herself, just once, to experience a man like Patrick MacNeill.

"I understand. I'll get back to you."

"Good. That's good." He paused a moment, as if there was

something else he wanted to say, and then unfolded abruptly from his seat. "Let me walk you to your door."

She glanced over her shoulder at Jack, still asleep in the back. "What about...?"

"I've got to shift him to our car anyway."

She waited, jingling her keys, as he lifted the sleeping boy from the car. "Go home. I'm fine. I don't need an escort."

Patrick adjusted Jack over his chest like an examination drape. The boy stirred and clung. "I'll walk you to your door."

She shrugged irritably. "Whatever you want."

He grinned at her over his son's dark head. "Is that a promise?"

Kate swallowed. Ridiculous that he could make her feel this way without touching her, with the child between them. "I'll let you know."

"Fair enough."

He followed her along the cement walkway, gravel from the cracks grinding beneath their soles, and then stood to one side as she unlocked her door.

"I'll be gone a couple of days next week," he offered abruptly. "Charter flight to the Outer Banks. My partner Ray doesn't want to be away overnight so close to his wife's due date, so I'm covering it."

It was none of her business. She found herself asking anyway. "What about Jack?"

"My brother Sean's between jobs right now. He'll come down and stay. Is it okay if I give him your number?"

She was gratified that he'd ask. The request didn't seem to fit what he'd said about—what was it? oh, yes—a stunt-roll relationship. "He really should call Dr. Swaim. Jack's not my patient."

"Yeah, but he likes you." He hesitated. "This isn't medical, Kate. I just want Sean to have backup. If it's not okay..."

"No, no. Please. He can call any time."

"Right."

Holding Jack against his shoulder with one large hand, Patrick dipped his head. Briefly, his lips touched hers.

"I'll call you," he said.

It sounded like a line. Wasn't that what her father had whispered in the driveway as he left, what a parade of boys had promised Amy? Hadn't her ex-lover said something similar just before he got the offer from Baltimore General and decided he didn't need her anymore?

But looking into Patrick's deep-set, dark blue eyes, Kate was tempted to believe him.

Of course, he wanted her help with Jack.

That was all right, Kate told herself stoutly. He wasn't trying to deceive her about his aims or his motives. He hadn't pretended his physical passion. He genuinely respected her rapport with his son.

Maybe this time. Maybe this once.

In spite of that flutter of hope, the following Wednesday, when Sharon Williams popped into her office and announced that Mr. MacNeill insisted on seeing her, Kate stiffened.

"Is Jack with him?"

"Yes, but—"

"Fine." Kate stood. "But I have rounds in twenty minutes. He's going to learn that I can't drop everything every time he blows in."

Sharon smiled knowingly. "I'm not sure this one can be taught, Dr. Sinclair."

Kate's spine straightened another degree. Maybe she was no man's dream date, but as a surgeon she'd learned to value herself and her time. She hadn't endured the slights and rigors of her male-dominated surgical training to let one cocky pilot dictate to her now. She marched down the hall, banged through the glass and steel doors—and stopped short.

For an instant, she was convinced she was seeing double. The waiting room appeared full of MacNeills. Patrick paced, fists jammed in his pockets, his wide shoulders and contained

intensity dwarfing his surroundings. She felt her heart trip into
double time at the sight of him.

But nothing could dwarf the man beside him.

Taller and younger than Patrick, his companion had the
same dark hair, longer and curlier, and the same male assurance. He wore a gold hoop in his ear, like a pirate, and exuded
cheerful good nature and unabashed sex. There were at least
three nurses craning for a look at him, and one patient's
mother was openly fanning herself.

Three months ago, such blatant good looks would have frozen Kate into a cold and inarticulate block of insecurity. She
discovered now that after knowing Patrick, his brother didn't
alarm her at all. No more than she would be afraid of a wolf-
hound after petting a wolf.

She tapped her pen on her clipboard. "So. Which Mr.
MacNeill can't wait to see me?"

Three dark heads turned. The shortest one dashed forward.

"Dr. Kate!"

A corner of her heart melted at the boy's exuberant greeting.
"Hey, Jack-o. Are you sick?"

"Nope."

"Pining for you," the younger man offered.

Kate smiled down at the boy's bright face. "I find that
difficult to believe."

"Okay," the pirate said agreeably. "Maybe Patrick's the
one pining."

The listening nurses goggled. Kate felt her cheeks flame.
With gossip breeding in the hospital like bacteria in a wound,
she'd always resolved to keep her personal life private. Not
that it had been much of an issue. Until recently, she hadn't
had a personal life. She swallowed. She still didn't have a
personal life. Patrick might want to go to bed with her, but
they hadn't even been on a date.

"Sean," Patrick said warningly.

"So it's me. I need a doctor. Take my pulse." He snatched

her hand, enclosing the pen with it, and laid it on his muscled chest, just above his heart. "What do you think, Doc?"

Kate lifted her chin, refusing to be flustered. "You feel normal to me."

"Not just a little hot?" His dark eyes were wicked, inviting her to share his joke.

"No. Sorry."

"You don't think maybe I need some bed rest?"

"You don't let go of her hand," Patrick growled, "and you won't be getting up for a week."

"Oops. Big Brother has spoken." Gracefully, he released her hand. "I'm Sean MacNeill."

She smiled, amused in spite of herself. "Kate Sinclair."

"*Dr.* Sinclair." Patrick stressed her title. "And she works here, Sean, so try for a little respect, okay?"

"Right. Sorry, Doctor."

Patrick's defense of her time and professional dignity won forgiveness and a concession. "It's all right. I've got a few minutes before I start rounds."

Patrick swept Jack's crayon box from the child-sized table, tucking it under his arm. "We wouldn't have bothered you except the Ape Man here wanted to meet you before I left town."

"Well, it's very nice to see you." Finally, she dared to look directly at Patrick, and her breath caught with sexual shock at the heat in his eyes. "All of you."

He smiled, still holding her gaze. "That's good to hear. I didn't want to send you screaming in the opposite direction."

Tension stretched between them like a soft cotton bandage. Kate reminded herself to exhale.

"Not yet."

"Am I missing something?" Sean asked plaintively.

Patrick collected himself. He didn't need his mischievous little brother taking notes on his love life and reporting back to their mother. "No. You wanted to meet her, you've met. Say goodbye, Jack."

The boy's eyes crinkled. "Goodbye, Jack," he parroted.

Kate laughed. Damn, she had a sexy laugh, deep and warm. She always looked surprised when it escaped, as if she didn't use it very often.

"Bye, Jack." She offered her small, practical hand to Sean. "It was nice to meet you, Mr. MacNeill."

"Yeah. A pleasure."

He held on to it a second too long. Patrick's brows flicked together in annoyance.

"Come on. Kate's got rounds. And we've got to go eat."

He jammed his hands into his pockets, resisting the desire to touch her. To kiss her goodbye. They had an audience. The simple, limited relationship he'd suggested to her didn't involve her colleagues at the hospital or his family.

"I'll be back next week." And then, because he couldn't help himself, he added, "You think about what I said."

She tilted her head, regarding him with cool challenge. "I'll think about it."

With Sean radiating curiosity, there was nothing more he could say. They left.

Patrick thought, he hoped, that was the end of it. It wasn't until they were seated in the warm, dark restaurant booth, with beers in front of them and a Cherry Coke for Jack, that Sean reopened the topic for discussion.

"Pretty thing," he observed.

Patrick tensed. He hadn't expected Kate's subtle appeal to register with Sean. The thought of his brother's perception made him uncomfortable. What he felt for Kate Sinclair—whatever he felt for Kate Sinclair—was none of his brother's business.

"Pretty enough," he agreed.

Sean sipped his beer, watching him. "Mind if I call her while you're gone?"

Patrick eyed him warily. "Are we talking about backup for Jack here?"

"No."

With a decisive click, Patrick centered his bottle precisely on a wet ring. "Then, yes, I mind. She isn't your type. She's a nice woman. A good doctor. And she's too old for you. Lay off."

Sean grinned, helping himself to fries from the red plastic basket in the middle of the table. "She's not your usual type either."

"Meaning?"

"Meaning…she's no Holly."

At the mention of his late wife, Patrick waited for the familiar twist of heart. It didn't come.

"True enough." In spite of his discomfort, he smiled. "The doctor's a damn sight harder to get along with, for one thing."

Sean swirled his beer. "Do you good. I used to wonder if you and Holly hadn't been stuck on each other since high school, if she would have been right for you."

Patrick's eyes narrowed. "What the hell are you talking about?"

"Well, it's no secret she thought the sun shone out of your—"

Patrick jerked his head toward Jack, busily scarfing down a bite-sized burger.

"Sorry," Sean said. "Hey, what do I know? I was just a kid. It's just she always seemed—I don't know—so soft."

Patrick set down his sandwich, stung by the criticism of his late wife. "She was young."

"Exactly. You both were. My point is, if you'd both been older when you'd met, would you have married her?"

"Of course I would have married her. I loved her." Too late, Patrick realized he'd used the past tense. He scowled.

Sean spread his hands appeasingly. "Hey, I loved her, too. We all did." He grinned, lightening the atmosphere. "Of course, agreeable women are my thing. Good luck with your doctor lady."

Under the joking tone, Patrick heard Sean's genuine affection. He felt a sharp, unmistakable tug of gratitude for his youngest brother. Almost nine years separated them. Yet the family ties were strong, the links of blood, of love, of shared experiences and commitments. John and Bridget MacNeill had raised their sons to stand back-to-back-to-back.

Patrick knew his isolation after Holly's death had worried his whole family. He'd felt the weight of their concern in his mother's looks and his father's silence, endured it in his brothers' teasing. But much as he hated to burst Sean's bubble, he couldn't let his brother take home the wrong idea about his relationship with Kate Sinclair.

He and Jack were a unit. The bonds forged in blood and pain wouldn't dissolve to admit anyone else.

"Look, I'll admit I'm working on getting her into—" His hand closed around the cool, sweaty bottle as he glanced at Jack. "—Getting to know her better," he finished lamely. "But that's as far as it goes. That's as far as it can go. She's got her job, and I've got Jack."

Sean's eyes danced. "Whatever you say, Big Brother. Whatever you want. Hey, I admire your taste. Welcome back to the land of the living."

Patrick frowned into his beer. "Shut up and eat your burger."

Kate went through afternoon rounds with a curious double focus. Not distracted. She would not tolerate distraction, in herself or her team or the students that trailed them from room to room. But Patrick MacNeill's visit scraped delicately at her customary protective coating, exposing her nerves, heightening her physical and emotional awareness. She felt almost like one of her patients, with the sensitivity of an open wound.

And so, in spite of the fact that nineteen of the unit's twenty-one beds were full, and the residents dragged, and the occupational therapist grumbled, she took her time on rounds. She rubbed the feet of the patient in Room 811, the only part of him unburned after a trailer truck collided with his pickup. She talked to Janet Heller for almost ten minutes, knowing that the woman was depressed by the decreasing frequency of her family's visits. She promised the nine-year-old in 816 a visit to play therapy if he'd take his meds for Nurse Williams.

She dealt with routine, too, checking fluids, dressings and pain meds, questioning residents, therapists and nurses, and reassuring anxious family. Exiting the room of an eighteen-year-old firefighter, she paused briefly by an intern retching in the hall.

Schooling her sympathy from her face, she repeated the hard-learned lessons of her own first year. "Don't let it get to you. You're no good to anyone if you can't keep your concentration."

He muttered into the basin as she passed. Calling her a name, probably. She shrugged. Maybe he wasn't finished throwing up yet. But it was good advice. She was struggling to follow it herself.

Patrick's blue eyes burned in the back of her mind. *You think about what I said.*

She couldn't forget it.

Sharon Williams followed her back to her office. "Got a minute?"

Kate straightened her shoulders. "Sure."

But whatever had driven Sharon to seek her out, she was in no hurry to discuss it. She hovered in the doorway. "You had a nice touch tonight. With the patients."

Kate smiled, appreciating the veteran nurse's compliment. "Our occupational therapist didn't think so."

Sharon shrugged, coming forward into the room. "Her? Oh, she doesn't like anything that keeps her from her dinner. She's as bad as a doctor that way."

Kate regarded her coolly, unsure if she'd just been insulted. Sharon grinned.

"I guess so," Kate said, relaxing. "You want to sit down?"

"Naw. Once I'm down I'll never get up." The big woman propped one hip on the corner of Kate's desk and sighed. "Cute picture."

Kate followed her gaze to the drawing of eagles taped over the filing cabinet. Her heart lightened, the way it did every time she looked at the darn thing. "Jack MacNeill drew that."

"Little Iron Man? Really? He's good. My kid is almost seven, and he draws birds like this." Sharon's finger traced a check mark in the air.

Kate nodded, waiting. She was pretty sure Sharon hadn't tracked her to her office to talk about kindergarten art.

"We sure have been seeing a lot of them lately. The MacNeills."

Kate's stomach flared. Uh-oh. She should have known Sean MacNeill's prodigal good looks and extravagant behavior wouldn't escape comment. Just what had the nurses in the waiting room seen? How much had they heard? And what were they saying?

"That's not surprising," she said noncommittally. "Isn't Peg still seeing Jack?"

"Every Wednesday. With his stitches out, he should be off the splint real soon."

So Swaim had removed the rest of Jack's sutures, and no one had even told her. Kate reminded herself she didn't want to interfere between her director and his patients, but she couldn't help her protective, proprietary interest in Jack.

"That's good. That's great. Um, how did it go?"

"Fine. Dr. Swaim kept all of his clinic appointments yesterday."

"Good," Kate said again, too heartily.

Sharon wandered over to the corner and began pinching at her yellowing philodendron. "He was asking about you."

Kate swallowed. "Swaim?"

"Mm. He wanted to know how often you'd seen the MacNeill boy."

"Just twice, I think." If she didn't count the surgery. Or the late night call to his room. Or her visit to his house or his jaunt to her sister's. "Why?"

''Apparently Mr. MacNeill questioned whether Dr. Swaim should do that surgery on the boy's face and ear or not.''

Kate rubbed a spot under her ribs where tension was beginning to burn. She was glad for Jack's sake that Patrick had listened to her. She was pleased that he trusted her judgment that much. But they weren't out of the woods yet. ''And?''

''And the Great White Doctor sounded pretty miffed that somebody was impugning his judgment.'' Sharon flashed a look over her shoulder. ''That's a quote.''

It was a warning. ''I see. Thank you, Sharon.''

''Don't mention it, honey.'' Brushing her hands, the nurse walked to the door. ''For what it's worth, I don't think they should do the operation either.''

''Did you say so?''

Sharon's eyes widened mockingly. ''And risk a reprimand?''

Kate sighed. ''Right.''

The tall nurse's warrior-maiden face softened. ''Look, it's not my place to say. It's none of my business. But you might want to steer clear of MacNeills for a while.''

''Even good-looking ones in the waiting room?'' Kate asked dryly.

Sharon sniffed. ''Maybe *especially* good-looking ones in the waiting room.''

''Thanks. I appreciate the advice.''

At least, Kate corrected herself, she appreciated the nurse's concern. She hadn't counted on Sharon as an ally, and the knowledge that the nurse thought highly enough of her to warn her was sweet.

But could she really stay away from the MacNeill men? Did she want to?

She thumbed an antacid off the roll in her pocket and sucked it thoughtfully. For almost twenty years, for all her life it seemed, she'd struggled to prove to herself and everyone else that she could make it as a surgeon. Her mother had always suggested she make the most of the brains God gave her, since He hadn't seen fit to bless her with looks. And she was good, dammit. Surgery defined her, empowered her, rewarded her as nothing and no one else ever had. Was the limited physical relationship which was all that Patrick offered worth the risk to her career?

Regretfully, Kate decided it was not.

Chapter 8

His lips were warm and firm and open. Perfect. His big, callused hands stroked over her shoulders to close gently on her breasts. In her bed, Kate shifted and sighed, her head tilting, her own hands fisting on the sheets.

The phone rang and woke her up.

Kate struggled to roll over, fighting sleep and annoyance and the seductive memory of Patrick's lips, Patrick's hands. Damn it. She wasn't on call tonight.

"Amy, this better be good."

"Sorry, Kate." The voice on the other end of the line was male and apologetic. "Not Amy, and not good, either."

Her heart thumped. *Patrick?* But no, this voice was rougher, younger, more like...

"Sean?" She identified him into the receiver.

"Yeah. Look, I'm sorry to be calling so late. I didn't know what else to do."

Worry propelled her upright. She shoved her hair out of her eyes. "That's okay. Is it Jack? Is he all right?"

"He's fine."

Oh, Lord. "Patrick?"

"Fine." Sean's hesitation hummed down the line. Kate bit back the impulse to fire questions at the phone, to diagnose the cause of his trouble. They weren't in her examining room now. "Look, I've got to ask you a favor."

"Go ahead."

"Could you watch Jack for me? Our dad's in the hospital, and I've got to get home."

"I'm so sorry," she said automatically.

She wasn't expecting this. *You agreed to be his backup,* she reminded herself, and was deeply grateful Patrick had introduced them at least. "Was your father sick?" she asked.

"No. He started complaining his chest hurt, and then his arm went numb. Mom's pretty upset. She made him go to the hospital after dinner, and, well, they admitted him."

Kate's mind raced. "Preexisting heart condition?"

"I don't know. We didn't think so." She heard his frustration, his fear, and sympathy welled in her at the change from the easy-going pirate she'd first met. "Con's with them," he continued, "but, jeez…I've got to be there."

She understood the claims of family, even a fractured one. And in a clan as close as the MacNeills appeared to be, the illness of their patriarch must strike hard. Kate yawned, struggling to think. She was off for the day. She could sacrifice a little sleep to watch Jack until Patrick returned. Surely it wouldn't take a pilot with his own plane more than a day to get back home.

"All right. Um, does your brother know?"

"Coast guard's radioing him. There are no phones on the island. I'm sure he'll call you as soon as he can."

Her sympathy ratcheted up a notch. It didn't seem right for family man Patrick to learn of his father's condition from strangers. Then it struck her. Did Patrick know Sean was handing over his son to her care?

"Maybe you should call his partner," she suggested.

"I did. Ray's taking over the charter return. But Shelby, his wife, is really pregnant. I can't leave Jack with her."

He sounded close to panic. "No, of course not," Kate soothed.

"You're my backup," Sean said plaintively.

In her memory, Patrick's deep voice echoed: *This isn't medical, Kate.* And she heard her own reply: *He can call any time.*

"Right," she said, resigned. "What do you need?"

"I've got a chance at a six forty-five flight to Boston through JFK," Sean said. "Gets me in around noon. If I could bring Jack over early…"

Kate squinted at her bedside clock. It was almost three in the morning. She rubbed her face with her hand, trying to wake up, her brain clicking over possibilities. "No, I'll drive out there. You shouldn't haul Jack out of bed. Besides, I know the way, and you don't."

His gust of relief made her smile. "Good. Great. Thanks. Thanks a lot."

Kate covered the receiver as she yawned again. "It's no problem," she lied. "What time do you need to leave?"

"Five?"

Which meant, Kate thought glumly, she'd have to leave her apartment by four. "No problem," she repeated.

She listened to more thanks before hanging up, pushed Blackwell off the bed, and headed for the shower.

Kate was both amused and disgusted to see that neither worry nor lack of sleep dimmed the incredible MacNeill good looks. Sean's eyes were bright, his hair attractively ruffled. His overnight stubble made him look more like a pirate than ever.

"I really appreciate this," he said, turning on his way out the door.

His black athletic bag swung, hitting her.

"Ouch." Kate rubbed her hipbone, feeling rumpled and tired. "Don't mention it."

"Jack's asleep," he repeated for the third or fourth time. "Important numbers are by the phone. Patrick has a message to call here."

"Fine. Now go, or you'll miss your flight."

"Right." She was enveloped briefly in a hard male embrace, her nose squashed to his soft shirt front. Surprise kept her immobile. "You're a doll, Kate. Patrick's a lucky bastard."

She blinked at the paneled door as it closed behind him, flattered, touched and bewildered.

Don't let it get to you, Katie Sue, she lectured herself. That boy would hug his grandmother if the old lady were helping him out of a jam. In fact, that's probably how he thinks of you, as a pleasant older woman he can wile into doing him a favor. His brother's current female domestic.

She must have been crazy to agree to this. Or tired and too susceptible to the MacNeill brand of charm. Patrick had asked her for backup, but he couldn't have anticipated interference on this scale. Would he even want her moving into his lair to watch his son? Did she want to be his nanny-on-call?

Kate had learned her lesson the hard way. Men found her attractive in direct proportion to how useful she could be. Hadn't Wade proven that when they were residents together, when she'd researched his cases and covered his shifts and warmed his meals and his bed?

All the same, she discovered, it wasn't totally unpleasant to be of use to the MacNeill men, to be included in their masculine family circle. At least she had no illusions about why they wanted her around. *If* Patrick really wanted her around. Wryly, she hoped she could live up to Sean's confidence in her as a baby-sitter. She was an excellent surgeon and a competent aunt, but the fine points of caring for a four-and-a-half-year-old boy for an extended time might be beyond her.

Rubbing absently at her stomach, Kate went into the kitchen to brew herself coffee and rustle up breakfast for Jack.

* * *

Cold cereal, she thought, surveying the boxes lining the pantry shelf. Perfect. Jack could pick his favorite and all she'd need to add was milk.

Satisfied with her solution to breakfast, Kate was hunting for spoons when the telephone shrilled. She flew across the kitchen to answer it before the ringing woke Jack.

"Hello? Um, MacNeills."

"Kate. Are you all right?"

The sound of that deep, smooth voice in the private morning hour made her heart hammer in her chest. She straightened her shoulders. "Yes, of course. Patrick, I'm so sorry—"

"How's Jack?" He interrupted her expression of sympathy.

"Fine. Asleep, actually. I checked on him about half an hour ago."

"Okay. I can be home in about four hours. If it's not too much trouble, can you give him breakfast? I'll pack for him when I get there."

He sounded distracted. Tense. Kate swallowed her annoyance at his abruptness, reminding herself that naturally Patrick was distressed about his father.

"Of course I can give him breakfast. Why do you need to pack? Pack for where?"

"Boston," came the clipped reply. "I'm taking him with me."

Kate's hand tightened on the receiver. "Why?"

She heard his sharp intake of breath, but he explained patiently, control stamped on his voice. "I just got off the phone with my mother. They're still running tests, but it looks like Dad's going to need an angioplasty."

So it was his father's heart. Her doctor's brain considered the options. "Stroke?"

"They don't know yet. Maybe not."

"When's the surgery?"

"Monday, probably. I can't let them face that alone."

His bleak tone tore at her. As a surgeon, she confronted countless families with good news and bad. But as a woman,

she felt totally inadequate to solace him. She struggled for
words that would help. "Sean—"

"Went up already. I know. And left you holding Jack. I
should break his neck. Kate, I'm sorry."

"I'm fine," she insisted, hoping he wasn't also thinking of
breaking hers.

"He shouldn't have bothered you."

"You gave him my number," she told him reasonably and
more confidently than she felt.

"Well, I shouldn't have."

His man-in-charge attitude was beginning to grate on her.
"For heaven's sake, why not?"

"You're too busy."

"I have the day off."

"It's still not right."

This was getting them nowhere. He needed help, and she
could provide it. "Why not? What do you think I'm going to
do to him? Admit him to the hospital?"

Silence.

"I meant," Patrick said tightly, "that I didn't want to impose."

"Well, you're not. Imposing, I mean."

"Sure?"

"Sure."

"I see." Did she imagine it, or was there the faintest trace
of amusement in his tone?

Kate bit her lip as second thoughts assailed her. "Of course,
if you feel I'm not qualified..."

"Come off it, Kate. You're the most qualified person I
know."

"I didn't mean medically."

"Neither did I."

Pleasure at the unexpected compliment bloomed in her
chest. "Oh. Well, thank you."

"Thank you. You'll do great. Jack likes you."

Another charged silence hummed through the line.

"So I'll see you in about four hours," Patrick said.

She heard the preoccupation return to his voice and thought of what faced him in Boston. He could cope, she reminded herself. He had lots of experience in coping.

And suddenly merely keeping Jack for a few hours until Patrick could get home didn't seem nearly enough.

Kate cleared her throat and took a risk. "Do you really want to take Jack with you?"

"Sorry?"

She plowed ahead over his surprise and her own self-doubt. "Well, it's just... He's probably had enough of hospitals. You'll be tied up with your parents and the doctors. He might be better off at home."

"Yeah, maybe. But there's no one to watch him. Shelby—"

"I could stay with him."

"Kate." He sounded shaken. "I can't possibly ask you to—"

The deep note in his voice gave her courage to continue. "You're not asking. I said I'd do it. I watch Billy and Jenny all the time."

"Yeah, and you don't need another parasite like your sister in your life," Patrick muttered.

"It would be better for Jack to stick to his routine." She didn't argue it would be easier for Patrick as well. "I can do his exercises with him. And you could concentrate on your mother."

She held her breath.

"You know, honey," Patrick said slowly, and now she could plainly hear his smile, "if this thing between us is going to take off, you've got to get over this habit of being right all the time."

"Is that yes?" she asked cautiously.

"That is yes and thank-you-very-much."

"Well." She exhaled, relief and pleasure relaxing her lungs. "All right."

His voice became brisk, commanding. "I'll fly direct to

Boston, then. Ray's coming out tomorrow to pick up my party, but if you need anything, his number's posted by—''

"By the phone," Kate finished. "I know."

"Right. My parents' number is there, too, but my guess is we'll be at the hospital. Medical authorization is on the mantel along with spending money. Jack's physical therapy schedule is on the fridge. Every hour on the hour, if you can manage it. You've got to help him with passive range of motion. If he—''

Enough was enough. The medical stuff she could handle. "Patrick."

"What?"

"I can take care of it."

He laughed briefly, almost embarrassed. "Yeah. Okay. I guess you can. Thanks, Kate."

She felt as if he'd cracked a door and let her slip inside. Warmth flooded through her. "You're welcome."

"I'll call you tonight."

This time she had no trouble believing him.

She was hanging up the phone when a shuffle behind her alerted her to Jack's presence. Turning, she saw the boy pausing in the doorway, his bear trailing from one arm, his blue eyes wide and wary.

"Dr. Kate?"

"Hey, Jack." She smiled, but he didn't reward her with his customary grin.

"Where's Uncle Sean?"

Uh-oh. She should have anticipated the child would be anxious without the reassuring male presence of father or uncle. "He had to go to Boston to see your grandparents," she explained gently. "So I came to stay with you for a while."

"Is he okay?"

"He sure is."

Jack scowled, looking so much like his father that her heart squeezed. "Where's Dad?"

"Your daddy's okay, too. He went with Uncle Sean." The

child's lower lip protruded further at this news. Obviously, he was picturing a MacNeill Men reunion that didn't include him. Kate decided they needed a diversion. "How about some breakfast?"

He scuffed forward. "Pancakes?"

Oh, dear. Cooking was not her specialty. "How about cereal?"

"But it's Saturday."

Kate nodded. "That's how I could come stay with you. I don't have to work again until Monday."

Jack ignored this explanation of her schedule, more concerned with his own routine. "But we *always* have pancakes on Saturday," he said, artfully earnest. "And watch cartoons."

Kate narrowed her eyes at this pint-size manipulative male in dinosaur pajamas. She'd worked with pediatric patients enough to know when she was being conned. And she truly didn't believe burning down Patrick's kitchen would be an auspicious start to a weekend of mothering his child. On the other hand, she sympathized with Jack. It must be tough to wake up and find your father gone, your uncle flown the coop, and some biddy in charge of your customary breakfast.

Kate nibbled her lip, considering. She'd told Patrick she could take care of things. Maybe her mother had regularly lamented her lack of domestic skills, but Kate was determined not to fail the MacNeills.

"Go get dressed," she said.

Jack balked. "Why?"

"Because we're going out for donuts, and you should have clothes on." She grinned into his brightening face. "Unless you want to eat in your pajamas."

"No way!" But he was smiling now, and excited. "I need socks."

She drew a deep breath. "All right. Let's find you some socks."

She *would* take care of things until Patrick's return.

* * *

Really, the day hadn't gone too badly, Kate thought, tossing crumpled boy's briefs on the laundry pile in the hall. The donuts had been a success. Jack had cooperated with his therapy. Kate had even had the chance to slog through some paperwork while he watched cartoons.

After lunch, they'd gone for a walk with the dog, and the boy had skipped and shouted and made up silly songs. It wasn't until bedtime that the strain of his father's absence affected Jack's sunny disposition, and then Patrick had called, making everything all right again.

Kate frowned and threw a diminutive pair of jeans on top of the dark load. All right for Jack, anyway.

After giving Kate a medical bulletin from the hospital and instructing her on Jack's bedtime routine, Patrick had spoken exclusively with his son. Kate told herself that Patrick's focus made perfect sense. The child needed his father's reassurance. She was just the baby-sitter. But as she'd coaxed Jack through his bath and another therapy session, as she'd flung dishes into the dishwasher and brewed her evening pot of coffee, Kate was aware of a percolating sense of grievance. Patrick could at least have asked how she was doing.

Scooping up a pile of dirty clothes, she staggered down the stairs to the laundry room off the kitchen. Obviously, Sean hadn't bothered with the wash during his two-day stint as Jack's caregiver, Kate thought virtuously. She found the laundry room as clean and as well-stocked as any operating room, stain stick, detergent and bleach marching with military precision on the shelf above the washing machine.

Maybe there were some advantages to moving in with an ex-Marine, Kate admitted reluctantly, measuring soap into the tub. But Patrick's father-knows-best routine on the phone had nettled her pride and hurt her feelings. Over fourteen years of medical training, and he barked at her like she was some recalcitrant recruit.

She stomped back up the stairs with a plastic laundry basket, fighting a yawn. Her scant night's sleep hadn't prepared her for a day in the company of an active almost-five-year-old. Maybe she'd better find an extra bed and turn in.

Easing open the door to Jack's room, she peeked in. In the glow of the night-light, she saw his dark head turned into his pillow, one white foot escaping the warmth of his covers. She was used to seeing children at the hospital, wakeful or sleeping. But there was something precious and particular about this boy sprawled trustingly in the tangle of blankets. Resisting the urge to brush back his hair, to touch his cheek, she tugged the sheet to cover his foot and slipped back into the hall.

She passed the white-and-black tiled bathroom. The next door opened on a bedroom, masculine and strangely impersonal in spite of the towel tossed on the floor and the framed family photos on the wall. Patrick's room? Ignoring the flutter in her stomach at the sight of the unmade bed, its pillow still indented from the weight of a man's head, Kate retreated to the hall.

That left one more room to explore. She opened the door at the end of the hall and flipped on the brass-plated switch. Light sprang up in the large room, catching her frozen like an intruder in the doorway. This, she realized, this was Patrick's bedroom.

I've got a perfectly good bed to take you to.

Square against the wall, tall between two wide, high windows, stood his bed. Solid posts and a bevelled top board framed thick, long slabs of golden oak, the burnished grain lustrous against the creamy walls. A crisp navy bedspread made it look neat; a twelve-inch mattress made it look soft. Kate had never seen a piece of furniture as inviting, or as intimidating, as Patrick MacNeill's bed. She was backing out cautiously when the bedside phone rang.

Kate jumped as if she'd heard a Code. No time to go downstairs, she thought. And then, scolding herself for her foolish reluctance to trespass, she hurried across the deep plush carpeting and answered the phone.

"MacNeills."

"You sound out of breath," Patrick said. "Is this a bad time?"

Kate sank nervelessly on to the wide, soft mattress. "No." She cleared her throat. "No, it's fine."

"Jack asleep?"

"Yes. Sorry." Mindful of his detailed instructions, she added, "He had a bath and brushed his teeth with the green toothpaste, and we read *Where the Wild Things Are,* and Finn MacCool made all the monster noises. I'll tell him you called, though."

"Why?"

Kate blinked. "Excuse me?"

"I already talked to my son, Kate. I'm calling to talk to you."

She was absurdly pleased. "Oh."

"Are you settling in okay? I suppose it's too much to hope Sean remembered to make up the bed in the guest room."

Disappointment pricked her. Patrick was being a good host, that was all, worrying over the comfort of his unexpected guest.

"How did you guess?" she asked wryly.

"I grew up with him, remember?"

"Well, don't worry about it." To prevent more of his directions, she added, "I'm sure I can find the linen closet. I even know how to make hospital corners."

"Not necessary. Take my bed. I put clean sheets on before I left."

Her hands stroked the navy coverlet. "I couldn't do that."

"Why not?"

"Because." Oh, heavens. "It's your bed."

His voice was deep and wicked. "But I like the idea of you sleeping in my bed."

Kate fought for a note of dry humor. "This isn't going to turn into one of those naughty phone calls, is it?"

"Do you want it to?" He sounded amused.

She put up her chin, forgetting he couldn't see. "Of course not."

"Because I don't have any experience with that kind of thing, but I could give it a shot."

Kate was embarrassed to realize that her heart was beating faster. "Don't be silly."

"I can't help it. I haven't done this before. So, what are you wearing?"

She bit her lip to control her smile. "Oh, please."

"Isn't that how I'm supposed to start?" Patrick asked in mock innocence. "Come on, help me out here."

Kate tried to ignore her racing pulse. "Jeans and a shirt. Hardly seductive."

"Honey, I've seen you in jeans. They'll do. Believe me, they'll do. Is the shirt buttoned?"

Involuntarily, her hand flew to her throat. "It's a T-shirt."

"Damn," he said, and there was so much genuine regret in his voice that she laughed. "What color?"

Her fingers stroked the soft cotton below her neckline. "Teal."

"What is that? Green? Blue?"

"Sort of a greeny blue, I guess."

"Uh-huh. And underneath?"

Against her sensible cotton bra, her nipples drew taut. Her face was hot. "Underwear."

He laughed softly. "That's real descriptive, honey. Guess I'll have to wait to find out in person."

She felt compelled to object. "I haven't said—"

"No, you haven't," he said roughly. "I just didn't figure that when I finally got you into bed I wouldn't be there."

There was an unexpected weariness in his voice, a fissure in his iron control. Instinctively, Kate responded to it, settling back against the headboard, drawing her legs up under her.

"How are things going, Patrick?" she asked gently.

"Fine."

"You sound tired."

"Yeah."

"How's your mother?"

"She's...okay."

Kate tapped her knee in frustration. "You know, getting you to talk about your feelings is like trying to make me describe my underwear. Can you tell me what's really going on, please?"

"I'd rather talk about your underwear."

She waited.

His breath blew out. "Fine. Things are a little tense up here. Mom wasn't expecting this, and she's upset."

"Are your brothers both there?"

"Yeah. Sean is flirting with the nurses, and Con is arguing with the doctors."

"Oh, that's productive."

She could almost see his shrug. "It's distracting, anyway."

"Is there something I can do to help? Talk to your father's doctors, anything?"

"No. Mom's pretty much got the medical angle covered. She works here, remember. Hospitals take good care of their own."

Kate nodded. "Well, if you think of anything..."

"Thanks. You're already doing more than enough. It helps knowing Jack is with you. It helps talking with you."

His confidence honored and scared her at the same time. Protected by the distance that stretched between them, they were drawing closer in ways she'd never anticipated. She took another cautious step forward. "How are you doing?"

"Fine. Like I told you, Dad's stabilized. There's not much to do at this point but wait for the surgery."

And Patrick was good at that, she thought with a tear at her heart. He'd had to be. Like an eagle forced from the sky, he'd trained his fierce, passionate spirit to withstand the confines of hospital waiting rooms. She could imagine how they all relied on him as the eldest. Silent, tempered Patrick would be an anchor for his worried mother, a rock for his shaken brothers, a stand-in for their stricken patriarch.

"The surgery's on Monday?"

"Yeah." He hesitated. "I know it's a lot, asking you to stay on another couple days. I could fly home tomorrow, pick up Jack."

"No," she said firmly. "Stay there. We're doing fine."

"What about your work?"

Kate pressed two fingers between her brows, rubbing away her worry. She'd have to juggle to cover Monday. "It's taken care of."

"Liar."

His perception disconcerted her. She wasn't used to having her needs considered or her pronouncements questioned. "I'll work something out. You just concentrate on your family. Good night."

"Yeah, good night." His voice roughened. "Sleep well."

Sitting on his bed, she pressed her thighs together. "I will."

He chuckled. "No, you won't. You'll think about me."

She resented the easy way he cracked open her defenses. Resented it, but couldn't resist it. "Dream on, flyboy."

"Oh, I will. I'll dream about you in my bed. It goes both ways, Kate."

With that, he hung up.

Just as well, she reflected. He'd left her speechless.

Cradling the receiver, she slid from the mattress. At least her legs still supported her. Her skin tingled. Her jeans chafed her thighs as she walked, and the soft knit of her shirt teased her shoulders. Hugging her arms across her chest to hold in her ballooning desire, she wandered across the room. And came face-to-face with a photograph of Patrick's dead wife.

From within her silver frame on top of her husband's dresser, a pretty dark-haired woman still round with recent pregnancy smiled shyly at the camera. With motherly pride and maternal joy, she supported the baby on her lap. Love encompassed them, as shining and plain as the halo on an angel. Her beaming eyes invited the photographer—Patrick, Kate assumed—into their magic circle.

Meeting the dead woman's expectant, happy gaze, Kate felt more like an interloper in Patrick's house, in Patrick's life, than ever.

Chapter 9

Patrick was still grinning as he hung up the pay phone in the hall. In spite of his reluctance to impose on Kate, he liked imagining the brisk lady doctor in his house, in his bed.

Bridget MacNeill came out of the waiting room. Her steps were firm. Not a strand of her salt-and-pepper hair was out of place. But the crow's-feet punctuating her expression appeared deeper than usual, and her smile was tired. Patrick frowned in concern.

She slipped her fingers into the crook of his arm. "How's everything at home?"

He covered her hand with his large one. "Fine. Jack's sleeping."

"Sean mentioned you have a—friend?—staying at the house."

He hedged, unwilling to expose his involvement with Kate to his mother and yet grateful for anything that would distract her from her worry. "Not a friend, exactly. Jack's doctor."

Bridget's eyes, blue as his own, widened speculatively. "Jack's doctor makes house calls?"

He was in for it now, Patrick realized. United in crisis, the family would once more feel free to meddle in his personal life. Resigned, he started to walk his mother back to the waiting room. "Remind me to kill Sean when we get to the hotel, okay?"

Bridget chuckled. "Now, Padraig, you know it's not his fault. None of you boys could keep a secret if I had a mind to get it out of you." Her fingers tightened briefly on his arm. "Except you."

Patrick shrugged. "That's because I don't have any secrets."

His mother sniffed, unconvinced. "Is she young?"

"Not old. My age, maybe a little more."

"Pretty?"

"I guess." How could he describe the potent combination of strength and insecurity that drew him to Kate, the soft body and hard-as-nails attitude, the crisp speech and compassionate brown eyes? "She's prickly as hell."

Bridget put her head to one side. "So, not that young, not particularly pretty, but still...special?"

Patrick narrowed his eyes at her.

She smiled sunnily, not the least bit intimidated. "I think she sounds wonderful. It's about time you found someone."

"Mom, you're way ahead of me here. We're not— It's not like that. Kate's just helping me out."

And he was just trying to get her into bed, but he wasn't confessing *that* to his mother.

Bridget nodded as if she understood. "That's very generous. I imagine with her job at the hospital— She is with the hospital?"

"Yeah."

"I imagine she doesn't have a lot of free time."

"No. But she makes time for her sister's family."

And that, too, was part of what drew him. He admired the way Kate shouldered responsibility without any thanks that he could see. He thought of the cans of tuna she'd carted to her sister's, the space blaster her nephew toted around. Her sense of commitment was as deeply ingrained as his own. Like a fellow Marine, he would trust her with his life. He could trust her with his son.

"She's got somebody to cover for her on Monday," he added. "After that, we'll see. I thought I might go home Monday night, once we know…"

Once we know if Dad's going to be all right, he thought but did not say. Memories of another hospital vigil beat at his brain, pounding to get in.

In the first weeks of Jack's recovery, his whole family had come down to be with them. Patrick had registered their presence, even drawn instinctive comfort from the gathering of the clan. But for him, reality had narrowed to the cot where Jack lay swaddled, battling for breath and life. Patrick had poured his own spirit into the fight, willing his own strength into his infant son. An exclusive bond had formed between them which even his family's love could not touch.

His mother turned, stopping him just outside the waiting room door. "I do wish that Lynn were here to support Con," she fretted.

Lovely, leggy Lynn was Con's high-priced fiancée.

Patrick shrugged. "He explained that. She had a scheduling conflict."

Bridget snorted. "What kind of conflict lasts for three days? And over a weekend, too." She shook her head. "I am so glad you came. So thankful."

"No big deal, Mom. I wanted to be here."

"They look to you, you know," she confided, gazing up at him earnestly. "They're strong, but they look to you."

He squeezed her hands. "Yeah, well, all those years I spent fixing their sandwiches and beating their heads in had to count for something."

"It's more than that, and you know it. Of all my sons, you're the one most like your father. If anything happens—"

"Nothing's going to happen, Mom. Dad's going to be fine."

Grimly, Patrick hoped he was right. He had already learned firsthand the fickleness of death and the cost of survival.

"Kate, you know I'd love to help you out," said Owen Roberts, the burn unit's attending physician. His telephone voice was faintly apologetic. "But those schedules were made up a month ago, and I've been covering for Gerry all weekend."

He was going to say no. Kate gripped the receiver tighter, torn between letting Patrick down and betraying her need to a senior member of the hospital staff.

"Couldn't Ernie fill in for me tomorrow?" she asked.

"Too much responsibility for a resident," Owen said firmly. "I know he can handle the admissions, but in an emergency we need another surgeon on call."

She couldn't argue with him, and she hated to beg. She tried so hard to keep her personal life completely separate from her professional role. Swaim was always quick to point the finger at women doctors who placed the demands of their families over what he perceived as their duty to the hospital.

But now Jack needed her. Patrick was depending on her. She had no choice.

"Please, Owen," she said. "I'll take the Fourth of July."

Owen chuckled. "Four days of fireworks accidents? You must be crazy. Or desperate."

Both, she thought. She glanced through the kitchen doorway at Jack, lying on his stomach on the family room floor, his sneakers waving in the air. The pieces of their interrupted board game were scattered around him.

"Please," she said again.

He sighed. "My wife will never forgive me. She wanted to go golfing tomorrow. What's so all-fired important? Got a hot weekend?"

Kate stiffened at the jocular insinuation and then forced herself to relax. She'd laid herself open to Owen's speculation by asking him for a favor. But there was simply no way she could tell the attending physician that she was disrupting the unit's schedule to baby-sit a patient. Swaim's patient.

"No, I... It's personal," she said.

She counted twenty heartbeats while he digested that one. "Okay," he said at last, reluctantly. "I'll see what I can do."

Relief made her gush. "Oh, thank you. I appreciate this, Owen, I really do. If—"

He cut her off, almost as uncomfortable with her uncharacteristic outburst as she was. "I know, I know, I'm a swell guy. See you Tuesday. I'll square it with Swaim. I hope it's worth it, Kate, whatever it is."

"Yes. Thank you," she said again.

Worth it? she wondered, hanging up the phone. Who could say? She didn't really belong here in Patrick's house, with Patrick's son.

Although sometimes, folding Jack's T-shirts into neat little thirds, seeing her razor rest beside Patrick's on the edge of his sink, she almost felt as if she did. But then the pile of paperwork she'd brought from the hospital spilled over into supper time, or she entered Patrick's room under the eyes of his smiling, dark-haired wife, and she knew that she did not.

He was coming home tomorrow. Her good deed would be over. She could go back to the hospital and her empty apartment, she would go back to being Jack's sometime doctor.

Rejoining Jack in the family room, Kate told herself she was relieved. She wasn't cut out for family life. Her own mother complained constantly that her older daughter lacked a woman's instincts. She'd never satisfied her sister's need for a confidante. She didn't have the time or temperament for a child, and she'd never been good at intimacy.

"My turn?" she asked, squatting on the floor.

Jack nodded and scooted over to make room for her.

Kate spun. "Six."

Together, they counted. "One. Two. Three.... Oh, darn," she said as her game piece ended at the top of a slide.

Jack giggled and swooshed it to the bottom of the board. "Dr. Kate?"

She watched him spin. "Mm?"

"Do you think I'm ugly?"

Her heart stopped with the brightly colored wheel. Shocked, s.·e stared into those solemn blue eyes, at that pointed chin and sensitive mouth. There was already a promise of strength in his shoulders and his one good hand that reminded her poignantly of Patrick.

Kate cleared her throat. "No," she answered truthfully. "No, I don't."

"I have a scar."

From somewhere in her medical training or her heart, she searched for the words to answer him. "You have a scar. Billy has freckles. Everyone looks different."

"If I have an op'ration will my scar go away?"

She weighed her reply, forced to balance her medical knowledge against Jack's ability to understand, her professional judgment against his father's decision and Swaim's likely promises. Lying would have been simpler.

"No. Just like an operation wouldn't make Billy's freckles go away. It could help," she added. "It could give your ear more shape. And sometimes the doctor can make changes in the scar's appearance to make it less noticeable. But one operation won't make a big difference to how you look."

The boy pulled on his lower lip, brows drawn together, digesting this.

"On the other hand," Kate continued, "the scar doesn't make any difference at all to the people who love you."

He twisted his neck to look at her. "Do you love me?"

Her heart wrenched and wrung. "Yes," she said, keeping her voice steady with an effort. "I guess I do."

Jack grinned. He flopped along the floor and rolled his head into her lap.

"I love you, too," he mumbled into her blue jeans.

She hadn't expected to hear those words. She hadn't known she needed to. They made her heart expand in her chest, crowding her lungs, stealing her breath, shattering forever the image created by her own mother's belittling words. Her hand lifted, hovered, and then touched his close-cropped hair.

Kate bit her lip. It was going to be pretty damn hard to maintain her professional distance after this.

Bridget cried in the arms of her oldest son. "It's so stupid," she sobbed.

Patrick held her, supported her. He understood her reaction better than she knew or he could ever show. "Ssh, Mom. It's okay."

She lifted her head from his chest, blue eyes seeking reassurance. "I'm just so relieved. He did say your father would be all right?"

Con, across the room, must have heard, because he left his discussion with the doctor to come over.

Patrick welcomed his arrival. Three years separated the brothers, but they'd won their share of school yard battles together. Patrick knew him as a methodical thinker and a vicious fighter. The middle brother in age, the middle one in height, he'd carved his place as the cool and brainy one, earning a scholarship to Harvard and a vice presidency at some hotshot financial group specializing in old money and new investments. In the past few days, while Patrick supported their mother and Sean played the clown to distract them all, Con had handled communications with the hospital.

Now he patted Bridget's shoulder. "As long as Dad watches his diet and takes his blood pressure medication, he'll be fine. The operation went great."

"Come on, Mom, don't cry. They're letting you in to see him," Sean said.

"Let's give thanks to God," Bridget said, smiling around at her sons. "And then I suppose I'd better thank the doctors."

Patrick released her. As she crossed the waiting room to talk to the surgeon, a huge weight lifted from his shoulders. His father would be all right.

The burden inside him eased, but nothing grew to replace it. He was empty. Numb. Even as Patrick clasped Con's hand and took Sean's punch on his shoulder, he felt curiously disassociated from his family's joy.

Con frowned. "How are you doing, bro?"

Patrick forced a grin. "Can't complain."

His brother's cool blue eyes regarded him astutely. "That's your problem. You never could."

It took Patrick a moment to decide that Con was joking.

"Anyway, it's all right now," Con continued. "Dad's all right. He'll be going home soon."

Home. Soon.

That was what was missing, Patrick realized. He needed to go home. Home to Jack. Home to Kate.

She'd neglected the stack of unread medical journals by the living-room couch to attend to the pile of unwashed dishes in the kitchen sink.

Kate pulled a face, wiping her hands on a dish towel. Who was she trying to kid? Household goddess was not her specialty. Patrick was unlikely to be impressed by her domestic skills whatever she did. Besides, she didn't really expect him home tonight.

She hung the towel on the oven door and refilled the dog's water bowl. The retriever, Silkie, sniffed politely at the water and then padded companionably after Kate into the living room, her nails clicking on the wide plank floors. With a sigh, the dog collapsed by the big navy chair. Patrick's chair, Kate deduced.

"Sorry," she told the dog. "He won't be back until tomorrow."

The retriever laid her golden head on her paws and pointedly ignored her. Amused, Kate pulled out a study on psychological assessment tools for burn survivors and settled on the couch to read.

The jingle of keys, the snick of a lock awoke her. Disoriented, she blinked at the black-and-white pages sliding from her lap. The retriever lurched up and dashed to the door, creamy tail flying.

The front door cracked open on a rush of fresh night air. Alarm stuttered in Kate's chest. Before she could uncurl from the couch, the opening widened, and Patrick MacNeill came home.

His broad shoulders were silhouetted against the golden glow of the porch light. Moisture gleamed on his short, ruffled hair and on the shoulders of his dark leather jacket. Dazed, Kate watched as Silkie flung herself at his feet in adoration.

Setting his flight bag just inside the door, Patrick crouched on his heels to praise the dog with his hands.

"Well." His potent smile lit his eyes as he looked over the dog's body at Kate. "Here's a welcome."

Heart hammering, Kate retreated into the cushions at her back. "She missed you."

Head to one side, he considered her. "Did she? How much?"

The teasing note in his deep voice deprived Kate of speech. Were they still talking about the dog? Vulnerable from sleep, she stared at him.

His expression altered. His eyes darkened as he rose and crossed the room to tower over her. With some vague idea of regaining her emotional balance, Kate started to slide her feet to the floor.

Patrick leaned over the couch. His hands came down on either side of her, one in the pool of light on the upholstered arm, one in the shadows at her back. Kate bit her lip. She felt trapped, and yet he hadn't touched her.

His face was cool and close. His breath was warm and scented with coffee. She could see the faint creases fatigue had carved at the corners of his eyes and his masculine stubble. The air jammed in her lungs.

"I missed you," he whispered. "Kiss me."

Hesitantly, she lifted her mouth. He didn't move. Tilting her head, she pushed down on the couch cushions and raised herself awkwardly. Her lips brushed his roughened jaw, his cool, firm mouth. She felt his intake of breath against her own mouth, and her nipples tightened in response. But he didn't crowd her, didn't grab her, didn't press her back into the couch. He angled his head and waited.

It was almost unbearably arousing, the promise of all that heat and power hovering above her. Close up, his face was blurred, his eyes almost black. A tiny bead of sweat streaked the upper corner of his cheekbone, just by his ear. She wanted to lick his skin. She pushed and tried again to meet his mouth.

This time she felt the drag of his lower lip, the slick warmth of its inner surface, before her balance betrayed her and she sank back onto the cushions. At the edge of her vision, his hand fisted on the upholstered arm. She made a sound of frustration and drew her legs under her, wiggling to her knees. She put her arms around his neck.

"Kiss me back, dammit," she said.

She watched that well-shaped mouth curve. "Count on it."

He took command of the kiss like a Marine battalion establishing a beachhead on a tropical shore: swift, efficient, and devastating. Kate felt her senses overwhelmed, her mouth invaded. He took it deep, drawing her up against his iron body, matching the demands of his hungry mouth with his hard hands. Behind her closed lids, she imagined rockets detonating against a night sky.

His lips forayed along her jaw, lingering with explosive results against her ear. She felt the resulting reverberations shower down her nerve endings to her fingertips. She curled them into his shoulders, relishing the resilience of his muscle, and heard him growl before his mouth plundered hers again, his tongue stroking and retreating and plunging deep.

She shuddered, struggling against the influence of his kiss, the impact of his touch.

"Wait," she said.

Patrick's arms tightened around her. His heart threatened to pound its way out of his ribs. Kate's chest rose and fell, pushing her full breasts into him with every breath.

"Wait?" he repeated.

"I haven't decided to do this. I'm not the kind of person who gets swept away."

He regarded her with affection, the double crease forming between her straight, dark brows, the way her teeth worried her bottom lip. "Honey, you were doing fine a second ago."

She stiffened. "Don't you make me laugh. I need to *think*."

Maybe she did. He was more inclined to go on instinct and snap judgment himself, but he could see her training didn't tend that way.

With one finger, he rubbed at the parallel lines over her nose, as if he could erase her fretting. "You're going to analyze this to death, aren't you?"

She glared. "What if I am?"

Nine years celibate, Patrick reminded himself. She had every reason and every right to think it over. Just because he wasn't feeling too reasonable himself right now...

He tried to think back to his first time with somebody new. There hadn't been anybody, really, since Holly in high school. He remembered that, both of them eager, and him almost as scared as her. But neither one of them had worn quite the look of longing and determination that battled on Kate's face now.

A gust of tenderness loosened the knot in his chest. She had to want this, he thought. If he wasn't coming to her with a whole heart and total commitment, he had to be certain at least that she wanted him the way he ached for her.

He released her. "Then I'm going to go make us both some coffee, okay? It's been a long day."

She scrambled off the couch. In her stocking feet, she barely came to his chin. "It's already made. Let me get you a cup. Have you eaten?"

Patrick smiled, touched and amused by her automatic attempt to take care of him. Hidden beneath that formidable intellect and doctor's ego lurked a secret nurturer. Maybe he could talk her into a therapeutic bounce on his bed?

Easy, ace, he cautioned himself. Kate deserved more, she deserved better, than that. He gripped the back of his neck with one hand, fighting fatigue, striving for control.

"I had lunch with my mom before I took off. Dad's doing well," he added as he followed her through the dining room.

"So you said on the phone. I appreciate your calling, by the way. Jack was a little anxious."

The familiar protective surge stopped him in his tracks. "Is he okay?"

"He's fine." She turned, her small, neat fingers closing around his arm. She tugged him forward into the kitchen. "I haven't starved him or anything. You, on the other hand, look like you could use a meal. Sit," she commanded.

He dropped into a chair, enjoying the unusual sensation of having Kate in his kitchen waiting on him. He suspected he'd better not get used to it. She poured coffee into a mug, hesitating only briefly over the location of the sugar bowl before setting both before him.

"There. You can have leftover pizza, if you want."

His stomach, subjected to five straight days of charter rations and hospital food, protested the very idea. But he didn't want to hurt the lady doctor's feelings.

"Pizza, huh? Jack must have been in heaven."

She paused, considering him over the top of the open refrigerator door. "Or I could make you a sandwich."

He grinned his gratitude. "A sandwich would be great."

With surgical precision, she constructed turkey and cheese on toast, heavy on meat and light on lettuce, just the way he liked it. He'd downed half of it before he remembered that he hadn't bought cold cuts before his trip.

"You do grocery shopping this weekend?" he asked casually.

Kate wiped nonexistent crumbs from an already shining counter. "Some," she admitted. "Jack and I had to go out anyway to pick up my bag and check on my cat."

Patrick nodded. "Did you take money from the mantel?"

"I— No, I didn't."

He raised his eyebrows. "You should have. Jack and I don't need charity. And you don't need another person taking advantage."

"I didn't mean to imply that you did. Were," she corrected herself in that brisk, snooty tone she assumed to hide uncertainty. "But you hadn't authorized any particular expenditure, and I didn't feel I had the right to take it."

The exactness with which she divided what was hers from what was his, as neatly as she'd bisected his sandwich, set his teeth on edge.

Patrick hadn't planned on admitting Kate into their lives. He wasn't ready to let anyone behind the barriers where Holly had once laughed and loved and lived with him. Once those defenses were breached, who knew what rage or grief would find its way over the walls? But he couldn't stand to see Kate set those limits around herself, as if she were of no account.

Patrick pushed his plate away. "You were buying food for my son. You were staying in my house. I figure that gives you some rights, Kate."

She twisted the dish towel in her hands, her big brown eyes wary and aware. "Does it?"

She was asking him for something, Patrick realized. For all her formidable self-sufficiency, for all his obligations to Jack, she needed to know that what they had between them was more than the physical release he'd offered her before. He didn't know how much more. But somehow the physical distance between them during his trip to Boston had provided room for their emotional closeness to grow. In spite of his uneasiness about letting anyone inside his iron barricades, it was surprisingly easy to give Kate the reassurance she needed.

"In my book, yeah."

Her smile flickered. She sat down opposite him. "Well. How's the sandwich?"

Patrick cleared his throat. "Good. It's great. Thanks."

She lifted one shoulder, and her soft, wavy hair fell forward on her cheek. He wanted to thread his fingers through it and tuck it behind her ear. "I owed you one," she said.

With an effort, he recalled the omelette he'd made for her. "No, you've got it backwards. That was payback for you helping out with Jack."

"Jack is my patient," she said earnestly, retreating to her doctor role. "Well, the center's patient, anyway. It's my responsibility to do everything I can for him."

He nodded. "I appreciate you coming out, all the same."

"No, I... It meant a lot, you asking me." She smiled wryly at her lap. "I'm not exactly Mary Poppins."

She was cheapening herself again. He didn't like it.

"No. But then, it's tough to find a nanny with a medical degree and pediatrics training." She blinked at him. "Look, Kate, it took a big load off my mind, knowing you were with him." He picked up the other half of his sandwich, stared at it and then put it down. "I thought I wouldn't get up there in time," he confessed.

Kate regarded the top of his dark head, unsure what he was telling her but more than ready to listen. "To see your dad?" she asked.

His mouth compressed. "Yeah."

She could hear the wealth of pain in his voice and the control he imposed over it, like an iron grating over a pit.

"But the surgery wasn't scheduled until Monday," she said quietly.

"I know. I guess I thought... I was afraid it would be like last time."

Last time? she wondered. Oh, Lord. *Last time.* His wife.

No wonder he had to go to his father, even if it meant leaving Jack with an interloper in his house. Horrible speculations made her stomach churn. ''Were you—away—when your wife had her accident?''

He turned his head to stare through the open doorway. She didn't think he saw the dining room. She didn't think he was going to answer her, either. But after a minute he nodded.

''I was on assignment with the reserves,'' he said. ''It took them sixteen hours to track me down. Holly's identification burned up in the crash.''

She heard stories like this all the time. She lived with them day by day. But she hadn't known about Patrick's wife. Compassion twisted her gut.

Trying to keep the horror from her voice, she asked, ''Was she— Did she make it to the hospital?''

His head jerked. *No.* ''They airlifted Jack. They couldn't tell who he was, of course, not until they'd traced the license plate, but they took him to Jefferson because of the burn center. Holly—'' His throat moved once, convulsively. ''—Holly never made it out of the car.''

Kate's eyes stung. Her own throat burned. She felt awful and inadequate, but she couldn't let the moment pass without offering some comfort. Lightly, she rested her hand on his big one, clenched on the tabletop. After a moment, he turned it palm up and held her fingers tightly.

''I am so sorry,'' she said.

''Yeah, well.'' He rolled his shoulders, still not looking at her. ''It was over four years ago.''

And he'd been carrying it around ever since, Kate suspected. The grief and the guilt and the anger.

''Did they ever catch the other driver?''

''Yeah. They got him on DUI manslaughter. Prosecutor called me personally to tell me so.'' Patrick shook his head. ''Hell, I didn't care. Holly was just as dead.''

Kate was silent, respecting his reaction, trying to absorb everything he'd told her. To learn of his wife's death and her murderer's fate from worried officials, to know that his baby son was sick and all alone in the care of strangers... She squeezed his hand.

"No wonder you had to go to Boston," she said.

His thumb rubbed the back of her hand in acknowledgement, creating a tiny spot of warmth. "Thanks for watching Jack," was all he said.

Her eyes misted at his gruffly expressed gratitude. She held the memory of his son's confession of love to her heart. "He's a wonderful boy. Thanks for asking me."

Patrick shook his head. He was already more indebted to her than he'd been to anyone in a long, long time, and she persisted in acting as if it were all the other way around. He grinned at her, deliberately lightening the atmosphere.

"You've got it backwards again, honey. But, hey, if you want to show me how grateful you are..."

She gave him her hospital look, surgeon-to-scum-of-the-earth. "Just eat the sandwich, flyboy."

But he saw the smile tugging the corners of her mouth. A warm and unfamiliar satisfaction filled him. "Yes, Doctor."

When he was done, she got up to clear his place.

"Leave it," he ordered. "You've done enough in here. Why don't you go put your feet up?"

He watched her consider that, her teeth fretting again at her lip. He wanted her to relax, sure, but more, he wanted to make out with her on the big, overstuffed couch. He wanted her to welcome him home again, to taste her, shallow and deep, to reacquaint himself with the generous curves of her body under the soft knit shirt she wore. He wanted to neck, the way he hadn't wanted since he was a randy teenage boy.

"I'm not sure. I have to be at the hospital early tomorrow." She tried a smile. "Rounds at seven."

He nodded to hide his disappointment, stuffing his lust back into its closet. "Fine. You go on up, then."

Standing alone in his kitchen, he listened for the pad of her footsteps crossing the dining room and going up the stairs. Silkie whined and thumped her tail on the hard linoleum floor.

"Tell me about it," Patrick muttered, and scratched her behind the ears.

He turned off the coffeemaker and the lights. He checked the locks on the doors, a holdover from years on military bases, trying not to think about Kate getting ready for bed upstairs.

What was it about the lady doctor that got to him so bad? It wasn't just the possibility of liftoff after four years of aborted missions and flying solo. Yeah, okay, that was a hell of a long time to go without sex, but before he'd met Kate his libido hadn't bothered him that much.

There was no denying her curvy body tempted him. A man could slake himself on those generous breasts, find ease between those firm, round thighs. But it was the whole package that attracted him, the unlikely combination of that soft, giving body and compassionate heart with her hard-edged intelligence and brisk determination.

Kate was probably the smartest woman he knew, certainly the most educated. He could only guess at the stubborn will that had sustained her through her years of medical school and training. She was tougher than his wife had been, more driven, and possibly less secure. The last woman in the world, he would have thought, to appeal to him.

But the past four years had put him through the fire. Maybe in Kate's tempered strength, he'd found his match.

Yeah, right. She was smart enough and tough enough to resist him, at least.

Grabbing his bag from where he'd parked it by the door, Patrick headed up the stairs. He checked in on Jack, sleeping peacefully on top of his covers, and forced himself past the closed guest-room door to his own room at the end of the hall. He set down the bag. Opened the door.

And saw Kate, wearing a blue scrub top and a determined

expression, sitting on the edge of his bed. Her legs were long and bare. He wondered if she had anything at all on under that top. And he wondered what the hell he was going to do now.

Chapter 10

Kate pressed her legs together on the edge of the mattress, hoping to make her thighs look thinner. Downstairs she could hear Patrick moving around, talking to the dog. Nerves jitterbugged in her stomach.

She was cold. The skin of her arms and legs bumped like uncooked chicken. But her cheeks were hot. She could feel the blood heating there, and beating in her throat and in her chest, and pooling warm and liquid in her lower body.

Look before you leap. Think before you speak. Analyze before you act.

She would not be foolish like her mother or trusting like her sister, both of them mothers and alone before their thirties. But how could she examine her options when all she could see was Patrick's intent face? How could she hear herself think over the drumbeat of her blood?

He was the worst man in the world for her. A patient's father, a grieving husband. A man too used to getting his own way and too aware of his effect on women.

But he had granted her rights, given her welcome, shared

his house and his son and a piece of his soul with her. She admired him, perhaps more than any man she'd ever met. His utter reliability, the way he supported his mother and loved his son and was simply there for every member of his family in a way that no one had ever been there for her— Oh, she liked that a lot. It made her want him. It made her want to be there for him.

Kate might have held out against her own desire. She could not resist Patrick's need.

She shivered, thinking of Wade Preston, the blond Apollo of Jefferson University Medical School. He'd told her he needed her. He'd even claimed to love her. But his need hadn't outlasted their shared residency, and his love hadn't survived the discovery of her background, so unsuitable for a doctor's wife in Baltimore.

This is different, she thought, rubbing her hands nervously on the goose-bumped flesh of her thighs. Wade, pledging his future, had been miserly with praise and stingy in bed. Patrick promised her nothing. But she suspected, with a newfound feminine instinct, that he would be generous with his passion. At the very least, he seemed really to want her. And she wanted him.

The door opened, and he was there.

Surprise sliced across his face, and something hotter surfaced in his eyes before his iron control returned. He retrieved his bag from outside the door and set it beside the dresser.

"Guest room's down the hall."

She swallowed. "I've been sleeping here," she said as briskly as she could.

He closed the door and leaned against it. The faint chink of the lock reverberated in the quiet room.

"I sleep in here," he said.

What are you going to do about it? his attitude proclaimed.

She hadn't exactly expected him to sweep her into his arms with cries of gratitude and gladness, but this cold, guarded response wasn't what she was looking for, either.

Kate stiffened her spine. She knew only one way to meet challenges. Head on. "Well, then, you'll have to share."

He continued to lean against the door, watching her with half-lidded eyes, his expression unreadable. Her heart hammered. "I told you I don't need your charity, Kate. Let's not do the comfort-the-poor-widower routine, okay?"

She thought she hid her flinch, the involuntary recoil from pain, but her already-heated face flamed.

"This isn't a routine for me. I wanted you, and I thought you wanted me." She stood. Deliberately, she flung his own challenge back at him, covering her hurt with proud words. "If that's not enough for you, if I misunderstood you, just tell me no."

He pushed away from the door at his back and caught her before she could take herself and her injured feelings out of the room. "Wait. Honey, hey."

His finger sought her chin and lifted it. She glared at him, hating that her eyes were wet and her nose was probably red.

He stroked her hair, her arm. "I'm sorry. I'm a jerk, all right?"

Kate wavered between relief and doubt. His big hand glided up her arm to her shoulder. He rubbed small circles at the base of her neck, gradually spreading reassurance with his touch. With one hand at her nape, he pulled her closer, enveloping her in his strength, his scent, his warmth.

"I thought you wanted time to think this thing through," he rumbled.

She let him draw her head down against his chest. "I'm a fast thinker," she muttered into his shirt.

His laugh quaked them both. He wrapped his arms tightly around her. "Smart girl."

Tentatively, she rubbed her cheek over his heart, absorbing the weave of the cotton, the rhythm of his pulse. He was big. So big and hard, built of solidly compacted muscle. Desire uncurled in her stomach.

"Not that smart," she forced out. "I didn't plan for this. I don't have any birth control."

"I do. I bought some in Boston."

Kate lifted her head to look at him, unsure whether to be pleased by his consideration or offended by his assumption.

Patrick shrugged. He wouldn't apologize for taking care of her. "Before I joined the Marines, I was a Boy Scout."

Her eyebrows raised. "Be prepared?"

"You got it."

She smiled, a sweet, wry curve to her lips. "I guess I do. Or I will soon, anyway."

Her surprising innuendo tickled and touched him. Her unexpected presence in his room thrilled him. Patrick wasn't certain what implication it had past this moment, but now that he knew she wasn't there out of pity, he for damn sure wasn't sending her away. For the first time in years, he was flying without filing a flight plan, and he couldn't bring himself to care. Not with Kate half-naked in his arms. He bent his head to taste her smile, to seek her sweetness with his tongue.

Her lips were soft and uncertain. They met his, parted, pressed, and then withdrew. She was trembling, he realized, and tightened his hold protectively.

"Cold?" he asked, hoping it was cold and she wasn't changing her mind. What did she have on under her cotton top, anyway?

"A little. I'm not very good at this," she added.

There was a rip at his heart that should have warned him that more than his body was involved here. He shunted the thought away, concentrating on the clinging silk of Kate's hair as it wrapped around his fingers, the quick stutter of her breath against his mouth. He ran his tongue over her lower lip and watched her eyes darken.

"Not good at what? Kissing?"

When she opened her mouth to reply, he took it again, gently, nibbling at it as if she were some ripe fruit. Peaches, maybe, sweet and juicy.

"No, you're good at kissing," he decided.

"Sex," she said, so firmly he nearly laughed. One look at her scared, resolute face dissuaded him. "I'm not much good at sex."

"Really?" he asked mildly. His mouth cruised from the determined point of her chin to the soft, perfumed hollow under her ear. He felt her pulse go crazy against his lips and smiled. "Why is that?"

"Well, I..." She arched her throat to give him better access, her eyes drifting shut. He noted that, rewarding her with a string of tiny bites down the sensitive cords of her neck to her shoulder. She shuddered. "I've only had one other, um, partner."

He blew softly on the damp trail left by his kisses, lifting the fine blond down on her pale skin. Against the thin blue top she wore, her breasts peaked. No bra, he thought, and nearly groaned.

"Same here," he said, angling for her mouth again.

She raised one hand against his chest, stopping and stroking. "You?"

"Yeah, me," he confirmed. He smiled down into her dark, shocked eyes. "You're just going to have to go easy on me, honey, okay?"

He kissed her open *O* of astonishment, gently urging her participation. He felt her start to relax, to return his kisses, and then she pushed again at his chest.

"But..."

Her active brain had clicked on behind her eyes, putting creases between her eyebrows.

"You're analyzing again," he observed. "Don't think. This isn't about thinking. How does it make you feel?"

His hands skimmed up her sides and down, the heels of his palms barely brushing her breasts.

He watched her throat move as she swallowed. "You want vitals?"

There it was again, that dry note she used as defense. He

brought his hands together, creating a deep cleavage between her breasts, rubbing his thumbs gently over their crests.

"Whatever you want," he said.

"Well, um…" Her eyes were dark and cloudy. "I'd have to say my temperature is definitely up."

"That's good." He circled the sweet, tight points of her breasts until they swelled against her medical top.

Kate breathed out through her mouth. "And respiration…that's probably up, too."

"Yeah?" he bent and captured one peak in his mouth, teasing it through the soft, overwashed cotton. He suckled, dampening the cloth, making it cling to the engorged nipple. Damn, she was sweet.

Her hands drifted to the back of his neck, encouraging him. Readily, he obeyed their silent urging, turning his head, laving the other nipple with attention. Her fingers tightened in his hair, sending bolts of heat to his heavy loins. He wanted to eat her up.

With his touch, he molded her, her ripe breasts, the column of her waist, the lush flare of her hips. He stroked down and reached up to her round, tempting buttocks. Panties. She wore thin cotton panties. He kneaded her through them, fighting the urge to rip them off and plunge to the hilt in her wonderfully female body.

He throttled the flow of images to his brain, trying to regulate the speed of his desire. Not this first time. After nine years, she deserved better than quick. He felt a strong responsibility to please her, to pleasure her, to short out her busy intellect with an overload of pure sensation.

Kissing his way down her body, he knelt and pressed his face to her stomach. She still trembled. No longer from cold, he was certain. Her lips were open and wet, her eyes slumbrous. Her hips swayed in unconscious invitation.

Slowly, he drew up the hem of her short blue top, exposing her tempting mound under plain blue panties, and the luscious curve of her pale belly, and the cute hollow of her navel. He kissed it and heard her sigh. He moistened a trail down the center of her abdomen and felt her gasp. He slid his tongue daringly under the frail barrier of cotton, moving the elastic out of the way with his fingers, and stopped at her choked protest.

He looked up. Her face was worried and excited, her lower lip caught in her teeth. Tenderness punched him hard. Clearly she wasn't ready for everything he had in mind. Maybe her medical education hadn't included such intimacies. He could push, he knew. And the sight of her through the thin cloth, the scent of her skin and her heady response, tempted him to touch, to taste. But he didn't want to make her uncomfortable. This first time, he wanted her with him all the way.

"You don't want to play doctor, honey, that's okay."

He stood, cradling her against his torso, giving her time to get accustomed to him and the feel of his insistent arousal. She wasn't used to this.

Patrick grinned into her hair. Hell, he wasn't used to this, either. If he got any hotter, he'd be finished before they got properly started.

How was it possible, Kate wondered, to feel both perfectly contented and almost unbearably impatient at the same time? She could have stayed forever on the bulwark of Patrick's chest, in the haven of his arms. And yet inside her, every molecule danced.

He felt so good, hot and hard, rough denim rasping her crumpled hospital top where he pressed against her belly. The surprising smoothness of his throat, the prickle of his beard, the movement of his breath, in and out, filled her senses. They streaked along her nerve endings like raindrops on a window-pane at night, leaving silver tracks of excitement in their wake. She felt awake, aware and very, very restless.

Her hips nudged his thighs. She slid her palms over the long muscles of his back, as if she could draw him closer, and mashed her cheek on a shirt button.

"I could take it off. My shirt," he said.

Oh, glory. Her mouth went dry.

"Maybe that would be a good idea."

He kissed her forehead and set her gently aside. Without fuss or show, he flicked open the buttons and pulled the shirt-tails free. And then, shrugging out of the sleeves, he looked at her, just looked at her, and the blue flame of his eyes melted her insides like candy.

"You want the pants to go, too?" he asked.

A more experienced woman could have made some sexy, teasing reply. A more confident woman would have stripped off his pants herself. Kate hesitated, despising her own inadequacy.

"Got to keep things fair," Patrick said.

Puzzled, she frowned.

"You let me see your legs," he explained.

Laughter bubbled inside her, washing away her doubt. "Then, yes, the pants should definitely go."

He shucked off his jeans and stood before her in nothing but navy blue boxers and soft yellow lamplight.

Her breath sucked in. She saw naked men all the time, she reminded herself. Old and young, sick and broken, she examined and handled and healed them.

But Patrick's body was special, broad and vital, fully mature and potently male. With a doctor's knowledge and a woman's appreciation, she admired the strength of his long bones, the power of his solid muscles. Dark hair covered his well-developed pectorals and dusted his abdomen and thighs. His arousal stood out boldly under his boxers.

Kate exhaled, returning her fascinated gaze to Patrick's intent face.

"All right?" he asked her quietly.

She knew he was asking if she were all right, but she couldn't find the courage to tell him that she had never in her life felt as right as she did at this moment. She wanted him, wanted this, with a surety that flowed from the marrow of her bones, and she couldn't find the words to say it. Even if she managed the words, she didn't know whether her feelings would be acceptable to him.

She smiled, forcing lightness. "I don't have much to compare it to. But you look perfectly healthy to me."

His eyes glinted. "I'll show you healthy," he promised.

He caught her close. Laughter shimmered and dissolved between them. She felt the slow rise and fall of his chest and heard the thunder of her own heart. Under her hands, his skin was hot. She flexed her fingers wonderingly on the texture of body hair.

He hissed. "Careful, honey."

Kate tilted her head to one side, considering. "Maybe," she said deliberately, "I don't want to be careful anymore."

His face stilled. His hands tightened. And then his mouth took hers.

He used his teeth to excite, his tongue to soothe. He made her crave his flavor. He taught her to follow his rhythm, in and out. Her breathing hitched. In and out. Distracted by the demands of his urgent mouth, she didn't register the movement of his hands under her loose top until they closed, warm and sure, over her naked breasts. Desire whipped through her, and she cried out.

The sound startled her. She struggled for composure, but it eluded her, battered away by his forceful mouth, his seeking hands.

"Patrick," she protested, "I don't think—"

"Good. Don't think, Kate." Relentlessly male, he moved against her, drugging her with the promise of his taut body. "Feel," he whispered. "Feel me."

She was helpless to do anything else. She thrilled at the wealth of sensation at her fingertips, firm flesh, smooth skin, rough hair. He slid his thigh between her legs, lifting her gently, and heat pooled at the contact. He pulled her top up, and the hair on his chest licked her breasts. With each fresh assault on her senses, her customary restraint slipped further. She felt it steal away, and passion rush in to take its place.

He lowered them both to the edge of the mattress, urging her legs to either side so that she straddled his lap. His big, warm hands cupped her buttocks. She gasped and arched into his waiting heat.

"Yeah," he muttered. "Like that."

He rolled with her, pulling at clothes. She lifted and tugged, smoothing his shorts from his tight hips, kicking her panties off one ankle, trying to get closer, needing to feel him skin to skin. He pressed and stroked, probed and caressed, drawing out her response, driving her from peak to peak. She couldn't breathe. She opened her mouth to tell him so and all that came out was a high, weak moan.

He swallowed it, his hands moving with deliberate power between her legs. He urged her up, up a steep mountain, into unknown terrain where her senses were clouded and her footing uncertain. Sensation pierced her as sharply as cold. For all her brave words, she was frightened by the force of it. Too high. She was too high, and afraid of falling.

His voice was warm in her ear. "It's all right, honey. I've got you."

She quivered, shaken by the thudding of her heart, by the pounding of his. Their bodies were sleek with sweat where they rubbed together. His shoulders gleamed. His hands were slippery. She closed her eyes against the vibrations set off by his hands.

Inhaling sharply, Patrick pushed her off the mountaintop.

And she flew.

Patrick covered her, body poised and screaming like a jet held on the ground. He knew he'd pleasured her. Now he waited until she dragged her eyelids open before he finished the job.

Her lashes lifted, and the open welcome in her eyes released his steely control. Lacing their fingers together, he thrust firmly inside her. She tightened around him like a fist, all wet, clinging heat, and forced the air from his lungs.

Need pulsed inside him. He held perfectly still, embedded

in her, immersed in pleasure so deep he couldn't string two thoughts together. One thought. *Think, you moron.*

"Oh, hell."

She touched his clenched and aching jaw. "Patrick? What is it?"

"Birth control," he rasped.

Brown eyes widened. "Do you have it?"

"In my suitcase."

He watched her face as she absorbed that information, her soft yearning plainly at war with her hard intelligence. She was a doctor, he thought. She wasn't going to invite him to take chances with her.

"Oh." Experimentally, she moved under him.

Patrick swore. "Don't do that."

She subsided, and that was just as bad. He could feel her against him and around him, her pebbled nipples, her moist sex. She smelled of citrus and woman, and he wanted her so bad he thought it might possibly kill him to leave her.

"Sorry," she said.

She didn't look sorry. She looked pleased and anxious and maybe a little amused. Her humor caught and tickled his. Four years, he thought, and his first time at the party he forgot to dress.

Carefully, taking his weight on his elbows, he separated from her. They both groaned.

"Don't move," he told her.

Her fingers pressed gently against his lips, caressed his throat. "You said that already," she remarked.

"So doctors are no good at taking orders."

"Excuse me?"

He grinned at her indignant face. "I'll be right back."

He felt her hand like a brand trail down his chest and side as he levered himself away.

"Hurry," she said.

Kneeling on the floor beside his bag, he looked up at her rosy body. She was flushed from his loving, naked in his bed.

A torrent of feeling sluiced through him: tenderness, appreciation and gratitude. And a good strong current of lust.

"Count on it," he said.

Sheathed, he returned to her, dropping another couple of packets on the bedside table. She wrapped him in her smooth arms and strong thighs, gloved him in her heat. He felt her stretch to encompass him and struggled not to lose it. But she was so tight, so hot and tight, he was blanking out. Concentrating fiercely on her face, he began to move.

He felt her tentative attempts to accommodate him, to pick up his rhythm, and strained to adjust his driving need. But her hands, her small, competent hands, were tugging at him. And then she did something complicated with her internal muscles and destroyed him.

He couldn't stop. He could barely breathe. He could only pound away at her, desperate, greedy, intent on his own completion. Grabbing fistfuls of her wavy hair, he fused his mouth to hers. She kissed him back, arching to take him, twining her legs with his. He felt the tremors begin again inside her, and battled for time, like a pilot fighting gravity in a wounded plane, shuddering with the speed of his descent and the force of his need.

When she convulsed around him, he flung back his head and went down in flames.

Kate sighed. Her body still vibrated in reflex rhythmic reaction to increased blood circulation and muscular tension. Knowing the physiological explanation, she discovered, didn't make those tiny shudders any less surprising.

Or lovely.

In gratitude, Kate turned her face into Patrick's throat and kissed his smooth, damp skin, stifling a giggle. Who would have guessed that at the advanced age of thirty-six Dr. Kathryn Sinclair would finally get it? Twice.

He stirred. "I'm mashing you."

She stroked a line down his back, tracing the strong curve

of his latissimus dorsi muscle, delighting in her right to touch and the heavenly weight of him pinning her to the mattress. "I don't mind."

"I'll move. In a minute."

"I don't mind," she said again.

He sighed. She felt the lift and relaxation of his torso all the way up and down her body, and something fluttered inside her.

He lifted his head, his eyes dark and intent. Kate felt another funny flutter. Was this softening change in her, this incredible lightness of heart and the sweet heaviness of her body, somehow visible on her face?

"You okay?" he asked.

She felt better than okay, better than she'd ever felt in her life. "I'm fine." She had to ask. "You?"

His slow smile curled her toes. "I'm wrecked. I'm going to need a long period of recuperation before I'm fit to walk again."

She was absurdly flattered. "Poor man." Unable to stop herself, she touched his cheek. "I'm a doctor. Perhaps I can help?"

Answering laughter sparked in his blue, blue eyes. "Maybe some exercises?" He shifted between her thighs, making her gasp. "I think I'd respond to a little physical therapy."

"I thought you needed time to recuperate," she said primly.

He rolled away, reaching for the nightstand. "To walk, I said."

She heard the foil packet tear, and then he pressed against her, slipped inside her.

She yielded around him, her hands reaching up into the short silk of his hair. "Oh, right, and this is no effort."

His face was suddenly so grave that doubt snagged her heart. But then he smiled and shook his head. "No effort at all."

Her breath caught and quickened as he moved again inside her in long, slow waves.

And it was just as lovely as before.

Chapter 11

Morning entered the room gently, in striped bars of dove gray through slatted windows. Patrick woke all at once, already hard and wanting Kate. He turned his head to find her. She slept with her cheek pressed to his pillow, her light brown hair tumbled over her shoulders.

The dim and private light, the peace of sleep, blurred her usual intimidating determination. Revealed between the rumpled hair and crumpled linen, her relaxed features were soft and surprisingly delicate. Her naked arm bore the imprint of his sheets.

His craving for her swelled. But with the hot and welcome rise of lust, emotion stirred, deeper than tenderness, more complicated than desire. Patrick refused to give it a name. After last night's uninhibited loving, he felt freer than he had in years. His mind was clear. His body hummed pleasantly with sexual tension, like a well-revved engine. He was reluctant to knot himself up by examining that elusive and troubling emotion.

A thread of hair had slipped forward onto her face. Caught

on her lip, it billowed with each soft puff of breath. Gently, he trapped the strand between finger and thumb and smoothed it behind her ear.

Above the pillow, her eye opened. The light in it thumped into his stomach like a fist. He didn't deserve to have a woman, any woman, look at him that way.

Kate's lips curved. "My hero."

"Don't say that."

The words came out more harshly than he intended. It didn't seem fair to let her read more into the situation than existed. He wasn't anybody's hero. He was just an overworked air jockey with a four-year-old son who needed him.

Kate's brows pulled together as her analytical intelligence woke behind them. He tried, too late, to soften his reply. "I didn't do anything special."

"Mmm." Languorously, she raised her arms above her head and stretched. The dangerous dip and pull of the sheet over her breasts riveted his attention. His mouth dried. Did the innocent lady doctor have any idea what she was doing to him?

He wrenched his gaze back to her face. Her brown eyes were compassionate and aware. Of course she did. If she had any doubts at all about his response, the hard evidence at her hip offered ready proof. She was too damn smart not to know of his desire and guess at his emotional turmoil.

He tensed, waiting for her to start the assault on his psyche. That was, after all, what medical professionals did. Even his family found it hard to leave well enough alone.

"*I* thought it was pretty special," she said, smiling. "But then, what do they say? If you want to get the job done, send in the Marines?"

Her teasing tone loosened the slipknot around his neck, the chokehold of guilt and responsibility. His muscles relaxed with cautious relief. She was okay, then. He could have her without some messy postcoital dissection of his *feelings*.

"All part of the service, ma'am."

Surrendering to the urge to touch, he circled her nipple with one finger and then spanned her soft breast with his hand. Her breath sighed out.

This much, at least, he could give her.

He replaced his hand with his mouth, savoring her scent and the flavor of her skin. He had always been a soldier, more comfortable with action than words, more sure of his desire than his emotions, more accepting of her woman's pleasure than that unsettling glimpse of her woman's heart.

To please them both, to distract them both, he took her fast and rode her hard. Deliberately, he lost himself in physical sensation, letting urgency drive away thought, concentrating on the wet, hot clasp of her body and her eager movements under him. He plunged in deep, purging his brain, filling his ears with the slap of flesh on flesh and her soft, welcoming cries.

But even as he drove them both over the edge of pleasure, even as his mind blanked and his body shuddered and emptied into hers, he could not rid himself of that troubling sense of deeper connection.

Lying in bed, Patrick heard the gurgle and hiss of running water and the squeal of the shower doors. Kate, he thought, getting ready for work. He narrowed his eyes at the digital clock beside the bed. 0600 hours. He hadn't slept long, then. They hadn't slept much at all.

He felt the pull of unused muscles, a twinge of unexpected conscience. He'd never slept with any woman besides his wife, not even when he was serving overseas. Now he had one in his shower.

The soap thunked to the tiles. He imagined Kate's rosy butt as she bent to retrieve it and had to shake away the impulse to join her under the warm spray, to slide soap-slicked hands over her curvy body.

Rounds at seven, she'd said. He didn't know her morning routine, but he'd bet the lady doctor was running late already.

Patrick frowned, scraping his thumb over his jaw. It would take some getting used to, being involved with a doctor.

Involved. He made a face at the dim room, as if someone could see him. What a word. He didn't have involvements. He was the marrying kind. He'd never been tempted to cheapen the memory of his marriage with a succession of one-night stands. *Semper fi* was the Marine motto. *Always faithful.*

And he had held true, first to his wife and his vows, and later to his grief. He'd had Holly, and then he'd had...

Nothing.

Jack.

Slowly, Patrick sat up, swinging both feet to the floor. How would his altered relationship with Kate affect his son?

You didn't think about that last night, did you, ace? You didn't think at all.

The running water stopped. Flinging back the covers, he stood. His gaze fell on his wife's photograph, smiling from its silver frame. Hell. Now he felt disloyal, almost as if she'd caught him in bed with the other woman.

He crossed the room, avoiding the eyes in the picture, and dug through his top drawer for clean shorts. Instinctively, he wanted to gird himself before Kate came back into the room. As if she hadn't already seen him naked. As if she hadn't already taken him into her body, blown his mind, and delicately peeled away at the armor covering his emotions.

As gently as possible, he had to find a way to get her out of his house. He pulled on the boxers.

And maybe Kate had had the same idea, because when she came out of the bathroom she was already zipped and buttoned up into one of those tidy blouse-and-khaki combos she favored. That gave him a moment's pause. She looked fresh and cool, her curling hair still damp, her face free of makeup.

She paused in the lit doorway, as if surprised to find him up, and smiled shyly. "Good morning."

Her hesitancy reminded Patrick that however uncomfortable he found this morning-after business, it was just as strange for her. Maybe stranger, given her touching confession about her lack of experience. Honor and kindness both dictated he make it as easy on her as possible.

And it wasn't that hard, after all, to slip his arms around her, to hold her fully-clothed body against his half-naked one until he felt her shoulders start to relax and her breath release against his chest.

He kissed her hair, which smelled of his shampoo. "You're up early."

"I need to leave for the hospital by six-thirty."

He'd expected to have to ease her along. He was taken aback by her apparent eagerness to go. "I'll make you some coffee."

"That would be nice."

For some reason, her polite acceptance ruffled him. He wished he could see her face. Maybe he hadn't slept with any woman since his wife, but he was pretty sure that after a night of steamy, mutually satisfying sex, Kate had a right to expect more from him than a hot cup of coffee on her way out the door.

"About last night..." she said against his chest.

Here it comes, he thought, and didn't know whether he felt dread or relief. Of course she would want more. And he had nothing more to offer her or any woman.

"I want you to know I understand that you're still in the grief recovery process," she said, all cool understanding.

His jaw unhinged at this analytical, early-morning dissection of his thought processes.

Precisely, she continued. "Please don't worry that I'll read too much into our...into last night. The stress of your father's illness after a long period of abstinence naturally made you reach out in a way that—"

Jolted, he gripped the back of her neck, turning her head to face him. "What the hell are you talking about?"

Her tongue darted over her lower lip, but her eyes were

steady on his. "I'm trying to tell you I don't have any expectations."

"Is that a fact," he snapped.

"Yes. You said you hadn't—that I was your first sexual partner since your wife passed on. It's only natural for you to feel ambivalent this morning."

Ambivalent, hell. He was suddenly, surprisingly angry.

"It didn't maybe occur to you that you should have expectations?" he bit out.

Now, why had he said that? She'd given him the perfect out. But he didn't want it. He couldn't make himself into a one-night Romeo, and he wouldn't treat Kate with less than the respect she deserved.

She blinked. "I beg your pardon?"

"Don't apologize. Call me names, slap my face. You gave me the best night of my life, and you're telling me I should pass it off as, what, therapy?"

She drew herself up, straight and cold as surgical steel. He admired her composure, even when it ticked him off. "You're deliberately misunderstanding me," she said.

"Only to make a point. Last night you said we weren't doing the pity thing."

"We weren't. We didn't," she protested.

"Then don't you think you deserve a little more than 'Thank you, Doctor, for the nice sex, I feel so much better now'?"

Even with the light behind her, he could see the color that flooded her face. But she pinned him with her cool doctor's gaze and asked in her clipped, light voice, "What did you have in mind?"

Frustrated, he dragged a hand through his hair. "This isn't about me."

"Isn't it?"

"Dammit, no. What do *you* want?"

"I told you last night. For just once in my life, I wanted

someone like you to want someone like me.'' She shrugged. ''I wanted you. Simple.''

It wasn't simple at all. His gut churned. But when she looked at him like that, with that small, wry smile, he was forced to admit that this new complication in his life was damn near irresistible.

''So where do we go from here?'' he asked.

Her eyes flickered. Maybe his lady doctor wasn't quite so composed as she wanted him to think. ''*I'm* going to work. I guess anything else is up to you.''

Fine. Let her see how she liked having someone invade her life.

''Dinner,'' he said decisively. ''Tonight. I'll pick you up.''

''That's not necessary.''

''You want to take your own car?''

''No, I mean, you don't need to buy me dinner. Anyway, doesn't the meal usually come before the sex?''

Her quick, defensive sarcasm entertained him. Annoyed him. ''If we get lucky,'' he drawled.

He saw the spark of comprehension, the answering laughter flame in her eyes, and suddenly the knot in his chest dispelled.

''I want to take you out to dinner, Kate. I want to spend the time with you. Say yes.''

''I...'' She chewed her lower lip. ''All right. I get off at four. Give me another couple of hours after that to play catch up, maybe?''

''Six,'' he confirmed. ''At the hospital?''

''No! My place.''

''Fine.''

He wondered how she'd react if he suggested they make love again before she left, and then grinned, shaking his head at his rampant libido and raging imagination.

He wasn't going to get that lucky.

''What is it?'' she asked suspiciously.

''Nothing.'' He bent his head and touched his lips to hers in brief promise. ''See you at six, Doctor.''

* * *

For once, she might clock out on time. She'd just look over the tests ordered for the little girl in 816, Kate decided, and her notes from this morning's team conference, and then she was out of here.

Anticipation sang in the marrow of her bones, a rising chorus of joy and desire that nearly drowned out the shouting voices of caution, the low notes of fatigue. Don't take it too seriously, she reminded her heart. Don't take him too seriously. However complimentary or confiding, the man's not looking for a lasting relationship. Just look at the way he stiffened up when he caught you coming out of his shower this morning.

She shook her head, dispelling her gloomy thoughts. She didn't get nearly enough sleep last night. Remembering how and why, her heart stuttered, and her body clenched deep inside. She could feel the foolish smile that curved her lips.

Maybe she wouldn't sleep tonight, either.

Yawning, Kate propped her feet on one of the lounge's molded plastic chairs and eyed the staff coffeepot. Whoever had poured last had left it to the next shift to brew fresh. The viscous sludge at the bottom looked bad, smelled worse and was nearly undrinkable. Even for her.

That was all right. She didn't need caffeine. Patrick MacNeill was already in her system, pulsing through her blood, waking every fiber and nerve, jolting her heart. Last night she'd taken an irreversible step, an unforgettable lover. A sudden memory shivered through her of his intent blue eyes and fiercely concentrated face as he thrust inside her.

In two and a half hours she would see him again. She wanted to pinch herself, either to keep awake or to make sure she wasn't dreaming. She struggled to review the situation with her usual professional detachment.

The best night of his life, he'd said. Could she believe him?

You deserve more, he'd said. Could she believe that?

No, she decided. No one and nothing in her life had pre-

pared her to accept that a gorgeous flyboy like Patrick
MacNeill, with his stormy eyes and lightning grin, his strong
sense of honor and his deep love of family, would attach himself permanently to brainy, plain trailer trash Katie Sue Sinclair.

She hadn't been good enough to make her father want to
stay. Her mother told her repeatedly she didn't have what it
took to hold a man. Even after Kate had clawed her way
through medical school, Wade certainly hadn't believed she
was deserving of more. But Patrick had made her feel beautiful
and wakened a longing as painful as hope in her heart. Lord,
how she wanted, just once, to believe she could have more.

"Hi, there, Kate." Owen Roberts, already in scrubs and
white lab coat, bustled into the lounge and made a beeline for
the vending machines. "You're here late."

Kate glanced at the clock on the microwave. Four o'clock
rounds didn't start for another half hour. "You're here early."

The burly physician slipped in his change and punched in
his selection. The machine whirred and chunked out twin
chocolate pastries.

"Wanted dessert," he explained. "Wanda's got me on a
diet. So…" Behind wire-rimmed glasses, his eyes regarded
her shrewdly. "How are you? Everything fine at home yesterday?"

Yesterday. It took a moment for Owen's concern to penetrate the fog created in Kate's brain by sex and lack of sleep.
He'd covered for her yesterday. Quick, betraying color
warmed her face.

"Yes. Thank you. And here?"

"Fine, fine." He hesitated. "Gerry was asking for you."

Kate's heart sunk. Gerald Swaim didn't approve of the staff
tampering with his precious duty roster. She could just imagine what he'd say if he knew his senior fellow was taking time
off to baby-sit one of his patients. Not to mention the night
she'd spent practicing her bedside manner on his patient's father. She fought to keep her face neutral.

Owen crinkled up his cellophane wrapper. "I wouldn't have said anything, but I thought you'd want to know. In case he mentions it."

He smiled at her tentatively, and Kate surprised them both by smiling back. For the first time, she wondered if their relationship as not-really-equals and not-quite-friends was as much the result of her own defensive attitude as the hospital's male hierarchy.

"Thanks, Owen. I appreciate it."

"Happy to help. We're lucky to have you on staff. I told Gerry you deserved a personal day."

She was grateful for the attending's unexpected support, but his championship made her nervous. "I don't think Dr. Swaim believes in personal days."

Owen twinkled at her. "Not for the interns, anyway. But you're a senior fellow. You've covered for him often enough."

"I'm also a woman. I can't afford to conform to some stereotype by neglecting my duties here for my so-called personal life."

Owen brushed chocolate crumbs from his fingers. "Perhaps it's not having a personal life that's the problem. Perhaps it's the patient you're getting personal with."

Dismay flared. So he'd heard about the MacNeills. Sharon had warned her. Gossip multiplied in the corners of the hospital like staphylococcus.

Control kept Kate's face blank, her voice even. If she couldn't compose her emotions any better than some first-year medical student, she deserved the attending's censure.

"I do my job."

"Very well, too. I just want you to have the opportunity to keep on doing it."

He spoke too kindly for her to consider his words a threat. He meant them as a caution, she supposed.

Before she could respond, Sharon Williams burst into the

lounge. "Dr. Sinclair? Oh, Dr. Roberts, thank goodness you're here."

"What is it?"

"Apartment fire. They're coming in now. Multiple victims."

Kate and Owen were already rushing through the door, down the corridor to the hydrotherapy room.

"How many?" Kate demanded, tugging a sterile cap over her hair.

Sharon ran beside her. "One adult female—the grandmother—and three children."

Children. Kate's stomach clenched. She hated it when it was children.

"Who've we got?" Owen demanded, scrubbing his hands at the sink.

"Ernie." Sharon named the senior resident. "He's meeting the elevator."

Gloving, Kate could hear them coming down the hall, running feet, raised voices. Water hissed into the two huge steel tubs which would receive the burn patients.

"Take a team," Owen ordered. "Ernie'll triage."

"Got it," Kate said briefly.

Necessity and training took over. Adrenaline pumped through her, sharpening her mind and senses. Emotions shut down. She could hear her voice and Owen's voice weaving through the children's screams, the grandmother's sobs, the nurses' soothing murmurs.

"Run a line."

"Get a heart monitor on her."

"I want a line on this kid. I don't care if you can't find a vein."

"Hold her. Hold her. Get the bench in the tub. The water's too deep."

"Dammit, where's the IV? He's going into shock."

"We've got smoke inhalation. We need to move to ICU."

"Start a trach."

Kate watched her own hands, moving with deliberate urgency, fighting slippery bodies and splashing water and death. As she battled, time blurred, each moment, each task, frozen in crystalline precision, whole minutes disappearing in the rush to accomplish it all.

Hours later, they were done, the wounds washed and dressed. Four survivors hooked to fluid lines and pressurized oxygen rested in a double-room suite, to take what comfort they could from each other's presence. The mother had finally arrived from work. Owen was with her now, trying to help her make sense of what had happened to her family.

Kate dropped her mask and stripped off her gloves. The ebbing emergency took all her energy with it, leaving her drained of everything but fatigue. A headache trembled behind her eyes.

"Kate." Sharon touched her arm. "You have a visitor in the waiting room."

She nodded, missing the nurse's next sentence in her eagerness to finish up her business here and go home. She regretted her haste a moment later when she thumped through the unit's doors and stumbled unprepared on Patrick MacNeill.

He was too big, too male, too healthy. Too much. His dark eyebrows lifted, and abruptly she realized how she must appear to him, disheveled, drenched and stinking of scorch and antiseptic soap.

She swore. "Dinner. I forgot. Sorry."

It wasn't an apology, Patrick thought, or even an explanation. She looked exhausted, brittle, brilliant, vibrating like a jet propellor blade. And none too happy to see him.

He stood slowly, spoke quietly, gauging her reaction. "I went to your apartment. When you weren't there, I called here. The desk nurse said you were almost finished up."

She rubbed two fingers just beneath her breastbone in a gesture he was learning to recognize. "We got the call right before I went off shift. I didn't even think... What time is it?"

"A little after six." It was nearer seven, but he wasn't going to belabor the point, not with her face as pale as a saint's in his mother's missal.

He'd almost called this dinner off. They needed some distance—okay, he needed some space—to figure out where things stood after last night. The only thing he was sure of was that sleeping with Kate hadn't eased his itch for her, or his mind at all.

She was a busy professional woman. She didn't need distractions any more than he did. But now all he could see was that she was tired, uptight, and alone.

"I'm sorry," she said again.

This time he heard the regret behind the defensive challenge. Unable to stop himself, he raised his hand to trail one finger down her damp, smooth cheek.

"Stop apologizing. You're not the only one with scheduling conflicts."

Those tiny twin frown lines formed above her nose. He nodded to a corner of the waiting room where Jack scrunched in one of the child-sized chairs, coloring.

She controlled it, but he caught her tiny start of surprise. Well, what woman would expect a lover to bring his kid along on what could be called their first date?

"Do you really think we need a chaperone?"

Damn, she was quick. But he and Jack were a package. The sooner she accepted that, the better.

Patrick shrugged. "I couldn't get a sitter."

She turned those too-observant brown eyes on him. "And you've been gone almost a week. You wouldn't want to leave him your first night back anyway. Hey, Jack." She spoke softly, a measure of tightness easing from her shoulders. "What are you drawing?"

The boy tilted his head and slanted her a smile, still half focused on his big white art tablet. "A get-well card. For Grandpa."

She strolled over, kneeling beside him to take a look. Their heads were nearly on a level. The sight of those two faces, so dissimilar in features and coloring, so alike in their expressions of assessing interest, jarred something loose in Patrick's chest.

"Great pterodactyl," Kate commented. "Orange is a cheerful color. How's your grandfather doing?"

"Okay, I guess." He looked to his father for confirmation.

"Better," Patrick said. "Fighting with the doctors to go home."

Jack swivelled in his chair, confiding, "I told Daddy maybe you could go take care of Grandpa, but he said you had people to take care of here. Did you make them better?"

Kate rubbed her face with her hand in the first overtly vulnerable gesture Patrick could remember. "I'm trying."

He remembered their conversation the night of Jack's surgery. Her face bleached under the cafeteria lights, Kate had argued she found her work rewarding. She needed to feel she made a difference in her patients' lives, she'd said. He wondered how it was possible to hold on to that hope in the midst of pain and frantic action. Who soothed her when her work was done? Who healed her?

Admiration for her moved him. Ignoring her slight resistance, he slid his hand under the fall of her hair and massaged her tightly corded neck.

"Sometimes it takes a while to get better," he said. "Even when the doctor does her job really, really well."

Jack nodded. "Like with my hand."

"Like with your hand," Patrick confirmed. They needed to get out of here. Jack needed dinner, Kate needed a break from the hospital, and he needed to take his hands off her before he embarrassed them both. "Anybody hungry?" he asked heartily.

"I'm starving," Jack said.

Kate pulled away. "I'm not exactly dressed for dining out."

He let her go. For now. "Yeah, well, with Jack along that romantic, let's-be-French restaurant I had in mind is out anyway."

She glanced down at her soiled blue scrubs. "I'm not even dressed for burgers."

"We can drive you home if you want. Wait while you change."

"Daddy, I'm starving to *death*."

Patrick suppressed a flicker of irritation at his son's near whine. They were already an hour past Jack's usual dinner time, and the boy had been remarkably patient waiting for Kate. He patted the pockets of his jacket for more snacks. "Have another cracker."

"I don't want a cracker."

"How about this," Kate proposed. "I have clothes here in my locker. Give me five minutes to shower, and we can go out for pizza."

"Yeah!"

"You want pizza?" Patrick repeated.

That faint flush he loved suffused her face. "He likes pizza."

He grinned at her defensive tone. "Pizza it is."

He'd never known a woman to get ready in five minutes before—Holly had liked her hair and makeup to be just so—but Kate managed it.

He smiled in approval when she returned to the waiting room, tidy in slacks and blouse, her shiny hair secured in a barrette. "All set?"

A burly doc in gold wire rims bumped through the doors behind her. "Kate, good job with the old lady. Did you talk to Ernie about—"

He checked, shrewd hazel eyes skipping from Patrick to Jack. Instinct had Patrick going on alert, his hands balling in his jacket pockets.

"Excuse me," the doctor said politely. "I didn't know you were busy. Mr. MacNeill, isn't it?"

He knew the guy. Roberts, that was it. Patrick nodded. "Dr. Roberts."

"That's all right," Kate said hastily. "Yes, I went over everything. He can page me if there's a problem."

"Wonderful. Well." The physician shifted his weight from foot to foot. "I won't keep you. Going out somewhere?"

"To dinner. Kate needs a break."

"Ah. Yes." His broad-featured face worked with brief, internal debate before he stuck out his hand. "Have a nice time, then."

"Thanks." Patrick shook, his gaze sliding to Kate. She was wearing her doctor's mask again, and the tension had returned to her shoulders.

He waited until they were at the elevator before he asked. "What the hell was all that about?"

Kate entered the elevator and turned, staring straight ahead at the sliding doors. "I'm not sure. If I had to guess, I'd say Owen's not going to report seeing us together to Dr. Swaim."

Jack hovered by the control panel. "Can I push the button?" he asked.

Distracted, Patrick replied, "Yeah, go ahead. Why would he?"

"Which one?" Jack persisted.

"L. For lobby. Why should it matter if he sees us together, Kate?"

"It shouldn't. It's just Swaim's been touchy about his practice lately. It's like he wants me to take over in surgery, but he doesn't want me taking any of his patients. It's weird."

"Have you talked to him yet?"

"Sort of."

"Is that yes or no?"

The doors opened on the lobby, and Kate strode through. Patrick kept up with her easily, one hand outstretched to Jack, trotting in their wake.

"I mentioned my concern, all right? He said I was imagining things, that he was simply a very busy man. But afterwards I noticed he started turning over a lot of the OR procedures to Owen and me."

She bolted out onto the lit sidewalk and whirled to face him. "The man is a surgeon. The head of the burn unit. I'm not going to embarrass him by questioning his ability."

"Or risk your job by ticking him off."

"Or risk my job. That's right."

She headed for the staff parking garage.

Patrick caught her arm. "Whoa. Slow down. The car's that way."

"I have my car."

He didn't say anything. He didn't let go of her arm, either.

Kate blew out a sharp breath, exhaling bad humor. "Oh, all right. You can drive me back to pick it up later."

He could. Or he could take her home and help her work off that temper in bed. Deciding she wasn't ready to hear that option yet, Patrick led the way silently to the Volvo and unlocked the doors.

"This is going to be fun," Jack announced, bouncing into the back seat.

Patrick glanced from his son's bright face to Kate's guarded one.

Fun. Right.

Chapter 12

Kate stared up through the windshield at the blinking red neon sign. "Bowling?" Her disbelief was evident in her voice. "We're not eating dinner at a bowling alley."

"Sure we are." Patrick cut the engine and unfastened his seat belt. "My old DI runs the place. Makes great burgers. And Jack can get a slice of pizza."

She relaxed slightly. "But we're not actually going bowling."

He angled himself in his seat to look at her. "Why not?"

"Well…" She searched for a reasonable objection. She was tired and tense and in no mood to make a fool of herself in front of Patrick Probably-Bowls-Strikes MacNeill. "Can Jack manage a ball, with his hand?"

Patrick grinned. "Jack still uses two hands. And we'll pull bumpers down in the gutters. He'll do fine."

"Great," Kate muttered. "Then I can be out-performed by a four-year-old."

Patrick paused in the act of swinging out of the car. "You can't bowl?"

She glared at him. "My sister can."

Amy could bowl. Amy could bowl and shoot pool and do any number of things that required time and money and friends. Kate had always been too stubborn, too broke and too shy.

"Time you learned, then," Patrick said. His grin broadened, and her heart actually fluttered. "You'll do fine. It'll take your mind off whatever's bothering you. You might even enjoy yourself."

She doubted it. But she let Jack take her hand and tug her through the sliding doors into the well-lit, echoing bowling alley. It smelled of floor wax, disinfectant and old shoes, with an overlay of popcorn and beer. Kate sniffed. Not disagreeable, she decided, after the stench of burns hanging in the hospital's sterile air.

League bowlers with matching shirts and polished bags practiced at one end. A children's birthday party chattered and crashed at the other. Patrick settled Kate at a center lane, while Jack pattered off to find a ball.

He eyed her feet assessingly. "You'll need shoes. What do you take, an eight?"

"Seven and a half," she replied without thinking.

He went up front to pay their charge, collect their shoes and place their food order. Kate eased back cautiously in her molded plastic chair, her attention captured by the three teenage boys in the next lane. They postured and cracked jokes, plainly showing off for the pretty girl bowling with her family on their other side. They reminded her of Sean. She smiled.

"That's better," Patrick said, setting a burger basket in front of her. Jack scrambled onto the seat beside her. "What are you thinking of?"

"Your brother," she replied, and had the pleasure of seeing his brows snap together in a frown.

"Don't waste your time," he advised.

She tilted her head, seized by an unfamiliar desire to test

her own feminine power. ''Why? Do you think I'm too old for him?''

Patrick scowled, handing Jack a napkin. He stuck a straw into his soft drink. ''No.''

Oh, she was enjoying this. ''I got the impression he liked me.''

''Yeah, he did. He does. But then, our Sean likes most women. He's commitment-shy.''

''Mmm.'' Thoughtfully, she selected a French fry and dipped it in ketchup. ''Runs in the family, does it?''

His eyes narrowed dangerously. ''Do you want a list of my commitments, Kate?''

Her heart jolted as if she'd just administered herself a shot of epi. Careful. She'd known what she was getting into when she'd decided to go to bed with Patrick MacNeill. He'd offered her pleasure, not promises. A shared respite from responsibility, not an added obligation. If the intimacy of the night had tempted her to think otherwise, she had only to remember the way he'd closed himself up from her presence in his house this morning. She'd been deceived once about a man's intentions. She'd be a fool to delude herself now.

''Not necessary,'' she said coolly. ''Unless you're trying to convince me to keep score.''

Amusement relaxed his face. ''You really haven't done this before, have you? It's done electronically.''

''Oh. No cheating, then?''

''No cheating.''

She wondered if they were still talking about bowling, but didn't have the courage to ask. ''Too bad.''

''You'll do fine,'' he assured her again.

''Daddy pulls down the thingies on the sides,'' Jack explained, speaking around a slice of pizza. ''To keep the score even.''

Not very even, a disgruntled Kate thought in the sixth frame. Her ball bounced off the bumpers, losing force, or glided along the side, never knocking down more than four pins. Jack had his own, two-handed style, rolling the ball from between his legs with surprising effect. His shouts of glee and whispered instruction relieved her embarrassment and made her smile.

But when Patrick played, her mouth went dry. The intensity he brought to their uncompetitive family game was positively indecent. Oh, he wasn't obnoxious about it. He joked, leaning back at the console, and patted and teased his son, and hunched over, making encouraging noises, when Kate got up to bowl. But when he stood and strode to the bottom of the lane, he drew every female eye, from the pink-haired lady spraying shoes at the counter to the teenage girl playing one lane over.

He walked like a warrior. Beneath his plain knit shirt, his shoulders were broad. His long back rippled with muscle. His concentration as he set the ball tempted every woman to imagine how that powerful attention would feel focused on *her*.

Kate knew, and the knowledge made her heart beat faster.

She clutched her soggy soda cup, trying to steady her heartbeat by analyzing the man's game. It was all a matter of technique, she decided. He had a smooth swing. Good balance. And a very nice, tight butt.

"Well, now, this is a pleasure."

Kate's face flamed. She turned. A graying black man in a bright purple bowling shirt smiled at her, extending his hand over the counter.

"Jimmy Burke," he said. "I run this place. I've been waiting a long time for Captain MacNeill to bring a lady around."

She wiped her hand hastily on her slacks. His grip was firm and callused, his forearm tattooed. "It's very nice to meet you. But I'm not his—I'm a doctor at the hospital."

The man's eyebrows climbed his high, domed forehead. "A doctor. Damn. Never pictured the captain with a medic."

"Yes, well, I'm sure he feels the same way," she agreed.

Patrick's back was to them. He waited politely for the blonde in the next lane to bowl before finishing his own frame.

With a wiggle, the teenager released her ball and sashayed to her seat, looking back over her shoulder.

"I can see why you'd be worried about finding him female companionship," Kate observed dryly.

"Oh, he's not like that, ma'am. Doctor."

"Kate," she insisted, smiling.

He acknowledged her name with a brief nod. "Thank you. Call me Jimmy. Anyway, he don't fool around. Patrick MacNeill was just about the most married man I ever knew. The rest of them couldn't wait to get out on liberty and drink and carry on."

She was fascinated and trying not to show it. "And he didn't go?"

The man laughed, displaying perfect white teeth. "Oh, he went. They all went. And being as he was going mustang— He didn't come in from college," he explained at Kate's puzzled look. "Sometimes a likely enlisted man will get tapped as an officer candidate and get a chance at flight school. That's what happened with Patrick. Anyway, maybe he needed liberty more than most."

She leaned forward, trying to absorb this new image of Patrick. "And...he was married, then?"

Jimmy Burke nodded. "About two years, I guess. To his high-school sweetheart." She must have kept the pang at her heart from showing in her face, because he continued with his story. "So every time his buddies would go into a bar and start to pairing up, like they do, Patrick would look them over, all the ladies, and pick out the ugliest girl there and buy her a drink."

Kate winced. "And I'm supposed to find this reassuring?"

Burke grinned. "Oh, yes. It was strategy," he confided, tapping his graying temple. "One of the reasons he made officer. See, he'd make that girl's night. She'd keep all the other pretty ladies away, and Officer Candidate MacNeill would get back to base without ever being tempted."

Kate pressed her lips together. Was part of her appeal her

own inability to tempt Patrick to emotional infidelity? "That's shameless," she said.

"No, it was smart," Patrick interrupted, coming over to sit beside her. She was painfully conscious of his arm, warm and heavy, draped along the back of her chair, touching her shoulders. He reached his other hand to Burke.

"Sir. How the hell are you?"

"It's Jimmy, now, Captain. I'm not your instructor anymore."

"It's Patrick, now, First Sergeant. I'm not in the Corps anymore."

Kate listened, both attracted by and excluded from this masculine exchange, reminded again how little she really shared of Patrick MacNeill's life. When Jack got up to bowl, she excused herself to watch, leaving the men to their conversation.

The boy danced in excitement. "Spare!" he crowed. "I'm beating you, Dr. Kate!"

Smiling, she tugged on the brim of his baseball cap. "Show-off."

Patrick unfolded his long body from his chair and came up behind them. "Are you being disrespectful to the lady, buddy?"

"No, sir." Jack tipped his head back, grinning at his dad. "I'm just beating her."

Kate laughed. "Don't sound so proud of yourself. I stink."

"I don't know," Patrick said. "Maybe you just need a lesson."

She eyed him warily. "A lesson?"

"Mmm. You're letting your arm cross your body before you release."

He was almost certainly right. And she didn't care, Kate reminded herself. But the hint of criticism raised her competitive hackles. "So?"

"So you want to bring the ball forward straight from the shoulder." He picked up her ten-pound ball like it weighed so many ounces and handed it to her. ''Here, let me show you.''

She could hardly object with Jack standing there, with Jimmy Burke looking on. But instead of demonstrating, Patrick wrapped his body around hers and guided her hand.

''Bring it back smoothly,'' he murmured into her ear, while she tried to ignore that his arm was warm and close along hers and his hips cradled her bottom. ''That's it. And then forward...like this...and release when the heel of your thumb is pointing at the center pin.''

The ball flew from her fingers, gliding almost straight down the wooden lane to crash into the number eight pin.

''Seven!'' Jack shouted, bouncing up and down. ''That's good, Dr. Kate.''

''There,'' Patrick said, his breath stirring the hair just behind her ear. ''Much better.''

Reaction shivered through her. She shrugged away, damning her susceptibility. She didn't want to respond to him on a purely sexual level, not when he kept so much of his mind and his life locked away from her. With a jolt of dismay, she discovered her heart was capable of misleading her more thoroughly than Wade Preston ever had.

''Let me see if I've got it.''

Grimly, she retrieved her ball from the conveyor. She could do this. She would do this. She was smart enough to master a simple game. Two steps, the way she'd seen him do it. Back from the shoulder, smoothly. Forward, straight. And with only a kiss from the bumper, Kate bowled her first spare.

She turned with a smile of triumph to meet Patrick's gaze, amusement and a hint of admiration in his blue eyes.

''Yeah, I guess you do,'' he said. ''And all by yourself, too.''

Her chin went up. ''Don't mess with me, flyboy. I've had a bad day.''

''Tell me about it,'' he invited quietly.

She opened her mouth to do exactly that before she realized

how inappropriate it would be with Jack there and the bowling
alley owner listening in. How inappropriate it would be, period. Patrick MacNeill had made it clear from the start he
didn't want her problems. He wanted a physical distraction
and help with his son.

"I don't think so," she said.

Something—frustration, fatigue, the lick of loneliness—
must have colored her voice. She caught the look Patrick ex-
changed with Burke, leaning over the counter behind them,
and was annoyed at her loss of control.

The owner straightened, elaborately breezy. "I'd best go
check on lane four. Those league bowlers get mighty thirsty."
He shook Patrick's hand again and nodded to Kate. "Ma'am.
Don't be a stranger."

She forced a smile. "Thank you. It was nice to meet you."

"My pleasure," he said before he walked away.

"Is it my turn?" Jack demanded, tugging at his father's
arm.

"No," Patrick said slowly, eyes steady on Kate's face.
"No, I'm thinking it's mine. Is that what you're thinking,
Kate?"

"I'm not thinking anything," she snapped. Experience had
taught her that much. The less you hoped for, the less likely
you were to be disappointed. The less you asked for, the less,
in the end, you gave away.

His dark eyebrows raised. "So what are you feeling?"

Don't think, he'd urged her last night. *Feel.* The memory
shivered between them.

Kate looked away, rubbing the spot beneath her ribs where
her cheeseburger burned. Feeling was dangerous. Feelings
were unreliable. What had feeling ever gotten the women of
her family but headaches and heartaches? She'd always prided
herself on her rational decisions, her dogged, methodical approach to problems. It was time to step back, to take a long,
cool look at what she wanted and what she could reasonably
expect from this man.

How did she feel?

Wretched. Besotted. Confused.

"Tired," she said.

"Do you want to go home?" he asked.

"But, Daddy," Jack objected, "it's my turn."

"One more frame," Patrick said, his gaze never leaving Kate's face. "And then we're going home."

"Not to your house," she said quickly.

Jack hefted his ball from the conveyor belt and carried it to the bottom of the lane.

"Why not?" Patrick asked.

"I don't have any clothes."

"What you're wearing looks fine to me."

"I have to feed my cat."

"You don't put out dry cat food for her?"

She did. Of course she did. Blackie would be fine. That wasn't her real objection, and Patrick knew it. She might have responded to his perception—she wanted to accept his invitation—but she was afraid of exposing her feelings to him while he still maintained his careful emotional distance. Not tonight.

"Jack—" she began.

"If Jack thinks anything about it—which he won't—he'll figure you're sleeping down the hall."

She needed to know what he wanted, what he was offering. "But I wouldn't be."

A gleam appeared in his blue eyes. "Sleeping? I don't think so."

She was unbearably tempted to give up, to give in, to go home with him. But she was dreadfully afraid last night had been a mistake. She was almost convinced he thought so, too. What had his sergeant called him? The most married man he'd ever known?

She thought of the photograph of Patrick's pretty wife, his remote courtesy that morning, and shook her head. "I can't."

"You won't."

"I shouldn't."

"Was it Roberts seeing us together?" he asked suddenly. "Are you worried about your job?"

"That's part of it." She wasn't sure if her new rapport with Owen Roberts extended to his keeping silent, or what it would mean if he didn't. But she didn't want Patrick to feel hedged by her concerns. Her mother claimed there was no surer way to drive a man off. Ten-year-old Kate, standing in the driveway watching her daddy desert them, had vowed fiercely never to confide her troubles to anyone again.

She shrugged. "Don't worry about it. It's my job. My choice. My problem."

Patrick's face shuttered. "I see."

Kate doubted it. But until she decided whether or not she could live within the posted limits of Patrick's life, it was easier to let him think she was covering her ass than to explain she was protecting her heart.

"Are you up to driving?" he asked.

She scowled. Her head pulsed, and there was a hollow in the pit of her stomach that neither the burger he'd fed her or the heartburn that followed had managed to fill. But she was an independent, competent, professional woman. Jack needed to get to bed soon. And Patrick, as always, would put his son's needs first. He ought to. She expected him to. Perhaps that was the part of him she admired the most. There was no way she would interfere with that, or encourage Patrick to see her as a drag on them.

"Of course I can drive."

"We'll take you to pick up your car, then."

The woman was retreating faster than an ambulance under fire, Patrick thought, as they cruised the highway back to the hospital. What the hell had happened to last night's responsive, eager lover? The street lamps lay a pattern of flickering black and white over the pale, set face beside him.

He depressed the gas pedal, picking up speed. Fine. He didn't need another dependent. It wasn't his place to worry over the shadows bruising those wide brown eyes, the creases dug in between those smooth, straight brows. Kate had made it clear she wouldn't welcome his concern or tolerate his interference. She didn't need him. He should be glad.

He was irritated as hell.

He glanced over at her, at her small, neat hands folded quietly in her lap and her face turned toward the window. Everything about her challenged him. He wanted inside that cool, analytical brain of hers, that hot, tight little body. Her snooty refusal to admit him really pushed his buttons.

Why should he care? He didn't want to divide his attention or divert his focus from his son. He didn't need a complicated and consuming passion. He'd brought Jack along tonight to demonstrate to her—to prove to himself—that nothing in his life had changed since he'd opened the door to his room and found Kate Sinclair half-naked on his bed.

Man, was he ever wrong.

The blue and white lights of the hospital glowed up ahead. They were almost to her car, and he hadn't said a word to break that self-sufficient silence of hers. Couldn't say a thing, with his son sitting up and listening in.

Patrick slowed at the entrance to the staff garage. "Which way?"

She delivered brisk directions to her parking spot. At nine o'clock, there was no activity in the shadowed garage and plenty of empty spaces. He hated the thought that she must regularly walk to her car alone. At least she had the sense to park under a light near the elevator. He found an empty slot three spaces down and pulled in.

Kate undid her seat belt. "Jack, thank you for letting me go bowling with you," she said warmly. Opening her door, she glanced back over her shoulder at Patrick. "Thanks for the ride."

The lady was brushing him off.

Patrick clenched his jaw. "Stay put," he instructed Jack, and got out of the car. "What's your hurry?"

Her head bent over her car keys. "You have to get home. So do I."

"So come home with us." Now where the hell had that come from? Panic nearly made him light-headed, like a pilot trainee at high altitudes. But that's what he wanted. Kate in his house. Kate in his bed. He forced a smile at her surprised expression, trying to soften the rawness of his need. "I'll buy you a toothbrush."

Just for an instant, he thought he saw an answering flame leap in her eyes. And then she shook her head, her soft hair falling to veil her face. "Not tonight."

He laid a hand on the car door, preventing her from opening it. "When? Tomorrow?"

"I'll sleep on it," she said coolly.

Frustration boiled through him. She was slipping away. Dammit. Damn her, and damn the need that raked his gut.

"Sleep on this," he growled, and reached for her.

The kiss was hot and hungry and rough. Way too much for persuasion, and not nearly enough. When he raised his head, she was shaking, and he was breathing hard. Releasing her shoulders, he waited for Kate to slice him into ribbons with her razor mind and scalpel tongue. She pressed her lips together. Oh, God. Was that hurt shimmering in her eyes?

Guilt flayed him. "Well? Aren't you going to say anything?"

She fumbled behind her for the door handle. "What would you like me to say?"

He was furious with her for failing to lose her temper. With himself for his failure of control. "You're pretty good at playing therapist. Why don't you spout that grief recovery bull you're so fond of?"

She lifted her chin a notch. "I'm a surgeon, not a psychiatrist. And I'm not your therapist."

"So what about your little theories this morning? How I can't handle intimacy with you because I'm still getting over my dead wife?"

"Is that what you think you're doing?"

"Hell, no." He dragged his hand through his hair. "I don't know."

Her eyes were bright as surgical steel. "Actually, I do have something to say."

Relief cracked his chest. "Fine. Say it."

Finally, she succeeded in opening her car door. She got in. "I don't need this. I don't need you. Go to hell, MacNeill."

The door slammed behind her. He stood there like a sorry ass and watched her red taillights as she drove away.

Chapter 13

"Daddy, do you like Dr. Kate?"

Patrick, pouring pancake batter, froze. He'd figured he owed his son their traditional Saturday morning breakfast after being away all weekend. Now a single drop fell and sizzled on the hot griddle.

He cleared his throat. "Why do you ask?"

"Well, I saw you kissing her. Last night."

Damn. Jack hadn't said anything when he got into the car. Patrick had assumed his son hadn't seen. Or maybe he'd hoped Jack wouldn't care. Or maybe, in the heat of the moment, he just hadn't thought at all.

Jack, standing on a chair beside him, reached forward to catch another drip on his finger.

"Watch it," Patrick said automatically. "You'll burn yourself."

Obediently, Jack slid his elbows back across the counter. "So, do you?"

Patrick wasn't sure he could explain the dynamics of his relationship with Kate in a way that an almost-five-year-old could understand. Hell, he didn't understand them himself. But he'd always tried to be honest with his son.

"Yeah, I do."

Jack nodded with satisfaction. "Good. I do, too."

Patrick hesitated. He didn't want the kid getting the wrong idea. Kate had been kind to Jack, but that was as far as it went. He and his son were doing great on their own. And the lady doctor had made it clear that she didn't want anything further to do with Jack's daddy. "She's a very nice doctor."

Jack gave his father a look, surprisingly adult in its scorn. "I like her better than any old doctor. I like her living in our house. I wish she could stay."

Uh-oh. Here was trouble. What had Kate said, that first night he'd kissed her? *Patients frequently develop crushes on their doctors.* Jack had fallen hard for Kate. But Kate was devoted to her career. The up-and-coming surgeon had no place in her sterile, well-ordered life for the MacNeill men. No patience with messy passions. No need for him. Resentment flashed through Patrick, overriding the nagging recollection that he'd been the one initially to set limits on their relationship.

He poured four uniform pancakes onto the griddle, buying time to let his boy down easy. "Just because we like a person doesn't mean they have to like us back in the same way. Or the same amount. Do you understand what I'm trying to say?"

"You mean she's mad at you?"

Patrick muffled a laugh that could have easily been a curse. "That, too. I just meant… Don't get your hopes up, buddy."

Jack held out his plate for the finished pancakes. "It's okay, Dad. She loves me back. She told me so."

"She loves you." That was a kicker.

"Yeah."

"She told you so," Patrick repeated. It took some getting used to.

"Yeah. When she was staying here." Jack waved his plate impatiently. "Can I have some pancakes, please?"

Wordlessly, Patrick slid four perfect circles onto his son's plate. All this time he'd been struggling to keep Kate out of his life with Jack, the lady doctor had already made a place for herself in his boy's heart.

"Besides, she wasn't mad when she said 'good night' to *me*." Climbing down from his chair, Jack pulled his plate toward the edge of the counter. He grinned, obviously enjoying the unfamiliar sensation of being one up on old dad. "But if she's mad at you, I think you should 'pologize."

It wasn't such a bad idea. Patrick was uneasily aware he was out of line last night. He figured his defensive reaction was at least partly Kate's fault. The woman got under his skin. She saw into his brain. And she was dangerously close to his heart.

He still owed her an apology.

He didn't know Kate's schedule. So while Jack poured syrup on his pancakes, Patrick called the hospital. The receptionist was evasive. Nurse Williams was blunt.

"We've got twenty-one beds and twenty-three patients," she reported. "Dr. Sinclair's got three surgeries scheduled this morning, and an abuse case just came in. I'll give her a message, Mr. MacNeill, that's the best I can do."

Patrick, already uncomfortable at the prospect of apologizing, declined to leave a message. Kate wouldn't thank him for broadcasting their association, he rationalized. Besides, what he had to say wouldn't sound right through a third party. It wouldn't come easy in front of an audience, either.

Hanging up, he studied his boy's dark head, bent over the plate of pancakes, and came to a decision.

"Hey, buddy. You want to have dinner tonight with Ray and Shelby?"

"Has she had her baby?"

Meeting Billy had whetted Jack's appetite for friends. Even a new baby was better than nothing. Patrick made a mental note to call Kate's sister and arrange a play date with the nephew. Better yet, Kate could make the call. "Not yet."

Jack shrugged. "'Kay."

So Patrick called Ray to confirm that his partner didn't have any flights scheduled for that afternoon. A few hours later, he dropped his son off at their house.

Shelby, swollen with child and bursting with impatience, welcomed them at her door with a hug. "I need the distraction about now," she admitted frankly. "And Ray can use Jack's help putting the changing table together. Don't you worry about a thing."

Patrick wasn't worried. He had it all figured out. Obviously, he'd screwed up. He'd never dreamed the restrictions placed on their relationship would hurt self-sufficient, self-possessed Dr. Kate Sinclair. He'd made no promises. She had no expectations. Correction, Patrick thought ruefully. She *said* she had no expectations. He should have known better.

Backing the Volvo out cautiously to avoid the garbage cans at the end of Ray's drive, Patrick considered Kate's confessed lack of experience. She'd confided her crazy insecurities about that sweet, curvy body of hers. He reminded himself a woman didn't do without sex for nine years and then go to bed and have it mean nothing. He'd done without for four, and it had meant plenty to him. Hell, he'd been immersed in her, lost in her, in her scent and her cries and the soft, wet clasp of her body. For a while there, he'd forgotten everything but the need to touch her, to take her, to have her.

Even now, negotiating rush-hour traffic on his way to her apartment, he wanted her. More than her body in his bed, he wanted the cool challenge of those intelligent eyes and the warm compassion of her smile.

Maybe that had scared him at first, he acknowledged. A man didn't change the emotional habits of a lifetime in one night. He was used to sleeping with his wife. Maybe Kate had had a point about his ambivalence. Maybe he hadn't been ready for another relationship.

But he was willing to risk it now. After all, Kate wasn't asking him to change his life or priorities. It was only reasonable that with her soft heart and hard experience, she needed more from him than occasional sex. Well, Patrick thought righteously, he could accommodate that. She could move in with them.

He waited for panic to hit with the scattering impact of shrapnel, and felt only a quiet, solid sense of rightness. His son would still be at the center of his life, but Kate would fill the corners very nicely. He wanted her. And Jack liked her. It would mean a longer commute for Kate, of course. She would need a new car. Maybe a Landrover ATV? Something safe and reliable for transporting her and Jack, but sporty enough to look at home in the doctors' parking lot.

Satisfied with his solution, he pulled in front of her building. He turned off the engine and sat for a minute with his hands resting on the steering wheel. Maybe he was nuts. He was buying her a car, and she wasn't even speaking to him.

He glanced at his wristwatch. Six o'clock. Her battered gray excuse for transportation was already taking up space at the curb, so she was home. But when he rang the bell, no one answered.

Fine. He'd had a mobile installed in the car so that Jack could always reach him on the road. Turning the ignition key, Patrick punched in Kate's number.

Her machine picked up. "This is Dr. Sinclair," it announced in her cool, clipped voice. "I can't come to the phone right now, but if you'll leave a message at the tone…"

Patrick opened the door of the car. With the headset tucked against his ear, he snapped a directive at her front window. "Kate, this is Patrick. I'm out front, and I'm not going away. You want to let me in, or you want to have this discussion at the hospital?"

This time, when he marched up the crumbling sidewalk to her door, it opened. She stood in the doorway with her arms folded and her eyes glittering in her white face. Tears? Guilt punched him in the chest. Had he done that? Left her hurt and defenseless?

She tipped her head to one side, considering him. "I'm sure this will come as a shock to you, flyboy, but not every woman is secretly thrilled by the Neanderthal act."

Ouch. Okay, hurt but not defenseless. He tried a smile, stepping forward to enter the apartment. "I'm not interested in every woman."

She didn't budge. "Oh, right. Just one. Only she's dead." Her eyes widened at the words that had escaped her.

Anger flicked through him. He fought to contain it. "Not dead, honey. Just real, real cold."

Her head dropped as she looked down and away. "I'm sorry," she said stiffly. "That was an awful thing to say."

He frowned. Twin grooves carved between her brows, and tiny lines bracketed her mouth. She looked every one of her thirty-six years. And yet, studying her averted face, he still felt the tug of lust, the more irresistible pull of concern.

"Let me in, Kate."

She stepped back, admitting him.

He'd come prepared for dinner and an apology. The wine and bread and cheese were still in the trunk of his car. Pulling the cellophane-wrapped bunch of grocery-store flowers from behind his back, he thrust it at her.

"Here."

She looked, if possible, more miserable than before as she accepted the bouquet. "I... Thank you."

"We need to talk."

She put up her empty hand, as if to hold him off. "Please. Not now."

The vulnerable gesture unsettled him. It wasn't like Kate to plead off a confrontation. Or to strike out cruelly, as she had a moment ago. Something had happened to wreck that brisk composure. Something was eating her, gnawing her from the inside out. Something more than him or them. Again, he felt that tug, as if she were drawing his heart out of his chest.

"What is it?" he asked quietly.

She shook her head.

"Is your sister all right? Your mother?"

"They're fine."

"Your job?" he ventured. He remembered she'd been upset last night when that other doctor had seen them together. "You haven't been fired or anything?"

"No. I almost wish I had."

He heard the tightness in her throat and deliberately kept his own voice easy. "Another bad day?"

She closed her eyes. "Yes."

"Do you want to talk about it?"

"Not particularly."

Patrick told himself that suited him fine. In his opinion, open communication was highly overrated. He respected Kate's desire to handle things her own way. All the same, he didn't like her pale, set look. And he wasn't crazy about being shut out like this, either. Maybe she'd feel better after a meal. That had worked the night before, at least until he screwed it up.

"Look, I've got dinner stuff in the car. Why don't I go get it while you put those flowers in some water?"

She nodded. But when he came back through the unlocked door a few minutes later, she was standing where he'd left her, her eyes squeezed shut and her mouth pinched tight, hugging his flowers to her chest.

Tenderness shook him. "Aw, hell, honey."

He set the bags on her desk table. Removing the flowers from her grip, he tossed them beside the groceries. With one finger, he tilted up her chin. "For someone who's always going on about sharing your feelings, you are one stubborn, silent woman, you know that?"

She didn't even glare at him. That as much as anything worried him.

"Come on, Kate. What happened?"

Turning her head from his gentle badgering, she said tonelessly, "We had a kid brought in today. A little boy, Jack's age."

Apprehension tightened Patrick's gut. The burn center saw kids all the time. "And?"

"You really want to know?" Finally, she opened her eyes, and the desolation in them startled him. "His stepfather doused him in gasoline and set him on fire."

He sucked in his breath. "That's horrible."

Kate shrugged. He watched her struggle for her usual composure, heard her retreat to her customary objectivity. "It's fairly common, actually. About a third of the pediatric patients we see are abuse cases."

The statistic staggered him. He could only imagine what the reality must be like. "What are you doing about it?"

She raised her eyebrows. "I'll spare you the medical details. The boy had third-degree burns over sixty-two percent of his body. Owen and I worked on him for five hours."

Patrick recognized the deliberate understatement and the dry tone. He ought to. He'd used the same defenses often enough. "I wasn't talking about his medical treatment."

"Oh." She rubbed two fingers between her brows, as if she could erase the lines of tension or smooth her tangled thoughts. "Well, the social worker took pictures, of course. The psych team is meeting tomorrow morning to discuss issues with the mother. With the stepfather arrested, the other children should be okay."

"That's good, but that's not what I meant either. What about you, Kate? How are you feeling?"

"I'm not feeling anything. I can't afford to feel anything."

She felt something, all right, Patrick thought grimly. It was tearing her apart. He didn't like it, didn't like not being able to fix things for her. He took her shoulders, but she was straight and stiff as a rifle under his hands. And as likely to go off, if she didn't find some safe release for the emotions churning inside her.

"Don't give me the medical line. You're off duty now. You don't have to play Super Doc."

She flashed. "Listen, flyboy, my Super Doc act kept that kid alive."

He preferred her anger to her distress. "Great. He's alive. Now cut yourself some slack. Cry, if you have to."

She jerked away from him. "I can't cry. I won't cry. Crying doesn't help."

He was used to being the strong one. Now he watched in equal parts irritation and sympathy as she paced her tiny living room. And understanding. God, how he understood. Her words were a bitter echo of his own soul's cry after the accident.

"Not the kid, maybe. It might help you."

She fetched up by the window, staring out as if her tidy living quarters were too small to contain her grief. "I can't afford to break my heart over every child who comes through the unit. How I feel isn't going to make anybody any better."

"So you don't let your feelings get in the way of what you have to do. But the feelings are there, Kate. You can't ignore them."

She whirled to face him. "You mean, like you do?"

It was a well-aimed shot, and it hit right on target. "We're not talking about me."

"No, we never do, do we?"

She was bitter, defensive. Right. And she still hadn't cried. Maybe talking wasn't such a good idea after all.

He crossed the room in two long strides, nearly stepping on the cat, and grabbed her. Her defiant face, her troubled eyes, tore at him.

"It didn't use to bother me," she snapped. *"Don't let it get to you.* I tell them all that, all the residents. You can't do your job if you let it get to you. Only I looked at this boy, this baby, and I saw Jack. I know what he's going to face. The process will be that much harder because he doesn't have a daddy like you to support him. His mother doesn't have it together, either. I'm in there trying to evaluate his wounds, and I came this close—" She held up her thumb and forefinger, half an inch apart, and shook them in his face. *"—This close*—to losing it. I don't want to feel this way. I'm no damn good if I let myself feel this way."

Frustration drew a noose around his chest. No damn good? She was the best thing that had happened to *him* in a long, sorry while.

He tightened his hold on her. "That's a load of crap," he said brutally. "Your patients deserve a doctor who will treat them with her heart as well as her hands and her brain. It doesn't make you less effective if you see them as people and not just as meat on a table."

She stared at him, shock plain on her face. And then, quite suddenly, tears welled, blurring her burning anger and her fierce intelligence. She cried.

Patrick gathered her against his chest, trying to absorb both her tears and her grief. If he'd had any illusions left that he could enjoy a limited, physical relationship with this woman, her tears destroyed them. His hand, as he stroked her soft hair, trembled slightly.

"He's so little," she wept. "They're supposed to take care of him. How can any parent do that to a child who depends on them for love?"

He didn't have an answer for her. All he had was the strength of his arms and the comfort of his embrace. So he held her, just held her, while she sobbed noisily and without pretense against his heart. After a long while, she quieted. Her breath flattened the damp fabric of his shirt.

Deep inside, where Patrick had thought it safely smothered, an ember of guilt burned, sparked to life by the honesty of her emotion and fanned by her breath against his chest. *So little.* He closed his eyes in pain, remembering another small boy, another burn survivor. So little, and so frighteningly dependent.

Kate shuddered, empty of tears. A new, delicate peace expanded to fill the hollow space inside her. Her nose, buried against Patrick's chest, was stuffy, and her throat was raw.

With her protective doctor's shell cracked around her, she felt
wet and naked as a new chick. And yet, anchored in Patrick's
arms, she also felt curiously weightless, and free for the first
time that she could remember of the burdens of her profession
and the weight of her own expectations.

"I love my son." The words grated out.

She tightened her arms around him, instinctively responding
to the rough need in his voice. "Of course you do."

"But I wasn't there for him, either."

She shifted to look up into his face. "What? When?"

"When he had his accident. When Holly died. I wasn't
there."

Indignation swelled, disturbing her fragile sense of well-
being. "That's not the same thing. You were on assignment,
you told me. With the reserves."

He shrugged, like a warrior resettling heavy armor. The gesture almost dislodged her hold on him. "Yeah. But the bottom
line is, I wasn't there when he needed me."

All her protective instincts surged to deny it. She was
fiercely angry he could think that way. "Don't you believe
it," she said. "Jack lived. I remember. The nurses called him
Iron Man, because he fought so hard to live."

Patrick's face had resumed its mask. She wasn't reaching
him. Kate punched his upper arm in frustration. "Do you
know how many patients we lose just when it looks like everything is going to be all right? Their immune system shuts
down or their metabolic rate goes up or an infection starts in
their wounds or in their lungs, and they just give up. Jack
never gave up. You wouldn't let him give up. I saw you in
his hospital room. I was just doing a visiting rotation, but I
heard the stories. He held on to life, for you."

Patrick's eyes met hers, cautious with the need to believe.
With fierce conviction, she said, "Don't you ever, ever tell
me you weren't there when he needed you."

His guard raised, revealing the wound that still oozed inside him. "I couldn't make the pain go away. I couldn't make him better. I still can't."

Her heart ached for him. But he didn't need her coddling. He needed to pull his head out of his hero hat and take a good hard look at reality. "So what? You do what you can," she argued. "You give him your love and support. Yes, Jack's scarred, but he's happy and secure, because of you."

"Dr. Kate." He touched her cheek, his touch a balm even as he refused her healing. His smile twisted. "Trying to make everything all better."

She blew out a short, exasperated breath. "Patrick, you can't possibly compare your absence from an accident with the deliberate decision to do harm."

She could see by his face that he still didn't believe her. Driven by the need to make him whole again, by the need to make him see, she named the thing that made her love him, the precious thing he gave his son. The one thing she'd never had. "The point is, once the authorities contacted you, you were there for him in every way that counted. *You* didn't walk away from a child who needed you."

She'd revealed too much. She knew it the instant the words left her mouth. She saw her mistake in the comprehension that deepened his blue eyes, heard it in the compassion that softened his voice.

"So who walked away from you?" he asked.

She didn't want his pity. She didn't want to confess to him what a failure she was. "Let's not do this. Let's not play my-scar-is-bigger-than-your-scar. You win, anyway."

"Fair's fair. Talk. Tell me, Kate. Who walked away from you?" he persisted quietly.

"My father." She blurted it out.

His strong fingers pressed comfortingly into the tight muscles of her shoulders. "How old were you?"

She pressed her lips together to control their trembling. She hated this, hated being reduced to a needy child again. It threatened the identity she'd created for herself as the all-knowing doctor, the almighty surgeon. "It doesn't matter."

He continued his slow massage. "How old? Do you remember?"

Too well. Too clearly. And saw again the shadowed interior of her father's car, the back of his head, the shape of his ears blurred by her tears. Had he looked back, just for an instant, when she blinked? *Daddy, I will be good.* "Ten. I was ten."

Patrick's hands paused a second and then resumed their gentle stroking. "His loss. He was a fool to give you up."

Clearly, he didn't understand. She confessed the rest. "Wade, too. My—my lover."

"And he was an idiot."

The conviction in his voice made her smile, in spite of the hurt at her heart. "So, according to you, the men in my life have all been brain damaged in some way, is that it?"

The corner of his mouth quirked up. "Looks that way, doesn't it?"

There was a shaking, aching hollow right under her rib cage. She had to ask, had to know. "And you? Are you a fool, too?"

His level gaze met hers. "No. No, a coward, maybe. Maybe I haven't wanted to take the risk of letting anybody down again. But I've never been called a fool."

Hope unfolded painfully inside her. At least when the time came, Patrick wouldn't walk away without a backward glance. She meant something to him. For now, that belief was enough. It would have to be. And it was more than she'd ever expected.

Tentatively, she raised herself on tiptoe to touch her lips to his jaw. He'd shaved before coming. The scent of his aftershave, masculine and spicy, tingled through her.

His voice rumbled near her ear. "Of course, with two brothers, I've been called a jackass a time or two."

Amusement swelled inside her, shiny and ephemeral as a soap bubble. No one freed her laughter the way Patrick did. For that alone, she would have loved him.

Loved him.

The realization burst the expanding giddiness in her chest and stole her breath. She couldn't love Patrick. She couldn't love anyone. Love led to disaster. Even if she discounted the lessons of her mother's example and her sister's misfortune, hadn't Wade's desertion taught her that?

Besides, Patrick didn't want her love. And yet, he held her so tenderly. He was so confident, so honorable and strong. He'd just shared the darkest corners of his heart with her, and there was nothing in him she could not admire. How could she not love him?

Kate rested her head on his broad chest, absorbing through their clothing the fit and feel of all those hard planes and angles against her softer curves. Not that she would ever tell him, of course. She would protect them both that much, at least. But what she could not tell him, she would show him.

She pressed her lips to the center of his chest, right over his heart, as her arms tightened around him.

"Kate?" His voice was rough.

She kissed his firm pectorals, which lifted with his breath. She nuzzled aside his shirt collar to kiss the ridge of his collarbone and the strong column of his throat.

He swallowed. "Kate, even a jackass could see where this is heading. Honey, are you sure?"

And this once, she was. For the first time, she allowed herself to feel the same ease and certainty in a man's arms that she experienced in the operating room.

"Sure." She nipped lightly at his earlobe.

He jumped. "Damn, Kate." It sounded like a prayer. Confidence flowed through her, as arousing as the scent of his skin, the hard planes of his body.

"Hold still," she said to him, as he had once ordered her, and they both smiled at the memory.

"I don't think I can," Patrick confessed.

His blood was hammering in his ears. Pounding in his veins. Pulsing low in his body.

She tipped back her head to look at him, amusement and a hint of challenge in her intelligent brown eyes. "Make an effort," she advised, and kissed him full on the mouth.

The flavor of her desire mixed poignantly with the salt of her tears. The taste of her, dark and desirable, went to Patrick's head like a jigger of Irish whiskey. He wanted to comfort her. He wanted to bring her satisfaction and find his own peace in her pleasure. But when he tried to take control, deepening the kiss, she drew away.

He raised an eyebrow in question.

"Come on." She tugged on his hand. "Come to my room."

Willingly, he followed her down a short, dingy hallway that needed painting to her bedroom door. Hell, she had him so hot, he would have followed her anywhere.

She stopped on the threshold. "I didn't make the bed this morning."

"Good. It'll save us unmaking it."

She smiled and opened the door. In spite of that second of doubt, she kept her bedroom as tidy and well-organized as her office. And about as impersonal, Patrick thought, sticking his hands in his back pockets. Nothing tacky or expensive adorned the shelves or walls. No money was wasted on frivolous decoration. The neat severity was interrupted only by a few photos in Plexiglass frames—he recognized her niece and nephew—and a silk-covered box on the dresser and a drawing of Jack's, taped to the mirror.

He grinned, pleased to find evidence of his son in Kate's sanctuary, and strolled closer. He recognized the white farmhouse and the shaggy blond dog. Two nearly identical black-haired, blue-eyed figures were labeled: Daddy. Me. The female standing next to them with the masses of light brown hair must be Kate.

She looked good in the picture, he thought, studying it. She looked right. She didn't need a label to belong.

She stood behind him, and her hands came around his waist to flow over him, disrupting his thoughts, disturbing the rhythm of his heart. He reached up and prisoned her distracting hands against his chest. He lifted them, one at a time, and pressed a kiss into the crease of each palm. She shivered against his back. Turning within the tender circle of her arms, he wrapped himself around her and sought her mouth with his.

Lush and moist, subtle and searching, the kiss inundated his senses. Her compact female body nestled close to his. The fragrance of her hair, the strength of her small, quick, clever hands, swamped him. She was everything he dreamed of. More than he deserved. And she was pouring herself out to him in her kiss. He scrabbled for his customary control and felt it slipping from his grasp, washed away by her sweetly generous response.

Cupping her breast, he teased the hard little point between his thumb and forefinger. She made a deep, assenting noise in her throat before she captured his wrist and pulled his hand away.

Patrick knew his confusion showed on his face. "Honey, what—?"

She wriggled her T-shirt over her head. The sight of her contained curves peaking against her bra dried his mouth. And then she undid the back clasp and slid the garment off her arms, and her generous breasts spilled free. He reached for her, impatient to touch her, to suckle her, to bring her pleasure.

She held him off with her hands against his chest. "Let me get your shirt off, too."

Bemused, he let his arms drop to his sides. What kind of game was she playing? Yet her sweet, serious face as she tugged the hem of his shirt free of his waistband convinced Patrick that for Kate, at least, this was no game.

When she glided her palms up his back, taking the shirt with them, her full breasts flattened against his abdomen, slid up his chest. All his blood rushed below his belt, leaving him light-headed. If he closed his eyes, he was afraid he would see spots dancing in the darkness behind his lids.

"Kate."

"Later." She tugged. He raised his arms, and she wrestled the shirt from his shoulders. "I'm busy right now."

His breath whooshed out as those busy hands occupied themselves with his buckle, button and zipper. Otherwise he might have laughed. "Honey. *Kate.*"

She paused a moment, uncertainty disturbing the sexy absorption of her face. "Am I doing this wrong?"

Patrick poised on a knife's edge. The image in the dresser mirror, her smooth, strong back bent as she attended to his zipper, her soft, curling hair spilling over her naked shoulders, made him desperate to take her.

He was used to being in charge of himself, of his response. And of hers. Now Kate, by her actions, was asking him to release his iron command. To give up control.

His jaw set. He could stop her delicious, disturbing seduction. He could laugh away her question, he could kiss away her doubt. He could pull her down on her unmade bed and love her until she was breathless and mindless and satisfied. But if he did, he realized, the question and the doubt would return.

She wasn't going to make him—she wasn't going to let him—work for their mutual release. She needed to give it to him.

"Wrong?" he repeated. "Hell, no."

Chapter 14

Patrick sucked in his breath. Held it, as Kate pushed his jeans down his thighs. He'd made love, many times. He couldn't remember ever being made love to before. A combination of expectancy and frustration dried his mouth.

She unlaced his shoes. Responding to her tap, he pulled one foot free, feeling off balance emotionally as well as physically. Her soft hair brushed his thigh. Unexpectedly, she turned her head and kissed the inside of his leg.

He hissed through his teeth. "Maybe we should move this to the bed."

Kneeling before him, she tilted her head to one side, as if considering his suggestion. "We could do that."

He relaxed cautiously. At least she was willing to listen. And then the muscles in his stomach jumped as she pressed warm lips against it.

"In a minute," she added.

She kissed him again, soft, inexpert, searing kisses, down the line of hair that bisected his abdomen to the place where it grew thick and coarse. Tension filled him to bursting. His hands clenched in her hair.

Kate looked up smiling, satisfied and shy at the prominent evidence of her effect on him. "Now," she said.

She rose and took his hand, linking her slim, smooth fingers with his. The connection seeped through him from their joined hands, along the network of his nerves and sinew, and settled deep into his bones. He was aware of her in every cell and fiber of his body.

She pushed him to sit on her narrow, rumpled bed, her touch lingering on his shoulders. He spanned her waist, pulling her close, as his mouth sought her breasts. Sweet. So sweet. And his.

She stopped him, stooping to brush a kiss across his lips. "Wait. Just a minute."

Another minute like the last one, and he'd never make it through whatever exquisite torture she had planned. But, hell, if she wanted to have her way with him... He dropped his hands.

Stepping back, she wiggled out of her jeans. She looked at him through her lashes and then, with a nearly audible gulp, pushed her sensible panties down as well. The combination of her shy uncertainty, her siren's body and her obvious resolution kept him riveted to the edge of the mattress.

She rattled open the drawer of the plain, pine nightstand and withdrew an unopened box of condoms. Recently purchased, he guessed. This was one more area where he was used to taking responsibility, one more duty she was determined to free him of. She unsealed the box, her face cool and serious, but he noticed with tenderness that her hands trembled. Her control was damn near as fragile as his.

When she had what she wanted, she approached the bed and, in a sudden movement, straddled his lap. His arousal leapt against her. His breath stopped. She leaned forward, her soft belly brushing against him, and his hands fisted on the bedcovers. Suddenly, she pulled away.

He groaned in protest. ''Honey, what—''

She waved the foil packet.

So he watched, torn between warmth and amusement and screaming frustration, as she tried awkwardly to sheathe his ready body. Her fumbling caresses shot sensation through his limbs and loins straight up to his brain.

She looked up at last, brown eyes rueful. ''I'm better with latex gloves.''

He loved her for her embarrassment, for her willingness to try. For him. For them.

He held out his hand. ''You want me to give it a try?''

''Please.''

She hovered, warm and near, while he protected her. Just as he was congratulating himself on getting the job done, her small, firm, competent hands stroked a line to his jaw and she held his head still for her kiss. Her lower body, hot and moist, nestled against his. His heart almost stopped. She raised her head. Their eyes met. He could see her, all of her, Kathryn Susan Sinclair, shining in her eyes, her bright intelligence and her deep compassion, her exacting standards and her naked need.

Answering need flared in him. Hunger roared in his ears. It licked like flame along his veins until he thought he might spontaneously combust.

She lifted slightly, still holding his gaze locked with hers. He felt her, wet and ready. Without his willing it, his arousal strained up, seeking entrance to her slick, tight body. Slowly, so slowly he almost exploded with want, she lowered to take him.

He was inside her, joined to her, eyes, loins and heart. And she was inside him, all the way in, under his skin, burrowing past his defenses to carve a place in his soul.

His arms lifted and came around her. His hands gripped her smooth, lush buttocks. Each stroke was a claim, each thrust a promise. He touched her, deep and deeper. He took her, again and again. And she claimed him, seized him, held him. Her muscles worked. She rose and fell, drawing out his response, milking his body. He could no more have withstood her than he could have flown his prop plane to the moon.

In a joining almost too intense for the body to bear, in a communion too deep for words, they moved together on her sagging mattress. And when at last he groaned and released deep within her, he felt her shatter around him and heard her whisper his name.

Kate's breasts still tingled. Her blood thrummed, and her body throbbed low deep inside. She felt, well, wonderful. Sexy, powerful. Loved. Was it too much to hope that he felt the same?

Patrick held up the bottle of wine, his blue eyes wicked with invitation. "So, are you going to let me pour you more wine?"

They were picnicking on bread and cheese, sitting on her bed. She was sitting, Kate corrected herself. Patrick sprawled, incongruously big and sexy in her neat, narrow room, broad and dark against the white sheets. He was quite naked. The curls covering his wide chest were damp with sweat.

Her gaze was irresistibly drawn down his ridged rib cage and muscled abdomen to his powerful thighs and the dark hair clustered thickly around his quiet sex. Her insides pinched with wanting him. Her heart turned over in her breast. He looked magnificent, animal, male. He'd fed her sumptuous bits of creamy cheese with his fingers. He'd dripped a trail of wine over her arching body and licked it from her skin. She was dizzy on more than alcohol, flushed with loving him.

She glanced self-consciously in the dresser mirror, where his flowers reflected their brightness back into the room. Her hair was a tangle, her face and chest were pink from Patrick's attentions. It was hard to worry about her appearance when his eyes darkened and heated with masculine appreciation. His bare foot rubbed hers.

"Honey, you'd better answer my question. I'm liable to get...distracted with you looking at me like that."

Wine. He'd asked her if she wanted more to drink. She put her hand over the mouth of her glass. "I can't. I'm on call," she explained regretfully. "You go ahead, though."

He shook his head, his quick smile gleaming. "Can't. I've got to drive back tonight. Shelby and Ray are only keeping Jack till nine."

And as simply as that, the world intruded on their retreat, and the reasons she'd feared getting involved with him in the first place jumped up and hollered for attention. They were two busy people, with other commitments and no time for an affair. Perfect for each other, he'd argued. *Neither one of us wants a complicated relationship in our lives.*

Only she'd screwed that up by going and falling in love with him.

She wouldn't regret it, Kate decided, folding her legs under her. She couldn't regret the way he made her feel, the precious closeness, the unprecedented intimacy. This time when they'd made love she'd felt him penetrate her very soul. She clung to the hope shaped in that moment of communion.

What they had was good. Better than anything she'd ever known. Better than most people found in a lifetime. She wouldn't press for more. She would give Patrick her love, and maybe in time he would see... What? That he couldn't live without her?

Get real, Katie Sue. She'd allowed Wade Preston to deceive her once. She wouldn't delude herself now.

"I guess you should hop in the shower, then."

"I guess I should." He smiled at her with slow heat in his eyes, and once again her heart did its absurd little flip-flop. "Join me?"

Don't press, Kate reminded herself. "I better not. You don't want to be late."

"Roger that." He swung his legs over the edge of the bed

and then leaned back to press a quick, hard kiss on her mouth. "You okay?"

She loved him for his expression of concern. "Very okay."

"Well, then." His blue eyes searched hers a moment longer. "Fine. What time do you get off tomorrow?"

Her heart started a slow thud in her chest. "Four."

"Dinner? My house, around six? Bring a bag for overnight."

He was inviting her into his house, into his life with his son. She fought to keep her joy contained, her voice matter-of-fact. "What about Jack?"

Patrick's vital grin flashed. "It was his idea. He likes having you around. Besides, I don't like you driving back and forth at night."

Even as she responded to his potent smile and the nearness of his warm, naked chest, his proprietary tone made her bristle. "I can take care of myself," she said.

"I know that," he said, surprising her. "But I figure you'll let me do it every once in a while because it makes me feel so manly."

She had to laugh. "Manly?"

"Yeah." He dipped his head to nuzzle her throat, and she nearly lost her balance on the bed. Her hands came up to catch his shoulders. "Manly. Macho. Virile."

"Virile is good," she managed breathlessly as he pressed her back against the sheets.

Heavy and hot, he covered her. "Glad you think so."

This time, he took charge. It was quick and rough and deeply satisfying. Kate surrendered to sensation, muscles lax and then tightening, tightening in a downward spiral that made him gasp into her hair. Afterwards they held each other, warm and close. She felt the thump of his heart under her palm, and felt her own constrict in her breast.

So he was late after all.

"Drive safely," she advised him at her door, when at last he was leaving, hastily showered and dressed.

His teeth showed in a brief smile. "I always do."

Kate could believe it. He wouldn't let another accident deprive Jack of his sole remaining parent. She wondered if providing his son with a second guardian was an argument for Patrick to consider marriage again, and then scolded herself for her pathetic attempt to rationalize a larger role in Patrick's life. They had that whole, wonderful, supportive clan of MacNeill men. Jack didn't need a proxy mother. Patrick wasn't looking for a replacement wife. They didn't need her.

She kissed Patrick goodbye and caught Blackwell before the cat dashed out the door after him. Alone in her apartment with its sterile white walls and her mountains of paperwork and her feline female companion, she reminded herself that this was it. This was her reality. Her chosen, hard-earned reality.

But in the aftermath of shared revelations, with her body still aching sweetly from Patrick's full possession, she couldn't help wishing for more. She'd always prided herself on her ability to reason, to deal in facts. But wasn't it reasonable to assume that things had changed after last night's closeness? Wasn't the intimate bond she'd felt a fact?

And so, even though Patrick's invitation was only for an overnight, she dreamed of a future in the farmhouse on the hill.

The visions clung, fragile and adhesive as spiderweb, when she went to the hospital the next morning. Surgeries weren't normally scheduled for a Thursday morning. But the child she'd admitted last night required her care. The dead skin remaining on his body had to be scraped away and the wounds covered with homografts before bacterial infection set in.

Standing at the stainless steel sink, Kate tore open the opaque foil packet to get at the sponge. It foamed in her hands, releasing the sharp, antiseptic smell of betadine. She concentrated on scrubbing between her fingers and under her nails, using the familiar routine to prepare her mentally for the task ahead. It was all very well for Patrick to urge her to treat her patients with her heart. This little boy needed her hands, besides, and every ounce of concentration she possessed.

The presence of Gerald Swaim, washing up at the sink beside her, tweaked at her attention. Had Owen Roberts said anything to him about her continued involvement with the MacNeills, father and son?

But when the director spoke, he too was focused on the case waiting for them in the OR. "I hear from Owen you did a good job yesterday."

Acknowledgement from Swaim was rare. Genuine pleasure filtered through her absorption and unease. "Thank you." Since a return courtesy was undoubtedly expected, she added, "I appreciate your standing in with me this morning."

The senior surgeon checked, as if he suspected her of some deeper meaning, and then inclined his silver head. "Always a pleasure to advise you on your technique. You have a nice, light touch."

Two compliments in one morning? Now Kate was suspicious.

Swaim turned his hands to run water under his nails. "I'll want you to assist on the MacNeill case next week," he added.

Her heart stopped. The water hissed into the sink. *The MacNeill case?* Jack? He didn't need that surgery. He shouldn't have that surgery. And yet against her advice and in spite of Billy's quick acceptance of Jack's scars, Patrick must have scheduled it. He'd ignored her opinion. She was so far outside the link he shared with his son that he hadn't even bothered to tell her his decision.

Hurt flared in the pit of her stomach. She swallowed it. Swaim was waiting for her answer. And Jack's well-being depended on her response.

Carefully, she rinsed the foam from her hands.

"Are you sure," she asked cautiously, "that the operation is in the patient's best interest?"

"Boy can't live with the scar."

"He can. He does. He's not severely disfigured."

"He's not your patient, Dr. Sinclair."

Kate winced at the posted limits. Damn. She didn't want to alienate the director. Not only was it politically unwise, she was reducing her chance to make him listen to her. And since Patrick would not, she needed to convince Swaim to delay this surgery. She reached for a sterile towel.

"I understand that. But don't you think it would be better to wait until Jack is older? Won't the results be compromised by his picking at the sutures afterward?"

"His compliance with his postoperative care is not our responsibility. It's our job to make him better."

She wanted to agree with him. Her whole career rested on her determination to succeed, to make things better for all her patients. Yet Patrick's words rang in her head. *Your patients deserve a doctor who will treat them with her heart as well as her hands and her brain.* "It's our job to treat the whole child."

The director of the burn unit glared at her. "It's not up to you to make that decision."

Heavy on the air hung the implicit threat: *It's not your job at all.*

Kate swallowed, sick at the risk she was taking. But there was one decision she could make. Had to make, in Jack's best interest and for the sake of her own integrity as a physician. "I won't do it. Please don't ask me to do it."

Underneath his sterile cap, Gerald Swaim's face stiffened. "I have to assume you are withdrawing from the procedure because of your personal involvement with the patient."

Bleakly, Kate reflected that if she were truly involved personally in Jack MacNeill's life, they wouldn't be having this discussion. "Are you asking me if I'm seeing Jack MacNeill's father?"

"I don't have to ask. I've been at this hospital a long time, far longer than you. I'm well acquainted with the hospital grapevine."

Her hands were shaking. She hid them in the towel. "I see."

Swaim's aristocratic face softened slightly. "To be frank with you, Kate, I understand your having difficulty performing the procedure if you've developed a friendship with the boy."

She looked up, in disbelief and hope. Was he actually prepared to accept her involvement and her judgment?

He went on. "Certainly, I prefer that explanation to the possibility that you're flouting my authority."

The hope died. He might be offering her an unexpected out, but for Jack's sake, she couldn't take it.

She twisted the towel in her hands. "My personal relationship isn't the problem. I don't think the operation is appropriate at this time."

Swaim's eyebrows climbed to the edge of his cap. "You're refusing to do it?"

Crazy, stupid, foolish risk. It flew in the face of years of purposeful effort and circumspect decisions. Officially, her fellowship ended in three short weeks. As a pediatric surgeon, Kate could write her own ticket anywhere. But to stay at Jefferson, doing the work she loved at the hospital where she'd trained, she needed Gerald Swaim's goodwill. She needed to be offered a slot as an attending physician.

Kate thought she'd proved her usefulness in the last few months, as the director left more and more of the procedures to her. But she was relatively young and still highly expendable. She didn't kid herself that she had any influence with the Board or the chief of surgery. If Gerald Swaim decided she was no longer useful to him, she was out.

"Well?" Swaim prompted impatiently.

Her mind skittered like a squirrel on the road faced with an inevitable collision. How could she refuse and risk her chance of staying at this hospital, near her family? And yet how could she agree, when doing so violated both her medical judgment and little Jack's trust?

Dammit, why hadn't Patrick consulted her before he agreed to this procedure? Why hadn't he listened to her?

Kate drew a short, sharp breath. "I... Yes."

Swaim stared her down. "You mean, you'll do it."

"No," Kate said miserably. "I mean, I refuse."

Swaim threw his towel into the sink. "You know you're not irreplaceable."

She lifted her chin, accepting both the judgment and the implied threat. "I know."

"I can still do the operation myself. Roberts can assist."

Kate didn't point out that Swaim had excused himself from such procedures for weeks. What good would it do? If Patrick were determined to seek this operation for his son, he would find some surgeon enchanted with his own abilities willing to do it. Whatever the risks to her job, whatever the hurt to her heart, she had to see Patrick and convince him not to go through with this.

"That's your choice, of course."

Swaim shrugged. "Very well. Let's not deprive *another* little boy of your expertise, Dr. Sinclair. Your patient is waiting. If you're ready...?"

Kate flushed. Swaim was being unfair. But because, in her own way, she was as good at repressing her feelings as Jack's father, she buried her hurt and anger and burning sense of injustice. She thrust her hands into her gloves.

"Quite ready," she said stiffly, and went in to operate.

The white farmhouse glimmered through her windshield like water at the end of a long, dry day, but Kate felt no freshening of spirit at the sight, no promise of relief. She bumped down the gravelled road, her throat tight and her gut churning. Half-sick with tension, she pulled in front of the house and cut the car's engine.

The door swung open. Patrick strode onto the porch, his shoulders broad beneath his white knit shirt and his voice warm with welcome. "Kate!"

She wanted to be angry with him. But faced with the reality of those wide shoulders and that potent grin, she had to fight the urge to lay her head against his hard chest and sob out her worries and complaints. He wasn't to blame for disregarding her judgment in the face of Swaim's advice, even if his dismissal struck at the heart of who she was. It wasn't Patrick's fault that she'd duped herself into believing that she meant something more to him than a second medical opinion. She was the one who'd misread their situation, weaving foolish dreams around a few shared confidences and some incredible sex.

Patrick hadn't deceived her. She'd deluded herself. It was a bitter pill to swallow.

She got out of the car. "Hello, Patrick."

He checked halfway, his shoulders tensing, before he continued slowly down the steps. "Problem?"

She remained by the car, resisting the pull of his closeness, resenting the advantage his height gave him. "You could say that." She glanced toward the house. "Where's Jack?"

"Watching TV. What is it?"

She fiddled with her purse strap. "Could we talk?"

"Sure." He raised his voice, his gaze never leaving her face. "Jack! I'm walking Dr. Kate down to the fence. Stay put, buddy."

A muffled shout from inside the house signalled Jack's compliance.

"Okay. Let's go." Patrick descended the last step, reaching for her hand.

Her insides aching, Kate pretended not to see. If he touched her, she would never get through what she had to say. His hand dropped.

"This way," he said shortly.

She fell in beside him, her sensible shoes silent on the soft, moist ground, her footing uneven. Somewhere overhead, a bird chuckled and was still. Before them, the field stretched gray and green in the late afternoon sun to the shadowed line of woods. The breeze, rich with dirt and growing things, stirred the branches of the trees and Patrick's hair, and cooled Kate's hot cheeks. But the sweetness of the scene did nothing to restore her peace.

Patrick propped his elbows and one foot on the split rail fence and waited.

"Well?" he asked at last.

Kate drew a deep breath, her hands tightening on her purse. "Swaim asked me today if I would operate on Jack's face."

He looked surprised. "I asked you that myself. Before the visit to your sister's."

"And I suggested it would be better to wait."

"Yes. But Swaim told me to go ahead and schedule the surgery."

"And you didn't think you should discuss it with me first."

He took his foot off the rail, straightening defensively. "I didn't see the need."

No, of course not. Wounded pride flayed her soul. The bitter memory of Wade's expedient desertion haunted her. Nothing Patrick could have said could have demonstrated more clearly how inconsequential she was in his life.

"Because I'm not Jack's doctor?"

"Well, yes. Swaim—"

"Or because I'm not his mother?"

Patrick was silent.

Her hand curled around the purse strap until her nails dug into her palm. "Then, what am I?" she forced herself to ask. "Somebody you sleep with, your girlfriend, what?"

He jerked his head impatiently. "I don't do labels, Kate. You don't need one."

But she did. Oh, she did. If not a label, then at least some assurance that he regarded her as more than a convenience.

Her heart tore. She staunched the internal bleeding and went on. She had to, for Jack's sake.

"Look, I know this challenges your father-knows-best routine. But speaking as a doctor, the risks of this surgery outweigh the benefits. Multistage reconstruction on the external ear alone is going to take three to four operations. Every time you put Jack under general anesthesia, you have to consider the outside possibility that he will die as a severe complication of the surgery. He should have some say in that decision.''

He turned away, rejecting even the idea. Rejecting her. ''He's not going to die.''

''Probably not,'' Kate agreed, fighting to keep her voice even. ''But do you really want to take that risk?''

He swung back to face her, blue eyes blazing. ''If the alternative is Jack living with the scar for the rest of his life—''

She stood her ground. ''Not for the rest of his life. For four or five more years, until Jack can decide what he wants done. Because he won't understand now that he won't wake up from this surgery as good as new. A surgeon, even a good surgeon, even me, might not make a difference a child can see and appreciate.'' She put her hand on his arm, pleading now. ''Wait until he's older. Wait until he can decide.''

His face was stony. ''He shouldn't have to face that kind of responsibility.''

Frustrated, she snapped, ''You mean, you don't want to give up that level of control.''

He shook off her hand. ''You don't know what you're talking about. He's my son. I have to make him better.''

She honored him for his caring. She agonized for him in his misplaced determination. But she couldn't stand by and watch him batter himself against the wall of things he could not change. ''You can help Jack get better,'' she agreed carefully. ''But you can never make it as if the accident never happened.''

He glared at her. ''Of course it happened. But Jack needs to get on with his life.''

He wouldn't tolerate her interference in his decisions regarding his son, Kate thought in despair. And he wouldn't see how those decisions were shaped by his needs as much as by Jack's.

"He is getting on with his life, his life with his face the way it is. You're the one who can't accept his scars. Maybe *you* need to get on with *your* life."

Patrick froze. "You're being ridiculous."

Her heart was beating so high in her throat it threatened to choke her. "Am I?" she asked quietly. "Then why can't you accept that things will never be the same? Why do you have so much trouble putting the accident behind you?"

"I have put the damn accident behind me. I've made a new life. I have this house and my job and my son. I have you."

His possessive claim now, even as he repudiated her advice, threw her into confusion. She took a deep breath, making an effort to respond calmly.

"To a point. But do you really want me, Patrick? Or do you just want a warm body who won't make too many demands on you, who won't interfere with your son?"

"Goddamn it," he roared. A crow, startled, launched from the old oak tree and flew away cawing. Patrick moderated his tone, but his fists still clenched at his sides. "What about last night?"

She pressed her lips together to keep her distress inside. Last night she'd been swept away in a mutual surrender of self, only to find after all that they were two totally separate people completely at odds. What good would it do to babble that she loved him, to demand that he love her, while he still regarded her as a satellite, far outside the orbit he shared with Jack?

Don't let it get to you, Katie Sue. Don't let *him* get to you. Think about Jack and what he needs.

"What about it?" she returned steadily. "So we proved I'm okay in bed. You can give up some control there."

His blue eyes blazed. "It was more than that, and you know it. I told you things I've never told anybody."

He had, and she did know it. It only made his exclusion of her now more painful.

"But not about Jack," she replied quietly. "I'm still on the outside looking in on you and Jack."

Patrick turned his head to stare out over the fields and far away. Black against the luminous pink-and-gray sky, his profile looked strong and proud and profoundly alone.

"I don't know what you want me to say. If you're ticked at me because I didn't take your medical advice, I'm sorry. You're a good doctor, Kate. I know that."

His unexpected offering moved and angered her at the same time. "Then why not listen to me?"

"I'm used to making decisions about Jack myself, that's all. I'd decided on the surgery months before we even knew you."

Kate wanted to point out that he'd been married before, that Jack had had a mother before. This Lone Ranger routine didn't cut it. But she didn't know enough about Patrick's relationship with his dead wife to challenge him.

Besides, she wasn't his wife. She wasn't Jack's mother. She was merely a handy adjunct to Patrick's life. Her problem, she accepted starkly. She couldn't let her foolish self-delusion interfere with getting the best possible treatment for Jack.

"You have to let go," she argued. "Of control. Of the past. You can't deny what happened to you and Jack. You can't erase it, from his face or from your hearts. You can only accept it and go on."

Patrick was still silent, staring out over the darkening ground. She wasn't reaching him, she thought in despair. In any way.

"Patrick?" she insisted softly. "Can you do that?"

His shoulders braced before he turned at last to face her. "I don't know. Kate, I honestly don't know."

Defeated, she dropped her head. She felt the betraying prick of tears and widened her eyes. Consciously, she reached for her medical persona, wrapping it around her like a lab coat to shield her lacerated feelings.

"Swaim is asking Owen Roberts to assist," she managed. "You should call him. Get a second opinion."

He straightened, tension and regret radiating from his coiled muscles. "I can do that."

She turned blindly. "I should go."

"Kate..." Once more he put out his hand. This time she genuinely didn't see until it was too late. "Jack's expecting you."

The words hurt. How could she disregard a child who wanted her? How could she run out on Jack? Yet she was falling apart. She had to get out of here. "Tell him something came up at the hospital."

He jammed his hands in his pockets. "Is that what you want me to do?"

What she wanted didn't matter any longer. He needed to decide what he wanted. Until he chose to put the past behind him and admit her all the way into his life, she would batter herself against the walls he'd thrown up to protect himself. His distant politeness was breaking her heart.

"Yes, please," she answered, equally polite.

He nodded, a brief, curt acknowledgement. "All right. I'll walk you to your car."

This time, Kate thought ironically, she was the one to drive away, when she would have given her soul for Patrick to ask her to stay.

If she didn't look back, it was only because her eyes were filled with tears.

Chapter 15

His second lesson of the morning was a disaster, a forty-something flight groupie more interested in landing a pilot than an aircraft. Patrick managed to get down to earth with his plane and his temper intact, and then took to the skies again alone.

He had no destination. Fuel was expensive and time limited. He was meeting Swaim at the hospital at two o'clock. So after radioing the distant Raleigh-Durham flight tower, Patrick settled down in a tight holding pattern over his own airstrip's signal cone, twenty-five hundred feet up, three knots above stalling. At the airplane controls, he had power and perfect freedom. He held them in check with his fingertips, making tiny, precise adjustments, never varying his altitude by more than twenty feet or his actual bank by more than a few degrees.

The disciplined focus kept at bay the storm of emotions inside him. Anger. Confusion. Doubt.

Who was he to decide what was right for Jack? When he and Holly married, he hadn't signed up for single fatherhood. It wasn't the kind of duty any man would volunteer for. But when his life erupted in a blaze of flame four years ago, he'd responded like any good Marine, taking charge, getting the job done. Who was Kate to tell him now he'd bungled? Prickly, opinionated, know-it-all doctor.

God, he missed her. Not eighteen hours since he'd seen her, less than thirty-six hours since he'd filled her on her bed—since she'd filled him, heart and soul and senses—and already he felt the lack of her like the phantom pain of an amputated leg.

Deliberately, he widened his perceptions to take in the round, flat dials and the bright, rolling Carolina landscape: dark pines, red clay, empty blue sky. Over his headset, he heard the anonymous voices of air traffic control, soothing and unobtrusive as music in a hospital waiting room.

One minute straight and one minute around. He timed his turn, scanning the instruments, scanning the sky. One minute straight. One minute around. He cross-checked his position on the second radio. Four minutes exactly.

Patrick nodded, calmed by the clear evidence that he was in control. In solitary, perfect control. And over the chop of the propeller as it cut the uneven air, he heard Kate's harsh accusation: *You don't want to give up that level of control.*

Damn woman. She'd even followed him into the cockpit. She'd entrenched herself so deeply, in his flesh, in his routine, in his heart, that he might never be free of her.

In the emotional wreckage after the accident, his duty had seemed so clear. Putting Jack first had been his way of keeping faith with Holly's memory. If he couldn't prevent the crash that killed his wife and maimed his son, at least he could sacrifice his own life to Jack's medical and emotional needs.

The wind veered as Patrick started another circuit of the radio signal. He made appropriate, sensitive adjustments to the throttle and steering column. For the past four years, he'd kept Jack at the center of his life in a holding pattern as rigidly controlled as the one he now executed over the landing strip.

The lady doctor was like an outlying signal, disturbing his concentration, pulling him off of his intended course.

She was a torment and a beacon. He didn't know how to respond to her. He was reluctant to lose control. He was afraid to lose direction. And yet…

He scanned the instrument dials, checking the drop of the Cessna's wingtip as he turned and banked again. One minute. The measurement was reassuringly precise. The exercise was restrictedly satisfying. Yet he wasn't going anywhere. Trust Kate, he thought dryly, to point that out. Kate, with her clear brown eyes that saw too much, and her wide, generous mouth that spoke so bluntly.

Maybe you need to get on with your life.

As if he hadn't struggled for four years to put the past behind him and make a life for Jack. Patrick frowned, bringing the plane back around. A life for Jack. There was the kicker. His anger wasn't really directed at Kate at all. He was mad at himself, because this softhearted, hardheaded, infuriating woman had made him realize finally that living solely for Jack was no longer enough. He wanted, needed, more.

He needed her.

Do you really want me? Or do you just want a warm body who won't make too many demands on you, who won't interfere with your son?

His mouth tightened. Over the fuel-rich carburetor mix, through the open air scoops and the Plexiglass flap on his left, the scent of the warm, damp earth rose from twenty-five hundred feet below. Patrick cross-checked the plane's position, correcting speed as he eased into the last leg of his circuit, suspended between the empty sky and the breathing ground.

Exhaling, he prepared to land, breaking radio silence. "At Dumont. Cessna November Two One Nine downwind, right turn, in the pattern for runway Two Seven."

While the radio cone provided a stable point for his holding pattern, its real purpose was to direct pilots en route.

Kate was right. It was time to go on. Not to leave his son

behind—he would never do that—but to find a new direction for their lives.

He suspected he'd found his heart's true destination in Kate Sinclair.

Gerald Swaim leaned back in his mahogany leather chair, his high-ranking-officer-face set in lines of disapproval. "I really don't understand your decision, Mr. MacNeill. We've discussed this procedure. You requested it."

Patrick let the man's tone pass for now. He had two objectives in this discussion, and antagonizing the director of Kate's burn center wouldn't help him achieve either one. "Well, now I'm un-requesting it."

Swaim placed his fingers together tip to tip, and then abruptly abandoned the gesture, dropping his hands to the top of his desk. "May I ask why?"

Patrick chose his words carefully. "Dr. Sinclair feels we shouldn't do anything until Jack can enter the equation. In a couple of years, if he can identify specific changes he wants to make in his face, we'll go for it."

"Of course, you're declining an elective procedure. But Dr. Sinclair is, after all, only a senior fellow. Perhaps you'd like a second opinion?"

Get a second opinion, Kate had said, her eyes shiny with tears she thought he couldn't see. Patrick's jaw tensed.

"I don't need one," he said firmly. "I trust Dr. Sinclair's."

Swaim frowned. "With all due respect to a colleague, Mr. MacNeill, I don't think you can rely on Dr. Sinclair's objectivity in this case."

Damn. Patrick straightened in his chair, watchful, wary. "Excuse me?"

"Given her personal involvement with you and with your son, can you really trust her judgment?"

Patrick struggled to contain his growing anger. This is Jack's doctor, he reminded himself. Kate's boss. He wasn't going to do anybody any good by taking the man's insinuations and shoving them up his... Yeah, anyway, it wouldn't do any good. "Yes. I can, and I do. Maybe especially given the way she feels about Jack."

Swaim assumed an expression of avuncular concern. "You know, it's perfectly natural for you to feel anxious about the potential risks of this procedure. Dr. Sinclair may simply be telling you what she thinks you want to hear."

Kate? The man must be joking. Patrick thought of the way Kate had checked up on his son after surgery, the way she'd come by his house at night when they'd struggled with his physical therapy. She'd braved Patrick's displeasure by pushing him to let Jack make friends with her nephew. She'd reorganized her work schedule to care for the kid when his grandfather had a stroke. She'd insisted on being there for Jack every step of the way.

Hell. He didn't need to wonder and worry about making Kate part of Jack's life. She'd already demonstrated both her ability to care for and her willingness to love the boy. All Jack's father had to do was overcome his grunt-stupid mule stubbornness long enough to admit it.

"No. She wouldn't do that."

"She might. If the two of you are personally involved, it might represent a conflict of interest. Something which, as director of the burn unit, would naturally cause me grave concern."

Patrick narrowed his eyes. Was this egotistical sawbones actually threatening Kate over her involvement in Jack's case?

"That's bull. She's always put her patients first. Everything she's done, every choice she's made, has been in Jack's best interest. In your patient's best interest. If you can't see that, you're blind."

Swaim appeared taken aback by this direct attack. "Not blind. But it's possible my vision has been obscured by..." He threaded his fingers together. "...personal considerations."

Patrick leaned both palms flat on the director's desk. "Like what?"

He pursed his lips. "I don't intend to discuss my private life with you, Mr. MacNeill."

"Why not? You didn't hesitate to drag mine and Kate's into this discussion."

The gray gaze slid away. "No. Well, perhaps I was wrong. Please don't misunderstand me. I have a great deal of respect for Dr. Sinclair's abilities. You might almost say I envy them."

As long as Swaim gave Kate her professional due, Patrick figured he should try to keep the conversation civil. Kate wouldn't thank him for ticking off her director. But his antagonism toward Kate just didn't make sense. She'd gone to bat for the man more than once, seeing his appointments and taking over for him in surgery. Why wasn't he grateful?

"Why 'envy?' Look, you've been Jack's doctor for four years. You're the director of the university burn center. I can see you being upset that I'm going with Dr. Sinclair's call on this thing with Jack, but she's no threat to you."

Gerald Swaim spread his pale, long-fingered hands out on his desk. He regarded them for a moment before he looked up. "I recently learned that I have Parkinson's disease, Mr. MacNeill. My hands shake," he explained in response to Patrick's puzzled look. "While the tremor can be controlled with medication, it is extremely unlikely I will ever operate again."

Hell. Illness of course excused the doctor's recent absences, explained his withdrawal from surgery. The man must be fighting for his professional life. Not to mention wrestling with his personal identity. A surgeon who couldn't operate? It would be like a pilot who couldn't hold the stick. Unwilling sympathy moved in Patrick's chest.

But pity wouldn't help Swaim. And letting him take his frustration out on Kate for damn sure wouldn't help her.

Deliberately, Patrick met Swaim's gaze. "All the more reason, then, for you to value having a good surgeon like Dr. Sinclair on your staff."

"Ah." The doctor's mouth twisted in a partial smile. "Yes.

Yes, you make a very valid point, Mr. MacNeill. Once I'm—limited—to administrative duties, I will, as you say, be very glad to have her on my staff.''

Amy held up her long-necked bottle of beer. ''We need to make a toast.''

Kate forced a smile. She appreciated her sister coming over on a Saturday night. Date night. Amy had brought the beer and the kids and her own airy charm. Billy, dangling a stethoscope for Blackwell to swat at, was a distraction, and brown-eyed Jenny a sweet comfort.

Dabbing the grease from a slice of pizza, Kate slid the paper plate in front of her nephew. ''How about, to your new job?''

Amy beamed with pleasure. ''I'll drink to that. To Newton's new Assistant Restaurant Manager.''

Solemnly, they clinked and drank. On her mother's lap, baby Jennifer arched her back and flailed her rounded arms.

Amy swung her bottle out of her daughter's reach with one hand, cuddling her expertly with the other. ''None for you, lambie pie.''

Jennifer dimpled, revealing four pearl teeth. Watching them, Kate felt a shaft of pure envy. What would it be like to bear a child of your own body? To know you were loved, unconditionally and completely? To share that magic parent/child communication and accept the responsibility of that child's care?

The memory of her own words pierced her. *I'm still on the outside looking in on you and Jack.*

And Patrick's voice, blunt and regretful: *I'm used to making decisions about Jack myself... I don't know, Kate. I honestly don't know.*

Her heart ached.

''Don't look like that, sweetie.'' Startled, Kate glanced up from the wriggling baby to meet her sister's eyes, surprisingly understanding, unexpectedly kind. ''Come on, now. We're celebrating. Let's drink to your new job. What is it again?''

The smile came more easily this time. Even with the hurt at her heart, Kate discovered, there was satisfaction in attaining a goal so long desired and so hard-won.

"Attending physician, burn unit."

"Cool." Amy lifted her bottle again. "To Jefferson University Hospital's newest attending physician in the burn unit."

"Thanks." Fortified by her second beer, Kate confessed, "I didn't think I would get it. When Swaim called me into his office yesterday, I thought he was going to tell me once my fellowship was over, I was through."

"But you work so hard! How could you even think that?"

Kate busied herself reaching for a slice of pizza, already regretting her uncharacteristic admission. "I made a mistake recently."

Amy leaned across the table to tap her son's arm. "Billy, honey, don't cram the whole thing into your mouth like that, you'll choke. The Perfect One made a mistake? I don't believe it. What did you do? Kill somebody?"

The Perfect One? Is that how her younger sister saw her? Kate shook her head. "No. No, I got personally involved with a patient."

"Oohh." Kate winced at the long, drawn-out note of discovery in her sister's voice. "With a patient…or a patient's father?"

The last thing—very nearly the last thing in the world Kate wanted—was to expose her pitiable love life to Amy's sympathy. Kate was the sensible, rational one, her life orderly and passionless. Miserably, she pleated her napkin, her single bite of pizza smoldering in her stomach.

"It's that good-looking MacNeill man, isn't it?" Amy asked shrewdly. "That Patrick."

"It doesn't matter who it is. It's over now."

"Oh, sweetie, I'm sorry. He was so nice looking, too. And I thought he liked you, I genuinely did."

You don't like me, she'd accused, that first night she went to his house.

Not at first, not much. You're good with Jack.

Not good enough, apparently. And did she really want them on those terms? Did she want to be Jack's surrogate mother, Patrick's substitute wife?

Kate stared sightlessly at her congealing pizza, recalling the way, three nights ago, she'd taken Patrick MacNeill into her body. The way he'd let himself be taken, body and soul. But she deserved more than sex, no matter how tender or profound. She deserved a man's whole heart and an equal place in his life. Even if Patrick couldn't give her those things, she would always be grateful to him for making her believe that.

"I think he did, too." She felt her lower lip threaten to get away from her and bent it into a smile. "Just not enough."

Amy's hand, winking with pretty silver rings, squeezed her arm. "Well, then, who needs him? You've got this great singles apartment and your little black cat and your nice new job… What are you going to do with all that lovely money?"

Kate shrugged, trying to be cheered by her sister's sunny interest. "I don't know. Start paying off my loans, I guess. Buy Billy new sneakers."

Billy's mother made a face. "He needs them. He's growing faster than kudzu. But on this assistant manager's salary, I can buy them. You put something aside for Mama and then get yourself some pretty clothes. Some killer khakis or whatever it is you wear."

The wall phone rang.

"I'll think about it," Kate promised, and stood to lift the receiver. "Hello?"

"Kate, it's Patrick."

His warm-as-whiskey voice lit a fire in her stomach. She pressed two fingers under her ribs, noting with a corner of her mind that her hand trembled.

"I know. I recognized your voice."

He gave a short, embarrassed laugh. "Yeah. Okay. Look,

I'm giving a birthday party for Jack next Sunday. He's turning five. I want you to come.''

Gladness leaped inside her, in spite of her best efforts to squelch it. ''Sunday?'' she repeated carefully.

''Patrick?'' Amy mouthed, sitting up in interest. Her sister's pleased, hopeful expression struck at Kate's heart.

All their lives, her mother and her sister had settled for whatever their men had left over to give. She couldn't do that. She wouldn't live hostage to Patrick MacNeill's ghosts. He was still haunted by the memory of his late wife, hung up on being both mother and father to Jack. The limited role that was all he would allow her would mess with her mind and break her heart.

She tightened her grip on the receiver. ''I'm sorry. I don't think—''

''Jack really wants you to come,'' Patrick said. ''You could bring your nephew. It would be nice for Jack to have another kid his age there.''

The clever way he used her own suggestions against her hardened her resolution. ''My sister can bring Billy.''

The boy stopped chewing to listen. His mother shook her head. ''Sunday? Sorry. Busy.''

Kate scowled.

''Jack specifically asked for you,'' Patrick continued persuasively in her ear. ''We'd both appreciate it if you could come. You're not on duty or anything, are you?''

''No.'' She lunged across the table to rescue Billy's glass from his elbow. Now, why had she told Patrick that?

''Good.'' He sounded relieved. ''That's good. Let's say three o'clock?''

''Oh…'' Kate wavered.

She should know better. She did know better. But how could she disappoint Jack? How could she deny her own hungry heart? She wanted to see them again. Jack *and* Patrick.

''Go, go,'' Amy hissed.

Kate bit her lip. How could she listen to her sister? How

could she risk repeating Amy's mistakes? Turning her back on Amy, Kate hugged the phone cord to her chest. "I guess I can bring Billy. I…might not be able to stay, though."

"Whatever you can manage will be fine. We'll see you then." His voice softened, deepened. "Kate, I—"

She couldn't bear to hear whatever he had to say, not with her willpower so low, not with her sister sitting there absorbing every nuance of expression.

"I've got company. I have to go." She hung up.

"So, it's over, is it?" Amy sounded amused. "Have you told *him* that?"

Kate stiffened. But when she turned, Amy's face was all sympathy.

"I didn't think I needed to," Kate said slowly. "He… It was pretty much his idea."

Amy shifted Jenny to her other thigh. "Did he say so?"

"No. But he doesn't want… He's used to doing everything for himself, for his son. He won't let me in, not all the way into their lives. And it hurts too much being on the periphery. Do you understand?"

"Oh, I hear you, big sister, but you better listen to yourself." She leaned forward earnestly, speaking over her daughter's head. "Because it sounds to me like you're in love with the guy. Maybe you should give it another chance."

Unexpected hope fluttered in Kate's chest. Was it possible Amy, with her vast romantic experience, saw something, knew something, Kate did not? "Do you think so?"

"Oh, I always think so." Amy lifted blond eyebrows, her smile self-mocking. "That's why I'm unmarried with two kids."

Kate sighed. If even her optimistic sister was doubtful, Kate's own dreams could only be wishful thinking.

Chapter 16

Kate watched as Janet Heller, with a betraying tremor, set the hand mirror facedown on her lap and closed her eyes.

Kate's heart squeezed in sympathy. She and Gerald Swaim had come to the woman's hospital room to evaluate the results of her most recent surgery. No matter how well they prepared their patients, every procedure raised unrealistic hopes. Along with disappointment, the burn survivor had to endure the fresh shock of each new repair.

After a moment, Janet looked up, her gaze seeking Kate's. "I'm never going to look the same, am I?"

Kate answered her, as always, patiently and honestly. "No."

Swaim stepped closer to the bed. "Dr. Sinclair actually did an excellent job. You'll see she placed the grafts to reduce the visible join. Most of that long seam falls under your jawline."

Both women ignored him. Janet Heller picked up the mirror and studied her appearance again. "It's better," she offered at last, tentatively.

Admiration for the woman's bravery swamped Kate's own

quiet satisfaction in her work. "Yes. And there will be other operations. The makeup nurse will work with you on ways to minimize the scars. It won't be your old face, but it will be a good face."

Tears rose in her patient's still beautiful dark eyes. "Yes. All right. Thank you."

Outside in the hallway, Swaim touched Kate's arm, a rare gesture in a man so reserved. "You did very well with her."

Kate smiled to acknowledge the unexpected compliment. Her cheeks nearly cracked with the strain. She hadn't smiled one whole heck of a lot this past week. Or eaten, or slept. Possibly she'd picked up a mild virus. She refused to consider that loss of appetite and sleeplessness were the classic symptoms of a broken heart.

"I thought the operation went well," she said cautiously.

"Yes, but I was referring to your manner in there. MacNeill was right. You do put your patients first, and you have a sympathetic way of engaging them which is very effective."

It took a moment for the reference to penetrate her tired brain. "Excuse me? You discussed me with Patrick MacNeill?"

"Yes. When he was in here to confer about the operation for his son." Gerald Swaim regarded her with what, in another man, might have been described as a twinkle. "He was quite appreciative of your abilities."

"Patrick MacNeill commented on *my* abilities?"

Swaim frowned. "Yes. As a doctor, of course. I wouldn't presume to inquire into your other, ah, into the other."

Kate couldn't believe her ears. Patrick MacNeill, Mr. Lone Eagle himself, had had the nerve to discuss her with her director. After dismissing her medical expertise as irrelevant to his personal life, he'd stepped outside his rigid boundaries to meddle in her professional life.

She was furious. She didn't need his intervention. And after closing her out of the magic circle he shared with his son, the man had no right to interfere in her job, no right to go behind her back to her boss, no right to disrupt her life and her thoughts and rob her of peace and sleep.

And she couldn't wait until Jack's birthday party on Sunday to see him and tell him so.

Patrick had planned Jack's first birthday-party-with-friends with all the care of a covert operation. His younger brothers had flown down to lend their support, to captain basketball for the kids and to drink beer with him. He'd laid in hot dogs and sodas and chocolate ice cream. Even the variables beyond his control seemed favorable today, he thought, satisfied. The sun shone. No one was sick. And Kate had said she would come.

Standing in the shadow of the porch, taping red and blue balloons to the railing, he allowed himself to hope. Once she was here, he was sure he could persuade her to stay. He just needed a chance to see her, to talk to her. And if that didn't work, he was damn near prepared to tie her up.

Jack raced around the corner of the house, Silkie barking excitedly at his heels. He thumped up the porch steps and cannoned into his father's legs.

"How long now, Dad?"

Patrick ruffled his son's short hair, smiling down at his excited face. The news that all three of his new friends would attend his birthday party had thrilled Jack. Patrick gave mental thanks, again, for Kate's perception. Once she'd opened his eyes to Jack's need for playmates, Patrick had found boys his son's age all over the place. He'd discovered the Emerson brothers, aged four and seven, living a mile up the road, and introduced himself to the boys' father as he stood pumping gas.

A play date had been arranged. The four-year-old reacted cautiously to Jack's scars, but once the injury was explained, the older boy, Alex, was more interested in Jack's trampoline. Since then Jack had been to the Emerson house twice to play with their awesome collection of action figures. It was another step, Patrick reflected, another letting go.

"How long?" Jack repeated, jiggling from foot to foot.

"Another hour. Sixty minutes. Why don't you go get the paper plates and things from the kitchen?"

"'Kay." Jack dashed off.

Patrick's brothers emerged from the backyard, the picnic table slung between them. They were dressed in jeans and T-shirts, although Con's shirt advertised a microbrewery in some chic section of Boston while Sean sported a rip at one knee and a gold hoop in his ear.

"Where do you want this?" Con called.

Sean, walking backward, grinned. "You don't really want him to answer that, do you?"

Con narrowed his eyes. "Just hold up your end, will you? Or I'll stick it someplace myself."

Patrick taped the last balloon and came easily down the steps. "Play nice. Over there," he directed them. "In the shade."

They maneuvered the table under the spreading oak.

Con frowned. "Is it long enough? How many kids did you say were coming?"

"Jack. Billy. The two Emersons. I figured four was plenty for a first party."

"Fine. I think we can take them." His brother's rare smile lit his face. "Seeing as how there's three of us."

"And we're bigger," Sean added.

It felt good to have his brothers here. Awkwardly, because these were things they never spoke out loud, Patrick said, "Listen…I appreciate you coming."

Con lifted an eyebrow. "Did we have a choice?"

Sean perched his butt on the table. "Are you kidding? Mom was so upset at missing Jack's birthday, she even made Boy Genius here take off from work."

Patrick looked at Con. His cool, logical brother had always been ambitious. Almost driven. Even when they were kids, the middle MacNeill had seldom missed a day of school. "You didn't have to do that."

Con shrugged. ''I wanted to come. It's not every day my only nephew turns five. Besides, I wanted to get away for a while.'' Deliberately, he turned the subject. ''So, you want me to load drinks in the cooler? What have we got, four kids, three adults?''

''Four and four.'' He hoped. ''Kate Sinclair is bringing her nephew.''

''Jack's doctor?'' Con inquired.

''Jack's attractive, female doctor,'' Sean answered for him.

''Interesting.''

''Off limits,'' Patrick warned them firmly. This afternoon was going to be complicated enough without having to arm wrestle his brothers for Kate's attention.

''Absolutely.'' Sean winked at Con.

Gritting his teeth, Patrick marched off to tie balloons to the mailbox.

Anticipation and dread closed Kate's throat and dampened her palms on the steering wheel. She was grateful for Billy, buckled in behind her. Her nephew was proud of Jack's present—a space blaster just like his own—and looking forward to a good time. Until Kate could get Patrick MacNeill alone and tell him exactly what she thought of his arrogant interference, Billy's enthusiasm would help cover the awkwardness she felt at attending Jack's family party as a non-family member. Patrick had denied her a label, but she had several bumping uncomfortably in the back of her mind. Temporary girl-friend. Easy lay. Fool.

She stiffened her spine against the car's sagging seat back. She would drop off her nephew and her gift, collect a hug from Jack, speak her piece and go. How difficult could it be?

She followed the dip and rise of the road into view of the white farmhouse and had her answer.

The yard was full of men. Big, handsome men. Kate blinked. Her gaze went immediately to Patrick, drawn as always to his aura of contained energy. He was laughing and lugging a red cooler down the steps. She recognized the tall, rangy pirate chasing little boys over the grass as Sean. A heart-stoppingly handsome giant with a lean, clever face propped up the porch, arms crossed against his spectacular chest. Another MacNeill, or she'd eat her medical kit.

Billy bounced in the backseat. "Oh, boy. Let me out, Aunt Katie."

She pulled in by the barn, careful to leave plenty of space under the basketball hoop. Billy popped out and raced across the lawn to join the zigzagging boys. Jack whooped a greeting. Kate got out slowly, taking time to put her emotions in order. She saw Patrick set the cooler on a picnic table and ducked back into the car to collect the abandoned gifts from the back seat.

"Kate. Thanks for coming," his deep voice said behind her.

In spite of her anger, her heart palpitated like a cardiac patient's or a girl's in the throes of her first crush. Taking a deep breath, Kate turned around, baring her teeth in a determined smile. "You're welcome. Thank you for inviting us."

His eyes narrowed slightly at her deliberate choice of pronoun. "Actually, I—"

"Kate!" Sean zoomed up, wrapped her in his muscled arms and whirled her in a circle, smashing her packages against her chest. "Angel! I need a doctor. These monsters are killing me."

The monsters, pelting up behind him, giggled in delight and tugged on his legs and the waistband of his just-right too-tight jeans. He set her down in the midst of the tangle of boys. Patrick caught the gifts as they fell. Roaring, Sean seized one child, tickled another, and charged back across the lawn with his nephew dangling under one arm and three other boys in hot pursuit.

Patrick's eyes were alight with humor as he handed her her slightly squashed presents. Jolted from her resentment, shaken from her pose of formality, Kate smiled back. And then remembered her grievance and the distance she needed to keep between them, and looked away.

"Kate, I—"

"You must be Dr. Sinclair." The big man holding up the house had left his post and strolled over. Both of his brothers, she was surprised to observe, were taller than Patrick. It was only Patrick's intensity that made him appear larger.

The giant offered his broad hand. "Con MacNeill."

She took it. "Call me Kate."

His grip was cool and firm, his blue eyes—so like Patrick's—intelligent and assessing. "I'm thinking Patrick surprised me. You're not what I expected."

"Yes, well, he certainly surprised me," she answered frankly. "I didn't expect you at all."

He smiled suddenly. If she hadn't felt so ruffled and uncomfortable, Kate thought she might have liked him very much. "Welcome to the family," he drawled.

He didn't mean anything by it. Kate was sure of that. But her certainty didn't stop the blood, hot and shaming, that rushed to her cheeks. What had Patrick told him about her? She was a respected member of the medical profession, not a convenient caregiver and bed-warmer.

Retrieving her hand, she lifted her chin and clutched her packages tighter. "Yes, well... Excuse me. I'll just go find a place to put these."

As she marched away, Patrick turned from contemplation of her pretty backside to scowl at his brother. "Thanks a lot, ace."

Con shrugged, unperturbed. "Well, isn't that why you invited her?"

Patrick ran a hand over his short hair. "I invited her because..." Because she belonged, dammit. "I wanted her to feel at home," he said to his brother.

"Mmm. Then you might have considered expanding your guest list some. You do realize she's the only female here?"

Patrick frowned, scanning the front yard. He hadn't thought... He'd never intended...

"Except for Silkie, of course," Con added smoothly.

Kate paused on the porch as Jack detached from the huddle around Sean. He dashed toward her. His blue baseball cap was knocked back on his head, his face flushed and beaming. Love for him obstructed her throat.

"Could you put my watch up in my room?" He tugged on the velcro band, almost stumbling in his haste up the steps. "I don't want to break it."

"Sure, sport." She knelt to help him. "It's a very nice watch."

His sneakers tapped an impatient tattoo to return to play. "It was a birthday present from Uncle Con," he confided.

"I'll make sure nothing happens to it," she promised gravely.

"Thanks, Kate."

Unexpectedly, she found her arms full of boy. His scarred cheek pressed to hers. His small, strong arms tightened around her neck. The scent of him, grass and sweat and child, stole into her lungs and lodged under her ribs.

He kissed her. "You're the greatest."

As she watched him run back to the action, his short figure blurred. Dammit, she was going to cry. In a house full of men, in front of Patrick and his brothers, before Jack and her nephew and assorted birthday guests, she was going to bawl her eyes out.

She sniffed. With a complete disregard for proper hygiene, she wiped her nose on her wrist and escaped into the house. The steps were cool and shadowed, the landing was quiet and empty. She heard the squeak of the mouse exercise wheel as she opened the door to Jack's room. The aquarium glowed greeny-blue on his dresser. The floor was an appealing little boy jumble. She stepped over Legos to place his watch carefully beside his bed.

Looking up, she saw it. Holly's picture. On the wall beside the bed, between a drawing of a dinosaur and a poster of Michael Jordan, was the silver-framed photo that once held pride of place on Patrick's dresser.

Kate's heart pounded in sudden, awful hope.

"There you are."

She whirled as if he'd caught her spying. "Patrick! I was just putting Jack's watch on his night table."

"That's nice of you." Did he actually have the gall to sound amused?

Flustered, she realized she still clutched Jack's gifts. She held them out. "I didn't know where to... Here. I'm afraid they got a little crushed."

He made no move to take them from her. "That's all right."

Why the hell was he standing there, blocking the way to the door? She felt like an idiot. "I got him an art set. I thought he could use it at the hospital."

"He's not going to the hospital. He's not having the operation, Kate. Not until he's older, like you said." He lifted the packages from her nerveless arms and laid them on the bed. "It's okay. He'll still like the art set."

Kate gaped at him.

He turned and took her cold and empty hands in his big, warm ones. "I decided you were right. Maybe I was stuck trying to erase the accident for Jack and me. I've decided we need more in our lives."

Her tongue was glued to the roof of her mouth. She loosened it enough to ask, "What?"

Patrick hesitated. "We had a long talk last night. About you coming today. I told Jack how I feel, and he said what he'd really like for his birthday this year is for you to be his mother."

Kate closed her eyes against the ache of dreams just beyond her reach. She was glad for Jack's sake that his operation was being delayed until the boy was older, that his father seemed prepared to get on with the business of living again. But she wasn't going to let relief over the boy's case blind her to the glaring and hurtful omissions in Patrick's declaration.

"You're good at that," she said painfully, opening her eyes. "Deciding."

"What do you mean?"

"Listen to yourself. You decided. You need. Jack wants. Somewhere along the way, you even figured you could interfere in my life."

Patrick's dark brows snapped together. "What the hell are you talking about?"

"You went behind my back to discuss my career with my director."

"I did not go behind your back. I had an appointment to discuss Jack's surgery."

"You meddled."

"Big deal. I went to bat for you. Just the way you've been going to bat for Jack ever since you met him."

Her pride was injured. "I'm not a five-year-old. I don't need someone to go to bat for me."

"The hell you don't."

His tone stung. His words hurt. Because the real hell of it was, he was right. There were times she was so put-your-head-down-and-bawl burdened and discouraged that she ached for another soul's comfort and support. But nothing in her training had taught her to ask. Nothing in her experience had convinced her to trust.

Doggedly, she insisted, "I don't need your help. I'm good at my job."

"You're great at your job. But it's draining you dry. You take care of other people all the time, Kate. You've got to accept that you need somebody to look out for you every once in a while."

She sneered. "And you're volunteering for the post."

"Damn straight I'm volunteering." He cupped her face, his palm callused against her jaw. "Marry me, Kate."

Temptation slammed her chest, staggering her resolution. She closed her eyes against the tide, willing it to recede. No woman could ask for a better refuge or stronger champion than Patrick MacNeill, a man whose passions ran as deep as his honor. But Kate could never accept his support while his heart was still captive to his son, while his honor still tied him to the memory of his late wife.

I told Jack how I feel, and he said what he'd really like for his birthday this year is for you to be his mother. Jack was at the center of Patrick's life. And Patrick would always do his best to get whatever Jack needed.

She shivered. "I won't marry you just because I'd make an adequate mother for Jack."

"This isn't about Jack."

Bravely, she opened her eyes to meet his heated gaze. "Isn't it?"

"No. Jack is fine. Sure, he likes you—he loves you—but he doesn't need a ready-made mom *or* a live-in doctor."

No, of course he didn't. The boy had his father, the best father in all the world. And she was forever excluded from that magic, masculine circle.

"*I'm* the one who needs you," Patrick continued angrily.

Her heart thundered in her ears. She couldn't have heard him correctly. "Excuse me?"

His warm hand slipped from her jaw. He turned from her, his shoulders square against the pale rectangle of Jack's window. "I need you, Kate."

Her breath hitched. "Why?"

He pivoted to face her. "Because you argue with me, dammit." His lightning grin relieved the grimness of his face. "You've probably noticed I can get a little…focused at times."

That was one word for his single-minded passion, his can-do, take-charge attitude. Kate could think of others.

"Bullheaded," she supplied.

He grimaced. "Yeah."

"Overbearing."

"Whatever." He jammed his hands in his pockets. "The thing is, I need somebody to make me face up to that. To stand up to me, as well as stand by me. You can do that, Kate. You have done it. You're a hell of a woman."

His blunt tribute moved her almost to tears. Yet he still
hadn't said that he loved her. More than she yearned for his
admiration, more than she craved his support, Kate needed to
depend on his love. Could she risk telling him so? The recur-
rent pain of rejection shook her like cold. She shuddered, remembering the back of her father's head as it blurred and
disappeared down the road. She felt again the awful, silent
tremors in her stomach at her medical school lover's betrayal.
When had her feelings ever meant anything to the men who
walked through her life?

Patrick's face, strong and open, swam in her vision. He
wasn't like them, she reminded herself. He would be honest.
He would be kind.

He could break her heart.

"What about your wife?" she forced herself to ask.

"Holly?" Patrick's gaze followed hers to the portrait of
Jack's young mother, hung over the boy's bed. "I loved Holly
for a lot of years," he said reflectively. "I fell into it when
we were kids, and it was a hard habit to break. I'll always be
grateful for the years we had. And for Jack."

Patrick stepped closer to Kate, his voice deepening, the heat
of his body raising the temperature of her own skin. "But the
man Holly could love died in that crash with her. The man
who was left…well, I don't think any woman could have
loved him. Angry and remote and all wrapped up in his kid."

Her heart was beating so fast and high in her throat it threatened to choke her. But she couldn't stand there and listen to
him malign the passionate commitment that first breached her
heart. She had everything to lose now by confessing her feelings. She had everything to gain.

"I did," she said, her voice shaking. "I do. I love you."

His hands, raising to frame her face, were so gentle. His
eyes, meeting hers, were so impossibly blue. "Sweet Doctor
Kate," he whispered. "You made me better. You make everything in my life better."

His lips, warm and certain, breathed new life back into her.

His arms, coming around her, were strong and sure. Joy seeped into her heart, shaking the foundations of her dry and reasonable existence.

"I love you," he said. "Marry me, Kate."

The joy bubbled up and sluiced through her, spilling onto her face in a smile. He kissed her eyelids, and the corner of her lips, and, at last, her trembling mouth. They kissed a long time. And what began in sweetness ended in hunger, so that her blood thrummed in her ears, and his chest rose and fell with his breath.

With a little gasp, she broke their kiss and buried her head against his shoulder. Rising through Jack's window, she could hear the sounds of their future, ball games and picnics and laughter. And when a moment later she lifted her face, she saw Patrick with their unborn children shining in his eyes.

She decided. "All right. I'll marry you. Let's go tell Jack he's getting a mother for his birthday."

* * * * *

Noticed anything different lately?

Like all those new flashes on your Silhouette Intimate Moments novels? That's because—just for you—we've created eight new flashes to highlight the appearance of your favorite themes. We've got:

Men in Blue:
Love in the line of duty.

The Loving Arms of the Law:
He's the law of the West, and
she's the lady he can't resist.

Families Are Forever:
Happily ever after—
with kids!

Way Out West:
Because there's nothing
like a cowboy.

So look for these new flashes,
only on the covers of Silhouette Intimate
Moments—available now!

Available at your favorite retail outlet.

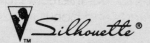

Look us up on-line at: http://www.romance.net   SIMTHEME1

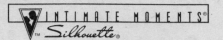

Separated as boys—
reunited as men—

THE SULLIVAN BROTHERS

are now discovering their need for family, as

KYLIE BRANT

presents the latest tale in her exciting series,

HEARTBREAK RANCH, #910

coming in February 1999.

Something sizzled between rugged rancher
Jed Sullivan and Julianne Buchanan—until
Julianne fled Montana for the big city.
Now she was back, and the attraction between
them blazed anew. But Jed had a secret, and
revealing it just might leave him with a
ranch—but no place to call home.

And don't forget to check out the first
book in Kylie Brant's intriguing
THE SULLIVAN BROTHERS miniseries:

UNDERCOVER LOVER, #882 (9/98).

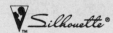

Available at your favorite retail outlet.

Look us up on-line at: http://www.romance.net

SIMSB

A marriage of convenience?

SPOUSE FOR HIRE

This January, don't miss our newest three-story collection about three resourceful women who hire husbands for a limited time. But what happens when these three handsome, charming and impossibly sexy husbands turn out to be too good to let get away? Is it time to renegotiate?

THE COWBOY TAKES A WIFE
by *Joan Johnston*

COMPLIMENTS OF THE GROOM
by *Kasey Michaels*

SUTTER'S WIFE
by *Lee Magner*

Available January 1999
wherever Harlequin and Silhouette books are sold.

HARLEQUIN®
Makes any time special ™

Silhouette®

Look us up on-line at: http://www.romance.net   PSBR199

INTIMATE MOMENTS®
Silhouette®

invites you to join the Brand brothers,
a close-knit Texas family in which each
sibling is eventually branded by love—
and marriage!

MAGGIE SHAYNE
continues her intriguing series

with

THE BADDEST BRIDE IN TEXAS, #907
due out in February 1999.

If you missed the first four tales of the irresistible
Brand brothers:
THE LITTLEST COWBOY, #716 (6/96)
THE BADDEST VIRGIN IN TEXAS, #788 (6/97)
BADLANDS BAD BOY, #809 (9/97)
THE HUSBAND SHE COULDN'T REMEMBER, #854 (5/98)
You can order them now.

Silhouette®

Available at your favorite retail outlet.

Look us up on-line at: http://www.romance.net   SIMTXBRD2

Available in February 1999

SHERRYL WOODS

AND BABY MAKES THREE
THE NEXT GENERATION

is back in
THE UNCLAIMED BABY

A STORMY NIGHT. A HANDSOME STRANGER. AND A BABY ON HER DOORSTEP.

"Sherryl Woods is an author who writes with a very special warmth, wit, charm and intelligence."
—*New York Times* bestselling author
Heather Graham Pozzessere

Also from Sherryl Woods,
look for these Silhouette new titles...

THE COWGIRL & THE UNEXPECTED WEDGING...SE, November 1998

NATURAL BORN LAWMAN...SE, December 1998

THE COWBOY AND HIS WAYWARD BRIDE...SE, March 1999

AND BABY MAKES THREE: FIRST TRIMESTER...By Request, April 1999

Available at your favorite retail outlet.

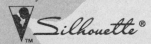

Look us up on-line at: http://www.romance.net   PSSWNG

COMING NEXT MONTH

#907 THE BADDEST BRIDE IN TEXAS—Maggie Shayne
The Texas Brand

When Kirsten Armstrong was falsely accused of murder, she turned to her jilted but still unbelievably sexy lover, Adam Brand—the only one who believed in her innocence. Would Adam help her outrun the law before a long-buried secret destroyed their happiness all over again?

#908 THE MERCENARY AND THE NEW MOM—Merline Lovelace
Follow That Baby

No sooner had woman-on-the-run Sabrina Jensen delivered her beautiful daughter than she was found by sexy oil tycoon Jack Wentworth—the presumed-dead father of her baby! But their family reunion was put on hold when Jack's double life caught up with them....

#909 HOME IS WHERE THE COWBOY IS—Doreen Roberts
Rodeo Men

Rodeo man Denver Briggs knew that his desire for April had never gone away. Then he learned her ten-year-old secret, and the rugged cowboy came face-to-face with the woman and child he longed for—and hoped to hold on to forever....

#910 HEARTBREAK RANCH—Kylie Brant
The Sullivan Brothers

Returning home after seven long years, Julianne Buchanan was shocked to discover that her father's ranch had been sold—to Jed Sullivan! Growing up together, they had long denied their attraction to one another. Would the hurt and betrayal she felt get in the way of their long-overdue happiness?

#911 THE COWBOY SHE NEVER FORGOT—Cheryl Biggs
Way Out West

When former lovers Kate Morgan and Shane Larrabee were reunited, the sparks flew as though time had stood still. He thought she had finally given up on her dangerous career as a cop, but he was wrong. And when Shane became the focus of her undercover mission, could she save his life before she lost him again—for good?

#912 SUDDENLY A FAMILY—Leann Harris
Families Are Forever

When he discovered he was the father of twin four-year-old girls, Zachary Knight found that his bachelor life suddenly went haywire. Then beautiful, sympathetic Antonia Anderson arrived and, with a compassion for children *and* sexy executives, offered to help him raise his newfound family. But when it came to love, did they have the courage to move ahead and greet the future together?